IMPACT OF EVIDENCE

IMPACT OF EVIDENCE

Carol Carnac

with an introduction by
MARTIN EDWARDS

This edition published 2024 by
The British Library
96 Euston Road
London NW1 2DB

Impact of Evidence was first published in 1954 for
The Crime Club by Collins, London

Introduction © 2024 Martin Edwards
Impact of Evidence © 1954 The Estate of Carol Carnac
Volume Copyright © The British Library Board

Cataloguing in Publication Data
A catalogue record for this publication is
available from the British Library

ISBN 978 0 7123 5525 4
e-ISBN 978 0 7123 6896 4

Front cover image © NRM/Pictorial Collection/
Science and Society Picture Library

Text design and typesetting by Tetragon, London
Printed in England by TJ Books Limited, Padstow, Cornwall

CONTENTS

Introduction   7
A Note from the Publisher   11

IMPACT OF EVIDENCE   13

INTRODUCTION

Among the hills of the Welsh border country, a little group of farmsteads is isolated by snow and ice, then floods. Late one afternoon, there is a terrible car smash on a crossroads in the hills. Old Dr Robinson is found dead in his big saloon car, which was thrown off the road by the violent impact and crashed down the steep hillside, which is now awash with flood-water. Local people are shocked but not surprised, since the elderly doctor was known to be a menace on the roads.

But why was there a second body in the back of the doctor's car? Who was the second victim, and how had he reached this isolated area? And if he was murdered, who did it, and why? The local policeman, Welby, also has an accident and soon two Scotland Yard detectives, Rivers and Lancing, arrive and battle their way across the floods. After they start on the trail of a clever murderer, they become involved in a sequence of strange and mysterious events. The atmosphere of the investigation is vivid, thanks to the author's authentic portrayal of the isolation of the neighbourhood and the daily struggle for survival of farmers working in very demanding conditions. In a night of dramatic events high in the lonely hills, Rivers uncovers the truth.

I've paraphrased the dust jacket blurb of the first—and only—edition of this novel, which appeared seven decades ago and has long been forgotten. But who was the woman who created this intriguing puzzle? The short answer is that Carol Carnac was a pen-name of Edith Caroline Rivett (1894–1958), who was generally known to her friends as Carol. Her first novel, *The Murder on the Burrows*, appeared in 1931, and launched a career of quiet achievement. At that time, it was not unusual for women authors to publish mystery novels (or indeed other work) under male or androgynous pseudonyms, because they thought that publishers would be reluctant to take on a novel written by a woman. So, for instance, Josephine Tey's first mystery was published under the name Gordon Daviot, and Lucy Malleson, another author of classic crime fiction, became J. Kilmeny Keith and then Anthony Gilbert. Carol chose the name E. C. R. Lorac—a combination of her initials and the reverse spelling of Carol. Lorac novels were, for many years, generally believed to be written by a man and her *Death of an Author* (also published in the British Library's Crime Classics series) contains interesting discussion about gender issues and authorship.

There were forty-eight Lorac novels, almost all of them featuring Inspector Macdonald of Scotland Yard, but in the course of less than thirty years this hard-working writer produced more than seventy full-length books in total; there were also short stories and stories for young people, such as *Island Spell* (1951), published as by Carol Rivett. Such productivity enabled her to live very comfortably, even though she was by no means a bestseller. Yet there is always a danger, when turning out two or more novels a year, that one will flood the market, with adverse results. This concern prompted several industrious authors to adopt alternative "brands" during the "Golden Age of Murder" between the wars. Carol was no exception and she launched a fresh series of books in 1936, this time under a female pen-name, Carol Carnac. The first Carnac detective was Inspector Ryvet (a play on her own surname) and twenty-two further Carnac novels appeared, fifteen of them featuring Inspector Julian Rivers.

The Carol Carnac books were rather less well known than those which appeared under the Lorac name, but they display similar characteristics, with a strong focus on setting. *Crossed Skis*, which has been published as a Crime Classic, is a story inspired by one of Carol's skiing holidays. The Lorac books had been published under the prestigious Collins Crime Club imprint from *Crime Counter Crime* (1936) onwards and in 1951, the Carnac books began to appear in the same list, starting with *It's Her Own Funeral*. Yet far from trumpeting the connection between the two series, Collins seem to have been happy to keep quiet about it. Perhaps there lingered a concern that over-productivity might tarnish Carol's reputation.

This theory may explain a minor mystery about *Impact of Evidence*. I was introduced to this book by David Whiteley, whose mother Lena knew Carol well. The family have given me a great deal of help with my researches and David has pointed out that, in many ways, the topography of this novel bears a strong resemblance to that of Lunesdale, which was where Carol's sister Maud and her husband lived. Carol moved there during the Second World War and set several of her books in the area, which she came to love. She became fascinated by rural society and the farmers' way of life, but avoided the mistake of presenting it in an idyllic way that didn't represent the reality. David has pointed out to me that in wintry conditions the road out of the top of Aughton, where Carol lived in a house called "Newbanks", bears a strong resemblance to Hollybanks hill in the book, which snow and frost might make impassable for a lorry. I wonder if her decision to set the story on the Welsh borders rather than in Lunesdale was an attempt to differentiate the book from Lorac's mysteries such as *The Theft of the Iron Dogs* and *Crook o' Lune*, and to reinforce the fiction that Carol Carnac and E. C. R. Lorac were two different people.

Whatever the truth, this is an entertaining mystery written in Carol's characteristic style. The book disappeared from view shortly after it came out, in the days when print runs were usually short, with many copies destined for the public libraries. At the time of writing, there doesn't appear to be a single copy of the UK edition available for sale online anywhere in the world. Seventy years after its original publication, I'm delighted to present *Impact of Evidence* to Carol's many fans of the present day.

MARTIN EDWARDS
www.martinedwardsbooks.com

A NOTE FROM THE PUBLISHER

The original novels and short stories reprinted in the British Library Crime Classics series were written and published in a period ranging, for the most part, from the 1890s to the 1960s. There are many elements of these stories which continue to entertain modern readers; however, in some cases there are also uses of language, instances of stereotyping and some attitudes expressed by narrators or characters which may not be endorsed by the publishing standards of today. We acknowledge therefore that some elements in the works selected for reprinting may continue to make uncomfortable reading for some of our audience. With this series British Library Publishing aims to offer a new readership a chance to read some of the rare books of the British Library's collections in an affordable paperback format, to enjoy their merits and to look back into the world of the twentieth century as portrayed by its writers. It is not possible to separate these stories from the history of their writing and therefore the following novel is presented as it was originally published with one edit to the text and with minor edits made for consistency of style and sense. We welcome feedback from our readers, which can be sent to the following address:

> British Library Publishing
> The British Library
> 96 Euston Road
> London, NW1 2DB
> United Kingdom

CHAPTER I

I

WILLIAM LAMBTON CAME BACK INTO THE COWHOUSE AND moved his milking-stool beside Buttercup—he always milked Buttercup last: she was an old cow, as cows go, and an easy milker.

"I see old Dr. Robinson's taken his car out again," said Lambton, as he settled comfortably against Buttercup's warm flanks. "That means he reckons there won't be any more snow. He's a good judge of weather, the old doc is."

"Well, he's not a good driver of a car," came Henry's voice from the far side of Jenny, the Ayrshire. "He didn't ought to be allowed to drive any longer, and that's the plain truth. He's a menace on the roads."

"Steady on now," protested Lambton. "That's exaggerating, son. He may drive slowly and he's too fond of the middle of the road, but I reckon he's safer than some of you lads, blinding along the way you do."

"Safe?" queried Henry scornfully. "I tell you he's nearly stone deaf—he can't even hear a tractor coming—he's half-blind, and it takes him a full minute before he can get his foot down on the brake. Has to sort out which pedal's which. If it wasn't that he was a neighbour I'd have reported him to the police long ago. He ought never to be allowed on the road at all. It's not only himself he'll kill one of these days: it'll be one of us, likely as not. That's a big car he's got, too."

"That's right," put in another voice. It was Kenneth, the hired lad, who chimed in this time. "Nearly smashed my bike he did, coming round Horn's Bend the last Sunday I was out. I went into the ditch—and he never even saw me."

"Now, then, live and let live," protested Lambton. "The old chap never drives far afield: just round our roads, that's as far as he ever gets. He likes to go up the brow to see the sunset, and his rheumatism won't let him walk, his knee's that stiff he can't manage the hills. You young chaps ought to make allowances and look out for him. You've got young ears, you did ought to be able to hear that old car of his half a mile away. And don't let me hear you say you're reporting him to the police, son. He's been our neighbour a dozen years and more, and I won't have you saying nought like that."

After milking was finished, Lambton left the fold yard and crossed the road to a field gate opposite, whence he could see right down to the river in the valley, some three hundred feet below. It was a chill afternoon in February, and the sun was just setting in a rose-pink haze behind the tors of Creffyn. There was snow still lying on the jagged ridges to the west, and to north and south the encircling hills were white. It had been a big snowfall—ten days of it—and for over a week Lambton's Farm had been virtually cut off: the tractor was the only vehicle which had been able to get up the hills to the main road, and it had been a hard job getting the milk away. A rapid thaw had set in two days ago, and now there was another problem—flood water. The melting snow from the hills had caused the river to rise in spate; looking down to the valley from his vantage point by the gate, the farmer could see that the river was still rising. That meant that the road to Brynneys' Bridge would be under water and the bridge would be impassable. There was another bridge farther south, but that meant fifteen miles of hilly driving.

Not that Lambton bothered about floods; he and his wife had experienced plenty of bad winters in the twenty-five years they had lived at St. Brynneys. The house was weather-worthy and well stocked with food and fuel—they could stand a siege, and still "lack nothing," in the farmer's phrase. Of course, they'd got to get the milk away—that was the first concern of a dairy farmer—but the contractors to the Milk Marketing Board had to do the collecting of it. When snow and frost made Hollybanks hill impassable for a lorry, Lambton and his lads would get the milk kits up the steep hill to the main road above: this road was the concern of the R.D.C., who did their best with a snow plough, so that the milk lorry could get within a mile of the farm.

So the weather didn't really worry Will Lambton; indeed, he felt they hadn't done so badly. There was always some snow, every winter, up here in the hills on the Welsh border. If there were heavy snow early in the winter it was a nuisance, because it tended to lie for a couple of months, half thawing and then freezing again, making the roads bad for weeks on end. It was much less trouble if the snow came late, as it had this year, in mid-February, because the thaw generally followed pretty quickly, and they felt the worst of the winter was behind them.

Lambton leaned comfortably on his gate, ruminating mentally, so to speak; casting his mind back to winters of long ago; he reckoned the winters had been harder when he was a lad, before the turn of the century. "Over fifty years ago since that winter the river froze... I'd just left school: fourteen I was and doing a man's job on the farm. Sixty-five next week, and not much to complain of—but the young 'uns think of us as the old 'uns all right." He shifted his bulk uneasily, for thoughts of old age had brought back Henry's sharp words about old Doctor Robinson. "Didn't ought to be allowed on the road: he's a menace..." The young chaps were over sharp these days. How old was the doctor? pondered Lambton. Seventy-five? He'd looked oldish when he came to Boars Wood, in 1940 that was, just after the war started. Mrs. Lambton had been none too pleased to have the doctor as a neighbour. "What does he want with a house that size, and him a widower with no daughters to keep house for him? If he's counting on help from me and Gwynyth he'd better think again—we've got our hands full already."

"What's he want to come here at all for?" had queried Henry (aged twelve in those days and already "ower sharp" in his speech). "St. Brynneys is no place for an old man like that. What'll he do?"

Lambton had replied sharply to his disrespectful son: "That's no business of yours, son. Don't you get thinking it's your job to arrange other folks' lives; and mind your manners—that's no way to speak of a gentleman like the doctor."

"He's just come here to be safe during the war, away from bombs and things," put in Gwynyth. "He'll pack up and go as soon as the war's over—you see."

But Dr. Robinson hadn't packed up and gone. He'd muddled along in the big house with such help as he could get from housekeepers: "Here to-day and gone to-morrow—and a proper pigsty, that house must be," had said Mrs. Lambton.

"I don't reckon he bothers over much about spit and polish—no man does, left to's self: he's got his car and his bees and his fishing and a bit o' shooting—a very fair shot he is, for his age and all," had replied Mr. Lambton.

Now, ten years later, the farmer couldn't help saying "Poor old chap." The doctor couldn't shoot any more—eyesight too bad: he couldn't fish—rheumatism too bad. The bees had died out several years ago, and now the boys were saying he oughtn't to be allowed to drive his car any longer.

Mr. Lambton turned away from the gate, but just at that moment his wife came across the road to join him. Mary Lambton was still a fine vigorous body: her auburn hair was grizzled now, her face wrinkled, but at sixty-three she was still sturdier than most women twenty years younger.

"Ah, 'tis a big water," she said, looking down at the turbid river. "That'll be over the road by Brynneys' Bridge—no market for us to-morrow. And there's more to come. With a quick thaw like this the streams will be in spate all down the Creffyn and the river flats'll be flooded before morning. Has Mr. Morgan driven those bullocks of his up? He'll be in trouble if he hasn't."

"I reckon he got them up before noon," replied the farmer; "the river was bank high along his pastures this morning. Better be getting in, Mother. It's a shrewd wind and no mistake."

They turned away from the gate, but just before they reached the fold yard there was a distant crash which brought them both to a halt. It was something between a clang and a bang—not a gunshot, not a tree falling, not a rumble of stones or a rock fall, but a noise loud enough to make Mary Lambton cry out:

"Dear sakes! Whatever was that now? Was it that old shed coming loose in the gale?"

"That wasn't a shed, Mother," said Lambton. "'Twas a motor smash away up top of Hollybank. Deary me—are those boys out? Henry did say he was going up to meet young Parsons…"

Before the farmer had finished his sentence, Henry came running over the cobbled yard, his big boots clattering on the stones.

"Hear that, Dad?" he called. "I told you it'd happen one day. I bet you any money that's the old Doc, and he's hit something good and hard. That was a car smash, that was—nothing else makes that sort of clanging din."

"Don't you dare talk to me about betting when it's human lives at stake," shouted Lambton. "You get the tractor out and hurry up about it. We'll go up Hollybanks and see what's happened."

"We can't get the tractor out—the magneto's gone wrong and I haven't had time to see to it," said Henry. "We'll have to take the Ford—and the radiator's empty to save a freeze up. Got a kettle on, Mother? I'll fill up with hot water. It'll be quicker to drive—quite a way away that is, I reckon—up by Horn's Bend again."

"I'll go up by the fields—it's shorter that way," said Lambton, but his son shouted back:

"Don't you be so silly. With the snow melting and all the streams in spate the ground's like a bog. I tell you it'll drag your gum boots off at every step. I'll get the Ford going in two twos. Hi, Ken—come and crank her…"

He ran off and Lambton followed with his wife. Henry was good with motor engines—he could always get the Ford started up from cold.

"I don't like it," said Lambton heavily. "That must have been a bad smash; it was right up top of Hollybanks, but we heard it as clear as if 'twere a hundred yards away."

"I don't like it either, Will," said his wife. "That'll mean someone's hurt—and hurt bad, likely. How're we to get a doctor out? The telephone lines are still down, and with the river rising like it's doing now the valley roads'll be under water in a few hours."

The telephone lines had come down during the snow. Now the snow was melting in a sudden thaw and the river was over its banks.

Lambton scratched his head unhappily. "We'll just have to do our best," he said.

2

Henry and Ken worked hard to get the Ford going. Ken cranked away until he was nearly puffed and the old engine started up, coughed, spluttered and died. Henry stood by the open bonnet, fiddling away with his clever fingers, but it was nearly dark before he coaxed the engine to a steady rhythm, and clouds of rain had begun to fall, sweeping up the valley before the west wind. "Rain... that's not going to make things any easier, there's still frost in the ground," said Henry, as he put the old car to the steep hill.

It was an awkward hill at the best of times and the steepest gradient was just on the bend—one in five, that bit was—before the gradient lessened and the road levelled out and ran straight for a few hundred yards, when it curved again to the crossroads at Horn's Bend. A wicked bit of road, that was, with a blind turn just where it joined the main road which swooped down from the Brynneys' Crest.

Henry was pretty sure what they were going to find. The old doctor had driven up Hollybanks, as he did every day save when snow or frost made the surface impossible; he had crossed the main road and continued to the crest of Hollybanks, where the rough farm road stopped at a clearing in front of the wood. There was a wonderful view westwards from this clearing, and room to turn a car. Then old Robinson had driven back to the main road—and crossed it without stopping to look and see if anything was coming. He'd done it before—Henry had seen him—and this time he'd done it once too often.

The Ford chugged its way up to Horn's Bend; the headlights were on, but they wavered a bit—the battery was sluggish with cold—and the rain made visibility worse. Just on the turn Henry rammed his footbrake on and then pulled the hand brake on, hard. It was a good thing that Henry's eyesight was keener than his father's—Mr. Lambton could see nothing through the blurred windscreen. A man's figure was swaying in the faint beam of the headlamps, swaying as though he were drunk: he staggered across the road to the hedge and seemed to vanish against the dark thorns. Henry called to Kenneth in the back of the car.

"Get them stones out and ram them behind the back wheels—we'll start going backwards if you're not nippy."

Ken jumped out—he knew all about this job on gradients like Hollybanks—manœuvred the stones into place and called "O.K." Only then did Henry dare get out of the car, saying to his father: "That's Bob Parsons. Looks as though he's had a packet." Then he called: "It's me, Bob—Henry. What's up?"

Lambton had scrambled out of the car and saw his son standing by Bob Parsons, holding him up as Bob leaned against the hedge bank, his face streaming with blood.

"It's old Robinson," he gasped. "I was driving down the hill, fast, and he ran his car right across me. I thought he'd brake when he saw me and I pulled out, but he accelerated and my jeep caught him sideways on and his car went over the bank. Oh, my God... I never had a chance to miss him..."

"You're in a proper mess yourself," said Henry.

"I was thrown out as I hit him—reckon I somersaulted right over his car," said Bob. "I must have blacked out for a bit, but I'm all right now. I was coming down to fetch you. I couldn't do anything by myself—his car's lying in the stream, on its side, and the doors are jammed. Come on."

"Look here, lad; you get in the Ford and sit quiet," said William Lambton. "We'll see to things as best we can. You're fit for nought."

Bob Parsons protested, but Henry seized him by the arm and shoved him towards the back door of the Ford. "Don't argue—there's bother enough without you being awkward. Get in and stay quiet."

As Henry pushed Bob into the back of the car, Ken started collecting gear from the boot with the aid of a torchlight: there was a hurricane lamp, which he lighted in the shelter of the boot, an axe and some iron bars. While Ken got the gear out, Henry went and examined the position of the stones behind the back wheels.

"Don't want the ruddy outfit to capsize backwards," he said gruffly. "It's bad enough as it is, and the damned road's like a kid's slide."

They went up to the crossroads, round the last bend, with two torches and the hurricane lamp.

"Better see if there's room to turn the Ford before I try to bring it up," said Henry. "Bob's jeep may be right across the road."

The old jeep was capsized in the ditch on the right-hand side of the road; its bonnet was close to the rough stone wall which had once edged the bridge over a stream—but the little wall had gone; there was a black gap where once the stones had edged the road. They went and looked over, down the steep hillside where a stream in spate had broken its banks and was cascading down over the sodden pasture. In the gleam of torchlight and lantern they saw the doctor's big old car, lying on its off side, the flood water tearing past it.

"Reckon he's had it," said Henry curtly.

He scrambled down to the car, saying to his father: "Hold the torch, Dad. I'd better try and lever the roof back—the door's all smashed haywire. Maybe one of these dam' silly sunshine roofs can be useful for once. Come on, Ken, you try with the other lever."

Up to their knees in a morass of clods and ice-cold flood water, they got at the roof, levering, bending, ripping, axe and bars forcing back the sliding top. Then Henry said: "You hold the torch, Ken, Dad's stronger than you."

The boy drew back thankfully, and Henry spoke to his father, his voice terse and quiet.

"His neck's broken, Dad. Needn't be afraid of hurting him; but we'd better get him out. With the flood that's coming down the whole outfit may be sunk."

Father and son heaved together. Henry had to smash the back of the driving-seat away before they got the old man's body clear of the wreck. Will Lambton's breath came in slow painful grunts, not from physical effort, for he was still a very powerful man, but from distress at the task he had to do. They lifted the broken body away from the flood water and laid it on the sodden grass while they got their breath. Suddenly Kenneth shouted from above them:

"There's some folks coming down the hill—on bicycles. That'll be Mike Dering and his missis. They went to St. Olwens this morning."

"Tell 'em to stop... they can lend a hand here," said Henry.

Michael Dering and his wife were the young married couple who lived in the cottage by Boars Wood: they worked for Dr. Robinson as housekeeper and gardener. William Lambton clambered back on to the road as the Derings jumped off their bikes, their oilskin capes shining in the torchlight under the teeming rain.

"'Tis a bad business," said Will. "There's nought we can do but take him home, poor old chap."

3

Henry, practical in all things, wasted no time over regrets or sympathy. "We'll have to get him lifted into the Ford. It's on the hill and I've got to get it up here to turn it. Dad, if you and Mike shove behind, maybe I'll get it going before it slips back. The road's wicked—this rain's made a worse muck of it than ever."

They turned back towards the Ford. "Bob's in the back, but he's fit for nought," said Will. "Maybe Mrs. Dering can tie his head up, 'twas bleeding sore."

When they reached the Ford, Will, Mike and his wife all went to the back and put their shoulders to the bodywork when Henry revved up the engine. It was commonplace to all of them in this remote spot, where ancient cars were the norm—"if she won't start, shove her," was the drill. The engine raced, the clutch engaged and for a sickening second the wheels spun on the treacherous surface, while the three human beings behind put out all their powers to hold the car long enough to give the wheels a chance to grip; then, just as they thought they were beaten, the car lurched forward on the grit which Henry had put down, and roared on up the bend.

"Lord, what a business... All right, Sue?" asked Mike Dering, and his wife panted:

"Yes. I'm all right—but I thought we were done."

"We would have been if it'd been anybody but Henry," said Mike. "No one else could have started the old brute on this—and that Ford's the only available car on the road this side of the river for lord knows how many miles."

They panted up the hill after the Ford. Henry had got it across the main road and Mike Dering ran up to guide Henry as he reversed at the crossroads. When he pulled up, Susan Dering opened the back door to see if she could do anything for Bob Parsons. He was lying back, his eyes closed, with a handkerchief tied roughly round his head.

"Here, let me fix that for you, Bob," she said. "I've got a clean handkerchief and a scarf. I'm so sorry about all this. I never thought the doctor would take his car out with the roads in this state."

Parsons' voice was very faint as he answered her. "If he'd only braked I could have got by. I think he muddled his brake and throttle, he just shot across..."

4

The three men went back to the doctor's capsized car. Henry jumped down, splashing thigh deep into flood water.

"Here, Ken, where are you?" he cried.

"I'm here," replied Kenneth. He was leaning against the back of the broken roof and his voice was shaking, his face green in the beam of Henry's torch. "There's another chap in there, Henry: in the back: he's lying in the water."

"Another—God, who is it?" gasped Henry.

"I don't know—you can't tell. You look yourself," jerked out the boy—and staggered away from the light.

In silence, save for the moan of the wind and the chatter and rush of flood water, Lambton and Dering joined Henry as he thrust his torch through the roof of the wrecked car.

"Ken's right," said Henry grimly. "I shall have to crawl inside… it's a good thing the chap is dead, he'd've been drowned anyway, this damned thing's going to fill up."

As though to add the last touch of horror to a situation already horrible enough, they heard Henry splashing and squelching in the water which was rising in the coachwork, dammed up by floorboards and rugs and carpets. He used his axe again, threw out cushions and rugs, and fragments of the coachwork and then wriggled half out again.

"Reckon you'd better haul me out, Mike," he said. "I've got hold of him but I can't lift him—go on, pull."

Lambton and Dering got hold of him bodily and pulled—it was the only thing to do. Kenneth was past helping—he was snivelling with the horror of it all and his hand swung the hurricane lamp in crazy arcs as he shivered helplessly.

They got the grisly job done at last, and laid another body beside the first—the body of a man unknown to any of them.

Henry pulled a flask out of his pocket. "I brought it for the casualties," he said gruffly. "They don't need it. We do."

He drank from the flask and passed it on to his father. "Have a good swig, both of you," he said. "We're not through yet."

Neither of the others refused. William Lambton never touched spirits as a rule, but he was thankful for the neat whisky, even though it half-choked him.

"Thanks for that," said Mike. "Where's the kid? Here, Ken, there's only a thimbleful left, put it down. It helps."

CHAPTER II

I

THEY GOT BACK TO THE FARM AT LAST. HENRY DROVE HIS GRISLY load with grim competence—two dead men packed in the back somehow, one injured man in front. Will Lambton had protested when Henry and Mike started manhandling the unknown casualty on top of the remains of the poor old doctor.

"'Tisn't seemly," said Will, in the archaic English which he always used in times of stress.

"That be damned," said Henry roughly. "If you think this old rattletrap's going to make another trip up Hollybanks to-night, you think again: she's missing on one cylinder now, and the battery's nearly conked out—and I don't blame her either. She's had fourteen mortal days of dead cold and she's had enough."

So Henry drove his load down to the farm, and Will Lambton trudged down the streaming hill with Mike and Susan and Ken. When they reached the level terrace which was the cause of the siting of the few steadings which made up the hill village of St. Brynneys, they found Henry at the farm gate.

"I've got Bob upstairs—Mother's seeing to him. Come in, all of you—Mike and Sue, too—and get warm, and have a toddy by the fire. That can wait."

"That" was the Ford, and its load.

"I don't like it, son," said Will Lambton unhappily, "but maybe you're right. Won't do no manner of good if some of us get pneumonia, and we're all wet through and chilled to the bone."

They went into the great farmhouse kitchen, where the open range glowed, almost red hot, with faggots stacked up the chimney, and a huge kettle sang on a crane. Mrs. Lambton came hurrying downstairs.

"We've got him in bed, packed up with hot bottles," she said. "Gwyn's with him. It's shock mostly, the cuts aren't that deep. Sue, my dear, come into the washhouse, I've got a fire under the copper and you can just step out of them wet clothes and put some of mine on instead, to save you getting your death. And then Will and Henry can change and have a rub down in here. Michael, Will can find you something to put on. Get out of them wringing rags, do—no one's going to be nice to-night."

They took Mrs. Lambton at her word. In a surprisingly short space of time they were all reclad in clothes which, if old and odd, were warm and dry, and Henry got busy with teapot and whisky. Michael looked around at the bizarre party. Will Lambton, shortish, broadish, Saxon of build and colouring, in a shapeless ancient homespun coat: Sue, slender and dark and supple, in Mrs. Lambton's best purple, tied round her slim waist with its belt, so that she looked almost medieval in the ample folds: Henry, short, fair, strong, with frowning resolute face, in freshly donned corduroys and windjammer jacket: Kenneth, a slip of a boy, in a dressing-gown he'd grown out of—and Michael himself, six foot of lean strength, in flannel bags too wide and too short, with Will's Sunday jacket above them.

"'Tis a shocking sad story and I'm sorrier than I can say," said Mrs. Lambton; "but crying's not going to help, and you deserve a good word, all of you, the way you've been struggling up there in the rain.

So have a hot drink, all of you, do, while I go up and get Bob settled, poor lad. He's that upset and I don't wonder."

"'Twasn't his fault," said Henry quickly, and Mrs. Lambton replied:

"It's no time to argue about that. Ken, up you go to bed. You can take the kettle and put your feet in hot water, else you won't sleep. Come on now."

When his wife had gone, Will Lambton turned to the others.

"What's to do?" he asked.

Henry knew what he meant and answered promptly: "The big barn's clear. We'll lay them both on the threshing floor. No object in carrying them to Boars Wood. The Ford's not going to start again till I've dried the plugs out."

"Didn't we ought to bring them in here?" asked Lambton, but Michael Dering said:

"Henry's right. Lay them in the barn. If the police could get out here with an ambulance—which they can't—they'd take them to the mortuary—and if it were me, I'd rather be laid on the threshing floor than on a mortuary slab."

"The police..." murmured Will Lambton.

"Yes," said Henry. "That's the next thing." His clear-headed common sense was already a jump ahead of his father. "The law says the police have got to be informed when there's a road accident... road accident, cripes... I'd say it was. The telephone wires are all down this side of the valley: we can't phone. The water's six feet deep over the road to Brynneys' Bridge—"

"And the flood's reached the St. Olwens' road," put in Michael. "Sue and I waded through with our bikes and just made it. It'll be thigh deep now."

"And I'm not doing any swimming to-night, police or no police," said Henry. "The only think we can do is to walk to Colonel

Wynne's and report to him. He's a magistrate—reckon he'll have to do."

"His phone's gone too," said William, but Henry replied:

"Who cares? We shall have done all we could do. The police won't get out here to-night and I reckon I'd like to say my bit right away—I'm not going to have Bob Parsons charged with manslaughter if I can help it."

"You're right there," said Michael Dering. "Colonel Wynne can hear our evidence before the police try tying us up in knots about it." He turned to Henry: "I'll walk with you to Maidencombe and see the Colonel. It's about six miles, isn't it? But he'll probably give us a lift back. He's a sportsman, and the floods don't reach the Maidencombe turning."

"Six miles—but it'll take a tidy time to walk it on a night like this," said Will. "Maybe they'll be all abed before you get there."

"Then they can get up," said Henry, who did not share his father's deference to "the quality." "O.K., Mike. I'll be glad to have you."

"Ought I to go back to Boars Wood and see the house is all right?" asked Susan.

"That you shan't," said William stoutly. "You've done enough to-night, my girl. You stay here with my missis. I'll just go along to Boars Wood and see there's no trouble—I'd rather be able to say I went, even tho' 'tis a fool's errand."

"O.K.," said Henry. "You go along there if you think you ought. Mike and I can do the rest—eh, Mike?"

"Yes. Two of us is enough," said Michael soberly. "If we could get a doctor out there's nothing a doctor could do—not for them. Let's get it over, Henry."

"Sooner the better," said Henry gruffly.

2

A quarter of an hour later, Henry and Michael turned up Hollybanks hill again. They had got dry topcoats on now: one was Will's old Home Guard topcoat, one was Gwynyth's new oilskins. They had sacks over their shoulders as well, farmer fashion, because sacks kept the rain from running down their collars. Both young men had been up since six o'clock, both had done a day's work before they started coping with the smash "up Hollybanks," but neither complained. The rain was coming down relentlessly, a curtain of rain, characteristic of hill country. All around them was the splash and chatter of streams in spate and from far below came a deeper note, where flood water was roaring over the final fall to the river.

"It'll get rid of the snow," said Henry phlegmatically.

"It'll do that all right—and get rid of some valuable stock as well if people haven't had their wits about them," said Michael. "I'd never have believed the river'd come up with such a rush." He paused, and then went on: "Henry—who the hell was the second chap in that car? Did you see anyone around during the day?"

"There's been no one in the village—not that we saw," said Henry slowly. "Look here, do you always go out, you and your missis, on Wednesdays?"

"That's the usual arrangement," said Michael. "Sue gets the old man's lunch ready and we bike to St. Olwens. Sometimes we go by bus to Market Rhyven and see a flick or what not. We didn't go out last Wednesday—the snow was too deep—so we were all the keener to go to-day. Sue gets a bit browned off if we never get near a shop. Why?"

"Well, could Dr. Robinson have fixed up for some chap to come and see him the day he knew you'd be out?" asked Henry.

"I suppose so—but why?" asked Michael. "We don't interfere with him—don't go snooping around or anything. Anyway, how did the chap get here—unless you're suggesting the old man went out and picked him up somewhere. There's a bus passes Brynneys' Bridge on Wednesdays."

"I don't know," said Henry. "It beats me. It's a rum go however you look at it; but I've always thought there was something rum about the old man. He's never had a soul to stay with him all the years he's been here."

"The more you think about it, the rummer it gets," said Michael slowly. "Either the doctor drove to Brynneys' Cross and picked the bloke up at three o'clock—"

"He didn't do that," said Henry. "He was pottering round in the garage half the afternoon, and he didn't get his engine started till after we'd begun milking. I was surprised he got it going by himself."

"Oh, he's very careful with his car," said Michael. "He keeps one of those lamps in the bonnet in cold weather, and he runs the engine for a bit most days. I've often looked into the garage after he's been pottering about, just to see it's O.K. His eyesight was getting very dim, poor old chap."

"He was much too blind to be allowed to drive," said Henry. "I've said so for months. I wish I'd done what I said—tipped the wink to the police so that he was told not to drive."

It was some time before they had breath to talk any more. Once up the hills, the wind met them full on, driving over the rough pasture, so that both men bent their heads to avoid the gale and the stinging rain. They trudged on doggedly for a couple of miles, and then turned right, downhill, now to the long valley of Maidencombe, at whose head Colonel Wynne's house was situated.

"Half-way—and the worst half done," said Henry. "Look here, Mike; reckon we'd better not get tied up in questions about who the second bloke is. All we need say is that we've neither of us ever seen him before. O.K.?"

"O.K. by me," agreed Mike. "I had a good look at him when we put him in the barn; I've never seen him before."

"And Bob's never seen him before, either," said Henry. "I made him look."

"What was Bob doing—I mean where was he going when it happened?" asked Mike.

"He was going to the Evanses, out on Slyne Pike," replied Henry. "They've been snowed up and they were short of food as well as fodder. Bob had got a load of potatoes and turnips in his van. He can get quite a load aboard in that box body he built at the back of his outfit. It was decent of him to think of it—he'd done the hell of a day's work before he got started."

"Bad luck on the Evanses, too," said Mike. "I reckon they're pretty short of food for themselves, to say nothing of their beasts."

3

Colonel Wynne was astonished, with reason, when he was told that Henry Lambton was asking for him at half-past ten that wild evening. The Colonel had been snoozing comfortably over a good fire, happy in the knowledge that his house was built on a site which no floods had ever reached. When his manservant told him that Lambton and Dering had come to report a car smash up at St. Brynneys, the telephone lines being down, the Colonel said: "Well, our line's down too… but ask them to come in, Thomas."

"Well, they're that wet they don't like to come through the house, sir: streaming, they are, as if they'd been in the river. They've walked here from St. Brynneys."

"Walked?" exclaimed the Colonel. "It must have been something pretty bad to have made them walk on a night like this. Where are they?"

"In the kitchen, sir."

"All right. I'll come. Get them a drink, Thomas."

Henry and Michael had left their coats in the porch; they stood near the kitchen fire, water running down their soaked clothing into pools around their feet. Looking at them, Colonel Wynne saw two young men who were so tired they could have fallen asleep as they stood. The Colonel was nearly seventy and Henry and Michael were only boys to him. He said quickly:

"Pull up some chairs and sit down by the fire, both of you. You look dead beat. Thomas is bringing you a drink. Now what's the trouble?"

With the stark clarity which never deserted him, Henry Lambton reported:

"Motor smash on the road just above Horn's Bend, sir. Two men killed—Dr. Robinson and another chap we don't know. The doctor ran his car straight across the road when Bob Parsons was driving his jeep down from Brynneys' Crest. Bob hit him—he couldn't help it. The doctor's car went through the wall over the stream and turned over. My dad and I went up and got the bodies out, and Mike Dering here helped us. We took the bodies to our place, and we've got them in the barn."

Colonel Wynne uttered shocked staccato phrases, but after getting his breath, Henry went on again steadily:

"We couldn't notify the police: nobody can get across Brynneys' Bridge, and if the rain goes on like it's doing now, with the melting snow coming down, we may be cut off by the morning—cut off altogether. My dad and I didn't want to have two bodies on the place for days and nobody knowing. So we came to you, sir. You're a magistrate. We couldn't think of anything else to do."

"Quite right, quite right," said the Colonel, "and a very fine effort on your parts, both of you, thinking of your duty as good citizens and coming out here on a shocking night like this. I respect you for it, make no mistake about that. Now you'd better have a drink—you're dead beat, both of you."

"Thanking you all the same, sir, I won't have no more to drink until I've said all I've got to say," said Henry bluntly. "If I drink whisky now I shall be as near drunk as makes no difference."

"Same here," said Michael. "It's hard enough to keep awake as it is, sir."

"Good lads, good lads—very sensible of you," said Wynne. "Now you've told me Dr. Robinson was killed—he was driving, I take it. What about the driver of the other vehicle?"

"Bob Parsons, sir, from Pine Quarry. He's cut about and shaken up, but he's not too bad. We've got him at our place. Bob was driving a load of food and fodder for the Evanses, up at Slyne Pike—they've been snowed up and they're short. Bob was driving fast, down from Brynneys' Crest: he had to drive fast because he'd got to get up the rise above the culvert, and if he hadn't gone at it fast he'd never've got up, the roads being what they are. The doctor just shot out of that farm track leading to Hollybanks wood: he was deaf, sir, and half blind with it. He ought never to have been on the road at all."

"Bad business, bad business, poor old chap," said the Colonel. "I noticed he was a bit tottery last time I was past his place—but who was the other chap in the car with him?"

"We don't know, sir. Never seen him, either of us."

"But what's his name?" demanded Wynne. "Didn't you look in his pockets?"

"Yes, sir. We looked, Mike and me. We carried him into the barn and laid him on the threshing floor—and we went through his pockets, whether we liked it or not. And there's nothing in his pockets, barring a few shillings and an empty packet of Woodbines."

"Nothing in his pockets!" exclaimed the Colonel. "That's a most extraordinary thing."

"I'd have you know Mike Dering was with me when I looked, sir," said Henry stolidly.

"It's quite true, sir," said Mike quietly. "I was there—watching."

"All right, all right," said the Colonel quickly. "I'm not doubting your word—but it's very odd."

"The whole thing's odd. That's why we came, sir," said Henry.

Colonel Wynne sat and looked at them, considering the situation. It seemed to him about as awkward as it could be: telephone lines down, the river in flood, roads under water—no reaching the police on the south side of the river, and to the north the hills still covered in melting snow, drifted nobody knew how deep. He turned to Michael. "Dering, isn't it? Let's think—you live at—?"

"Boars Wood Cottage, sir. I do—did—Dr. Robinson's garden, and my wife cooks for him—did, I mean."

The Colonel blinked... gardener... the chap didn't sound like it. His voice was an educated voice. Hastily concealing his surprise, Wynne went on:

"The bridge your end is out of action. What about St. Olwens' bridge?"

"There was eighteen inches of water over the road when my wife and I came through it at four o'clock, sir," said Mike. "We waded through, pushing our bikes. That was flood water from the thaw. Now the rain's come down that dip in the road will have three feet of water over it, and the river's rising all the time."

"It's the hell of a business," said the Colonel. "That means we're cut off on this side—and the road over the top may not be passable for days; they say the drifts are twelve feet deep." He looked again at the two young men, his lips twitching a little. "Oh, well—that's my headache now—you've handed it to me all right. Now I'll take a short formal statement—names, times, registration numbers and so forth."

Once again Henry gave the required information; his father had heard Dr. Robinson's car pass the farm at five o'clock, when they were milking. It was about half an hour later they heard the smash, but it was well after six before they reached the crash—they'd had a job starting the old Ford.

Colonel Wynne wrote the facts down in his large legible hand, made Henry and Michael read the statement and then they both signed it.

"Very good," said the Colonel formally. "I commend you both for what you've done, and I shall tell the police so. Now I'll drive you back to Brynneys' Crest. I'd better not come down the hill or I may never get up again. I'll try to get the police out to-morrow; it's their duty to reach you, and they'll have to punt over the floods if that's the only way. And now—what about that drink?"

"I won't say 'No'," said Henry, and Michael suddenly grinned. "I've never been drunk yet, sir, so I hope I'll keep up my form."

Colonel Wynne smiled back at him, though he was sorely puzzled. Michael's speech had been of the simplest but there was something about his voice and bearing which wasn't like a working man's. To Wynne's old-fashioned service eye, Dering was officer type, not private.

4

A steaming toddy apiece—whisky, lemon, hot water—was dispensed by Thomas, who was then told to go and get the car out. As Henry finished his drink, Colonel Wynne risked a question.

"Look here, Lambton, off the record and between ourselves, have you any idea at all you'd care to suggest? I'm thinking about the doctor's passenger and the fact that he had nothing on him to show his identity and that none of you know how he came to be in your parts."

"I don't know," said Henry slowly. "I could make up a story—same as anyone else—but it'd be guessing."

"Why not guess out loud then?" asked Wynne. "I won't repeat what you say. You can trust me for that."

Henry's fair face was flushed and drowsy, his speech not quite as clear as usual, but his eyes were as intelligent as ever.

"'Take one with you,'" he quoted—and Wynne recognised the allusion all right. "The doctor may have got muddled," went on Henry, "put his foot down on the accelerator instead of the brake—or he may not. If that bloke in the back was there to make trouble—well, the old chap may have thought, 'This is it—I'll take him with me.'"

He broke off. Wynne turned to Michael Dering. "You've been working for Dr. Robinson, so you must know him a bit. Any guess from you? This is all very irregular, but we're all three human beings. I've just stood you a drink—and I didn't do that to loose your tongues. I don't abuse hospitality, lad."

"That's all right, sir," said Michael. "But I didn't know Dr. Robinson. I've worked for him for six months and so has my wife, and we don't know anything more about him than we did the day we came. He never talked to us. Perhaps if a chap's as close as that, he's got something to be close about. I don't know—but Henry's guess is as good as anybody else's."

He turned to Henry. "I'd never have believed it of you, never have thought imagination was your long suit—but you may have got something there all the same."

Henry looked stolidly into the blazing fire. "The old man lived there thirteen years," he said slowly; "he was our neighbour. When I first saw him, when I was a kid, I wondered why the heck he came to

St. Brynneys at all. I've been wondering ever since. We're like Mike: we don't know him. Nobody knew him. That's all from me."

"Well, come along—I'll try to get you home somehow," said the Colonel.

They got into the Bentley—Henry and Michael in the back, the Colonel and Thomas in front. Before they had driven the three-mile stretch along Maidencombe valley, both Henry and Michael were fast asleep, but they woke up at once when the car pulled up on Brynneys' Crest.

"I can turn here," said Wynne, "and you've only about a mile to go. I can't afford to come down in case I get stuck; if my car packed up too, it'd put the lid on it. The trouble is that the frost's still in the ground and the rain's turning to ice."

"You're telling me, sir," said Henry. "Thank you for the lift—and good night."

They trudged off into the rain and Wynne turned his car by a field gate, slowly and carefully. Then he said: "I'm going along to inspect the smash, Thomas. You can stay in the car if you'd rather."

"If you're going I'm coming with you, sir," replied Thomas.

They lurched through the lashing rain, down to the turn and to the smashed bridge over the culvert. The flood water was coming over the road now, as well as under it. In the light of their torches they saw the jeep with its box body, its front wheels wrecked, its springs smashed: they looked over the broken bridge and saw the old Buick, half submerged now.

"Beats me why Parsons wasn't killed too," said Thomas.

"The hood's rotten—he must have been thrown right up through it," said Wynne. "If the fabric had been sound he'd have been killed. Well, we've done all we can do. Let's get home while the going's good."

CHAPTER III

I

WHEN THOMAS TOOK THE COLONEL'S TEA IN NEXT MORNING, he found his master already sitting up in bed, smoking a cigarette. Thomas had been the Colonel's batman in 1914, and he'd been with him ever since.

"Good morning, sir. Still raining—hard as ever."

"Harder—if possible," said Wynne. "But I've got to get across the river somehow, the sooner the better. If this goes on, the bridges may go."

"Yes, sir. Len's been down as far as the approaches to St. Olwens' bridge. The bridge itself's all right, but the approach road's under three foot of water. The car's not going to help, but I'm game to wade. It's not more than waist-deep."

"Very sporting offer, but I hope I shan't have to take it," said Wynne. "I think I could get Major through it. He's often taken me over the river when it's low—he doesn't funk water."

Major was the Colonel's old charger; he was a tall horse, over eighteen hands. His jumping days were long over, but he still took his rider uphill and down dale, picking his way skilfully and cautiously, over ground which no other horse would have negotiated safely.

"That's an idea, sir. I've always said if Major was put to it, he'd swim."

"I've no doubt he would," said Wynne. "Get out my waders, Thomas. Might as well keep as dry as I can—and breakfast in twenty minutes."

The Colonel looked like nobody's idea of a horseman when he was finally kitted up for his adventurous jaunt: the rain was still coming down relentlessly, and Thomas spread out the Colonel's oilskin cloak over Major's haunches, like an old-fashioned cavalryman's. The tall horse twitched his ears and raised his nose questioningly as he faced the rain, but set out sedately and steadily.

Colonel Wynne knew that the roads in Maidencombe had one advantage over the St. Brynneys' roads: the frost up in the hills had been much harder and the roads were still frozen under the surface. Here, in the valley, there were no ice patches for the horse to slip on. When they reached the flooded stretch, a couple of hundred yards from the bridge, Major halted, whinnied, and showed that he had no enthusiasm for the job, but after a few words of encouragement he waded in and kept going, very slowly, picking his way with care over obstacles under the flood water, for the ground was thick with mud and rocks washed down by the spate. At one point he stopped altogether just before the water reached his belly. He was shivering now and he whinnied again, a higher-pitched note which made the Colonel unhappy. Then, very deliberately, he struggled on, until the water became shallower. When he stepped clear of the flood on to the bridge proper he neighed loudly, almost a trumpet call of a neigh, stood and shook himself and then went on to the farther side as sedately as ever.

It was mid-morning when the Colonel reached the village of St. Olwens. He stopped at a farm on the outskirts of the village, and the farmer took Major into his own stable, beside a huge carthorse whose warmth was like central heating. It wasn't until his horse was unsaddled, rubbed down and given a hot bran mash that Colonel Wynne went on to the village constabulary.

Here, he learnt, the telephone was working again—the one line for miles round that the Post Office men had repaired since the havoc wrought by the snow. Jones, the elderly constable, received the Colonel with deep respect, but the latter wasted no time in debating the inevitable topic—the weather.

"There's a peck of trouble up at St. Brynneys, Jones. There was a motor smash last night on that shocking bit of road below Brynneys' Crest—two men killed and one injured. Young Henry Lambton walked out to my place to report it. As you know, all the telephone lines are down our side, and we're virtually cut off. The approaches to the bridges are under water and the snowdrifts up in the hills make those roads impassable, but we've got to get those bodies down from St. Brynneys somehow."

The constable looked nonplussed. "I ought to get out there and take statements," he began, but Colonel Wynne cut in:

"Use your head, Jones. If you got there yourself, how could you bring the bodies back? One bridge is out of action, and St. Olwens' bridge has three feet of water over the approaches on our side. No motor vehicle can get through."

"Could a farm cart and horses do it, sir?"

"No. It couldn't. It'd bog down, and farm horses wouldn't face it. I rode through it myself—Major brought me through. He's the only horse I know who would have done it, and the water's still rising. But those two corpses can't be left in Lambton's barn till the floods go down. We've got to have an inquest and a burial order."

"Yes, sir," said the constable, who evidently felt he was being faced with the impossible.

"Well, I'm going to cut out the usual formalities and speak to the Chief Constable," said Wynne. "There's no time to lose, because things are getting more difficult every hour. Major Trevor can get the military to send out an amphibious vehicle—a Duck. There are several of them at the training camp on the Wyvern reach. We can manage with vans our side—my estate wagon can get out to St. Brynneys, but it can't cross the river. Now I'm going to use your phone—and here's the statement about the accident those two chaps gave me last night. I'll see to it the coroner thanks them for what they did. It's not many young chaps who'd have walked out to Maidencombe last night to report an accident, especially after the sort of job they'd had."

"Yes, sir, indeed," said the constable, whose slow-moving mind had been hard put to it to take in the Colonel's quick clipped speech.

2

Colonel Wynne was thankful when he at last got through to Major Trevor at Loucester,* the county town. The Rural Exchange was in chaos, with lines down and connections unobtainable. The Colonel heard them try one junction after another—Gloucester, Hereford, Ross, Monmouth—before they connected him, for the snow had been widespread and repairs impossible.

"That you, Hugh? Thank God for it. We're in a mess out our way and I want some help quickly."

Wynne and Trevor were old friends, and the Chief Constable grasped the salient facts quickly.

"Yes, I follow. I'll get through to the C.O. at once—before he's sent all the Ducks out."

"Good. Tell them to keep this side of the river and pick me up at St. Olwens' constabulary. I'm not going to attempt to ride back, it's not fair on the horse. I've told my chaps to bring the van as near the

---

* Loucester, pronounced Losseter.

bridge as possible, and I'll take some sacks of flour and other food back with me. They'll be in a poor way up in the hills. The van can bring the bodies back to the bridge. Send out the best of your chaps you can spare, Hugh. It's a queer story and it may take some sorting out."

"Right. I'll square it up with our Super—he's got some intelligent fellows in his C.I.D. section. I'll ring off now, Charles, and get through to the camp. If you think of anything else, ring me again in half an hour's time. The telephone system's all haywire, lines down everywhere."

Colonel Wynne sat back and smoked a cigarette after that. He was a very conscientious man and he wanted to think things out. Fortunately Hugh Trevor knew the river Aske, and he hadn't asked tom-fool questions about boats. There weren't any boats, for the Aske wasn't a boating river—it was a turbulent mountain stream, racing over a rocky bottom, with rapids and waterfalls and jutting-up rocks along the whole reach from Brynneys' Bridge to Wyvern. In the summer it sometimes shrank to a mere trickle, with deep pools, beloved of anglers. When there was rain in the hills, the Aske would rise suddenly, in a matter of hours, fed by the streams which raced down the mountain sides. Consequently it was a very dangerous river, and those who knew it didn't take any liberties with it.

Wynne had often seen the Aske in spate, often seen it rise and flood the water meadows from side to side of the valley, but he had never seen a flood of such magnitude as this one. The river had been bank-high all January—it had been a very wet month. Then came the ten days of heavy snowfall and the sudden thaw, and the water couldn't get away fast enough. "I doubt if there's a boat anywhere between Brynneys' Bridge and Wyvern," thought Wynne. "I suppose we could have made a raft and poled it across to the bridge, but I'm damned if I should have liked punting corpses that way. No. Let the National

Service lads do a useful job—and we've got to keep communications open somehow. If this sort of thing goes on, every house our side of the river will be short of food. None of the tradesmen's vans will be able to get across. Now what ought I to buy? Flour, sugar, tea... the grocers will know."

3

At Lambton's farm the usual jobs had been done that morning, at the usual time. Henry woke up soon after six, as usual, and by seven o'clock the cows were being milked. Later, as the daylight strengthened, Will Lambton crossed the road and looked down to the flooded valley. Memories in the country are long; stories of storm and flood were handed down from one generation to the next. It was in his father's time, Will remembered, that St. Brynneys had been cut off for fifteen days, with flood water over all the low-lying roads. St. Olwens' bridge had collapsed that time—the arch on the Maidencombe side had been swept away—but they had rebuilt it just as it was before.

"Never seen the like of it, not in my time," said Will to his son as he went back to the farm. "Reckon that bridge'll come down again. The timber the water's taking down will dam the arches, same as it did before, and then something's got to go."

"Why didn't the silly fools rebuild the bridge properly?" asked Henry disgustedly. "That approach road should ha' been built up on a causeway and another arch added."

"Well, that bridge has stood for hundreds o' years they say," said Will.

"A fat lot that helps us," said Henry. "Better tell Mother to get the separator out. The milk lorry can't get here to-day and the lord knows when things'll be straight again. Thirty gallons of milk we've got waiting. It's got to be made into butter or else go down the drain."

Butter. The word took Will Lambton aback. They hadn't made butter at St. Brynneys since the Milk Marketing Board started collecting the milk about twenty years ago.

"Butter," he muttered. "That takes me back, that does. Mother won't like that. Never rains but it pours, seemingly."

"It's a proper mess," said Henry.

They went into breakfast. The big barn doors were closed: nobody had been inside again, nobody had let their eyes rest on the barn doors, but at the back of everyone's mind was the thought of those two bodies—and their minds jibbed away from a problem which had no precedent to help them to solve it.

Mrs. Lambton had got the usual good breakfast for them—porridge, followed by fat bacon from their own pigs, and fried potatoes with it.

"It's like to be hard day," said Mary Lambton. "Make a good breakfast. It'll help you through."

"How's Bob?" asked Henry.

"He's bad, son. Feverish—chill, I reckon. But 'tis no manner of use fussing. We can't get a doctor out and we've got to do our best as we are."

"I'd better go along to his place and see to things," said Henry. "There's his birds want feeding, and he's got half a dozen pigs."

"Michael thought of that," replied Mrs. Lambton. "He's going along as soon as he's had his breakfast. He and Sue went home as soon as they got up. I'm that sorry for them, they've not been settled here for long and they've got that cottage real home like, and now they'll be out of a job, and turned out of the cottage as likely as not."

"It's a proper mess all round," said Will gloomily. "There's the milk can't be got away. Henry reckons butter's the only thing to do with it."

"Sakes alive! D'you think I haven't got any wits left?" demanded Mrs. Lambton indignantly. "I thought of that before you did, Will. Gwynyth and I got the separator out as soon as we saw the floods, and we've got the copper fire going already so's to have boiling water to scour it out. Not that it hasn't been looked after. No gear's ever allowed to spoil in my dairy. And it'll do Gwynyth good to learn to make a proper batch of butter—not the little tiddly bits we've made for ourselves these years past."

She broke off. "'Tisn't the butter I'm worrying about," she went on slowly. "It's those two poor souls in the barn. I can't leave them like that, Will. 'Tisn't Christian or decent."

"See here, Mother," said Henry. "I've told Colonel Wynne about it. He said he'd be along to see to things as soon as he could manage."

"Maybe he did, son. He's a good Christian gentleman, the Colonel is, but I'm not going to let him think we're no better than heathens ourselves. Your father can get them long trestles set up, and lift the poor souls off that floor. Then I'll see to it. It's not the first time I've done what I could for the dead."

She turned away, tears running down her face, and Will said:

"You and me'll do it together, Mother. 'Tisn't much—but it's all we can do."

Mrs. Lambton wiped her tears away with her apron. "That's settled then," she said. "Gwyn can get the separator going, Michael's gone to see to Bob's place. Henry, you'd better get the tractor right, and clean them plugs, or whatever it is, in the Ford. We don't know what we may have to do before the floods go down. There's some folks this side may be in proper trouble—the Evanses, and poor old Taffy Williams out on Caerlyon. He'll be out trying to find if any of's sheep are still alive. Deary me, 'tis hard on the shepherds."

"I can't stop looking at it, Mother. I never did see anything like it," cried another voice. "The valley's just one lake, rising every minute it is."

"Now don't you waste time staring, Gwyn," said Mrs. Lambton briskly. "You can do the washing up for me before you start on the separator. Bad weather means one thing on a farm, and that's hard work."

Gwynyth Lambton was a sturdy girl, not fair like Henry and her parents, but dark, with a vivid colour and bright dark eyes—a throwback in colouring and features to some Welsh forebear.

"Farming's all hard work, I reckon," she said. "No wonder folks say, 'How ever d'you live out there?' One thing I'll never be, and that's a farmer's wife. Now don't you start lecturing me, Mum. I'll do the washing up all right, and scour the separator and feed the hens and make the swill for the pigs, and then feed the calves and then fetch the milk into the dairy; and then we'll see."

"If you work as hard as you talk, my girl, you'll soon be through," said Mrs. Lambton, "and get a rice pudding on, do—a big one. The men need feeding this weather."

4

They got the trestle tables set up in the barn—tables that had been used for many a harvest home party. The bodies were lifted on to the tables and finally covered with clean sheets. Before she left them, Mrs. Lambton stood and looked steadily down at the two dead men. The old doctor looked almost noble, his harsh features refined by the alchemy of death to the similitude of carved ivory, his white hair smoothed back, a tiny bunch of snowdrops under his folded hands. Mrs. Lambton had shed no more tears; she was doing a job which women in lonely farmsteads count as their duty, and she did it as well as she knew how.

"He looks peaceful, poor soul, happier than he did when he was alive," she said softly. "I've often thought he looked wretched—but that's all done now, whatever 'twas."

The other victim of the smash was a sorry sight. Mrs. Lambton had bound clean linen round his head, to hide the cuts and contusions which discoloured it.

"Did you ever see him before, Will?"

"Never." The farmer stood and stared unmoved—this was a stranger whose death meant nothing to him. "He's no countryman," he said slowly. "He's a townsman—and not much loss to anyone, I reckon. What beats me is how he got here. There's no sign of another car, nor bike, nor such like, and you'd never think he could 'a walked out here in those shoes. Town shoes, those are, and worn through at that."

He drew the sheet up over the battered face. "'Tis a puzzle right enough." He paused and then added: "I hope the Colonel gets out soon. If so be he's not here by afternoon, we'll have to move them to Boars Wood—carry them on the trestles. We can't leave them here."

Mrs. Lambton knew what her husband meant: un-coffined bodies could not be left for very long in a barn.

"We'll wait and see and hope for the best," she said quietly. "The Colonel knows all that. He'll get here somehow, and bring them as ought to come."

They went outside again into the rain and closed the barn door behind them. "And how anyone's going to cross St. Olwens' bridge to-day I just don't know," said William. "That bit o' road's deep enough to cover any car by now, and enough muck along with it to bog down a wagon."

"You'll see, the Colonel will manage somehow," said Mrs. Lambton.

CHAPTER IV

I

COLONEL WYNNE'S STRATEGY WORKED PERFECTLY. BY MIDDAY an amphibious vehicle had ferried him over the flooded approaches to the bridge in company with a County C.I.D. inspector and his attendant constable, together with stores of food of all varieties. The Colonel had said frankly that housekeeping wasn't his long suit and that the tradespeople had better send anything that might be needed for several households cut off by the floods.

"Make a proper job of it," he said. "This sort of thing only happens about once in a lifetime."

The Colonel's credit was good, and the load was considerable; the "amphibious vehicle" could have taken stores for a battalion, but the estate van was less commodious. "Keep the rest here; I shall be back in an hour or two," said Wynne. "You can run a sort of shuttle service for us to-day—and to-morrow we'll see how things look."

As they started their drive up to St. Brynneys, Wynne discussed with Welby, the C.I.D. inspector, the main facts of the story which Henry and Michael had told him last night; then he added: "I'd like to say this. The Lambtons are excellent people, straight all through; you can believe what they tell you because they're innately truthful. I've known them for years and I have a high regard for them."

"Very good, sir," said Welby. "And now about Dr. Robinson—you knew him too, I take it?"

"Well, I did and I didn't," said Wynne. "When I drive that way—for fishing or a bit of rough shooting—I generally stop to have a word with the Lambtons. I called in on old Robinson when he first came to Boars Wood in 1940, but I didn't get the feeling he welcomed company; the reverse, in fact. He liked his own company. I never went into the house again, but I've met him often enough; he fished and shot in the roughs and he was a keen naturalist. But when all's said and done I feel I agree with Henry Lambton—I didn't know Robinson. I never heard him express any opinion about anything, barring fishing and the weather, and so forth. He was a very reserved old chap. The other young fellow, Dering, said practically the same as Henry."

"Dering; he's the gardener, isn't he? Do you know him at all, or where he came from?"

"No. I'd never spoken to him before. He's been there six months, but I've never happened across him—but the Lambtons seem to like him so he must be a good neighbour."

"Right. Now the chap who drove the jeep—Parsons; can you tell me anything about him?"

"He's been at Pine Quarry for three years. It's a smallholding—ten acres, of which six are pasture. He bought it when old Stephens died—it's a freehold. I think another chap lived with him when he first came, but he couldn't stand the loneliness and he went off somewhere else. Parsons is a very hard worker; raises a lot of table birds and markets them: eggs, of course, some pigs and a few grazing beasts, and he grows some potatoes and root crops. He also acts as carrier—he'll take and fetch anything in that box van he built on to his jeep. I've seen a bit of him; he's grazed a horse for me—and done well by it; provides us with table birds and is generally useful. He told me he went on the land when he was demobbed—he's about thirty-five and served in the Commandos and later got a farm job to learn a bit. I have a yarn with him occasionally—he's a nice straightforward chap and a very hard worker. Ah... this is Brynneys' Crest—you'll be able to see what happened last night."

For the next quarter of an hour, Welby noted the layout, commenting on the dangerous nature of the crossroads. Wynne told him the roads had been much worse last night, with the rain glazing into ice on the still frozen surface. By now the thaw had penetrated an inch or so and there was no ice.

"In my opinion, Parsons couldn't have stopped his vehicle on that slope," said Wynne. "If he'd braked hard he'd have gone into a skid and probably capsized. Here's his jeep—what's left of it. They're tough vehicles, aren't they? An ordinary car would have crumpled up like a concertina. He shot right through the hood. I suppose the canvas took some of the shock but I'm surprised he didn't break his neck."

"I've known a driver shoot through a sound hood and survive," said Welby. "The fabric's rotten in that one. Army left-over, I suppose."

He stood and looked down at the doctor's capsized Buick. As Henry had prophesied, it was now more than half submerged: the torrent was scouring the ground from under it and the heavy car was sinking into a morass.

"We can't do anything about that until we can get a crane up here," said Welby. "You know I'm surprised the jeep didn't go right over on top of the other... Of course the front wheels were bashed in when it hit the Buick... May have rebounded a bit... I see his hand brake's on... You can never tell what'll happen in a bad smash like this... I'd better go over and have a look at the other one."

He plunged down over the edge and splashed around for a few minutes in the misery of ice-cold water and sludge, and then clambered back.

"They must have had one hell of a job last night," he said. "It took some pluck to tackle it." He glanced at Wynne and then added: "I wanted to make quite sure no one could have opened that back door. It's jammed tight; the bodywork crumpled on impact."

Wynne stared at him for a moment. "I didn't think of that one," he said slowly.

"In our job we have to think of everything," said Welby. "If we miss anything, it's always the thing we miss which matters. Very good, sir; let's get on. This is a rotten job for you, what with the rain and the cold."

"It's a rotten job all round," said the Colonel; "but I'm as inquisitive as any other normal fellow, and I tell you frankly I'm puzzled to death. Not over the collision—those cars tell their own story—but over the passenger. Can't make it out at all. Where did the chap come from and how did he get here?"

2

They went straight to Lambton's farm; Henry had just finished his repairs to the tractor's magneto, and he, his father and Ken were standing by with sacks over their heads while the tractor belched smoke and roared out the full blast of an old T.V.O. engine. When he turned his head and saw the Colonel and his two companions Henry's stolid face lightened. "That's something to be thankful for, anyway," he said audibly.

"We're that thankful to see you, sir," said Will Lambton heartily. "'Tis trouble all round and no mistake; step inside, sir, out o' this dirty weather."

"This is Inspector Welby from Loucester," said the Colonel. "He'll be wanting to take a formal statement from all of you; but first—better see the casualties." He spoke to Welby and the latter nodded. "In the big barn," said Henry stolidly.

"All right; we'll go there first," said Welby, "and I'll see you afterwards."

"You lads can get the stuff out of my van," said Wynne. "I loaded up with flour and groceries and so forth—I thought you might be short, and other folks as well."

Henry and Ken went about this job with alacrity and the Colonel went into the farmhouse kitchen to have a word with Mrs. Lambton and a warm by the fire.

"I'm very sorry about all this distress you've been put to," said Wynne. "Life must have been difficult enough this last fortnight without all this extra work and worry."

"If it's the weather you mean, we take it as it comes," said Mrs. Lambton serenely. "'Tis a good house, this one, no worry about flooding, however bad it be in the valley; we're warm and dry and we've lacked nought. Will and me are sore troubled about the old doctor and the other poor fellow. All you can say is 'twas soon over—they could hardly've known it happened."

"What about the other driver—Bob Parsons? You've still got him here?"

"And likely to have," said Mrs. Lambton. "I think it's that concussion as they call it; he seems all moithered. And if I might say so, sir, I hope the police officer won't be worrying Bob with questions; he's not fit to talk. He's drowsy like, and I doubt if he knows what he's saying."

"Ought I to get a doctor out?" asked Wynne. "I expect we could manage it."

"Bless you, no, sir. It's quiet he needs, quiet and warmth. I've tended my own men folk when they've been and hurt themselves. I know about head wounds—we get all sorts of accidents on a farm, with the tractor and wood felling and all the heavy jobs they do. We don't trouble the doctor to come out here much—experience teaches a woman to be a nurse, and most times it's her own mother-wit she's got to rely on."

A few minutes later Welby came in, with Bowen the constable, followed by Will Lambton, Henry and Kenneth. "We'll all sit down if we may, Mrs. Lambton," said Welby. "I don't want to be too long and I think the simplest thing would be if I read out the statement Colonel Wynne wrote, after the evidence given to him last night by Henry Lambton and Michael Dering. It seems to me to cover the ground pretty thoroughly, but you can tell me if there's anything you want to add or alter. Do you agree?"

The three concerned all nodded agreement, and Welby read out the Colonel's report.

"That's right," said Will Lambton, when the Inspector had finished. "Couldn't be better—much clearer than I could say it, and I reckon he's got it all in."

"It's O.K. by me," said Henry. "That's what happened—barring a few details which don't matter."

"Add anything you remember," encouraged Welby. Henry pondered a moment; then he said:

"I'd like to say I knew it was a motor smash the minute I heard it. There's nothing else could make a sound like that hereabouts; and I knew it must be the Doctor, because he'd gone up Hollybanks not long before. He oughtn't to have driven a car—not these past two years, he oughtn't. He was deaf and getting half blind and he only thought of himself. His road sense had gone long since, like an old dog's does." He paused a minute and then went on: "Because I was certain it was a smash, I put some gear in the boot of our Ford—an axe and some iron bars, and some cable for towing—only we couldn't use it. Ken and I levered the roof back with the axe and bars—that's how we got it open, 'twas the only way of getting him out." Again he paused, looking straight at Welby. "I thought I'd like to say why I took the axe and bars, just in case of any awkward questions."

His voice was gruff and dour, and Will Lambton said: "Well, I never! What's in your mind, son?"

"That's all right," said Welby quietly. "He's telling me he used his head, that's all. I'll have that written down, Bowen, as near to Mr. Henry Lambton's own words as you can get it. Now then—about Dr. Robinson being a dangerous driver—are you all agreed about that?"

"Yes," said Ken, speaking for the first time. "He just drove as though there was only himself on the road; he had me in the ditch on Horn's Bend, and my bike too—and he never even saw me. Anyone seeing the wings of his car could tell—he was always biffing something."

"I'm afraid 'tis true," said Will Lambton. "He drove slow enough, but he never looked out for no one else."

"If you all knew this, why didn't you report it?" asked Welby. "The traffic police can't be everywhere, but they'd come and look into any complaint about bad driving, especially in the case of a very old driver."

"'Twas my fault," said Will Lambton. "Henry, he wanted to report it, but I said No, the doctor's a neighbour—and, anyway, he only drives round our roads; he doesn't go into town nor drive along them big main roads any longer. But 'twas my fault. Michael Dering, he was at me not long since: 'Tell the doctor he oughtn't to drive himself no longer,' he said—but 'twasn't easy. The doctor wasn't the sort you could say a friendly word to, not in the way of advice. Very short, he was. But 'twas my fault. I know't, and the blame's mine."

"Well, that's clear enough," said Colonel Wynne. "Any jury would accept that—and understand it."

"That's for them to say," said Welby dryly. "Now I think I've got all the points I need, so far as you three witnesses are concerned—and I'd like to add my word to Colonel Wynne's—you acted with great promptitude and did everything within your power, and nobody respects you more than I do, when I think what the conditions were last night. And now about the driver of the jeep—he's upstairs, I understand."

"Yes, he is. He's in Henry's bed—that being warmed and ready," said Mary Lambton, her resolute voice clear and deliberate. "And he's not fit to be asked questions by no one, police or no police. A real knock on the head he got and it's that concussion afterwards; he don't really know what he's saying. And I might as well say what I've got to say and done with it. You're talking about reporting, Inspector. If you wake Bob Parsons up now and ask him questions, I'll report you to the Chief Constable. We've had enough work and worry about this, and we're ready to stand up for ourselves, having as much common sense as most."

Much to Colonel Wynne's relief, Welby did not take umbrage; he laughed, quite good humouredly.

"All right, Mrs. Lambton—he's your patient and I don't want to retard his progress or upset his nurse. It's my duty to go upstairs and see him, but I don't want to question a sick man who may not be responsible for what he says. In any case, he has already stated that he collided with Dr. Robinson's car, so that's quite clear. Now, if you'll take me upstairs—?"

The blind was drawn in the small bedroom where Bob Parsons lay, his head swathed in bandages, but Welby could tell a sick man when he saw one. Parsons turned over restlessly and Mrs. Lambton said:

"You lie still, Bob. 'Tis quiet you want."

"There's Bess up there; I must go and see to her, she'll be in a state with me away all this time," said Bob. His voice was difficult to hear, thick and drowsy, but Mrs. Lambton replied at once:

"'Tis all right, Bob; you haven't got to worry about Bess. She's with Michael and Sue. They'll look after her. Now you try and have a sleep, do."

His eyes closed again, and Mrs. Lambton smoothed the sheets, patted his shoulder, and turned to Welby. The latter nodded and walked quietly out of the room.

"Who is Bess?" he asked, as they went downstairs again. "I thought he lived alone."

"Bess? She's his sheep dog; he left her chained up and that's about the last thing he remembers doing," replied Mrs. Lambton. "He'll be better to-morrow; they're often mazed after a knock on the head; his pulse is all right and he's not so hot as he was. Michael Dering's been up to Bob's place to feed his stock, and he brought the bitch back with him."

"I'll go along and see Dering now," said Welby. "I'll get Colonel Wynne to show me the way." He paused and then added: "You've had a lot of work and distress over this, Mrs. Lambton. I'm very sorry."

"Well, that's kindly said, Inspector, but we're used to hard work here—and we'd 'a been ashamed to do less than we have done," she replied.

3

Colonel Wynne walked with Welby along the streaming road.

"The next house on the left is Boars Wood," he said, "and the Derings' cottage is beyond that. The Doctor's garage is on the right here—just opposite his gate. He asked permission to put it up there because it's level ground. As you can see, his garden's above the level of the road."

"Yes—the whole place is on the hillside," said Welby. "Just come inside that garage, Colonel. I'd like a word with you."

"Right." Wynne stepped into the shelter of the wooden garage; its sliding door was right open, but as it opened to the east, the rain had not driven in.

"Every picture tells a story," commented Wynne, pointing to the uprights of the garage on either side of the entrance. They had both been splintered and knocked about by the bumpers of the car and it was obvious that the driver who had garaged his car here couldn't judge distances—or else was very careless.

"Yes. He couldn't have locked this door, could he?" said Welby. "The door post's all askew." He went inside and lowered his voice. "This business isn't as simple as it looked at first sight, Colonel. If my judgment's anywhere near right, the unidentified corpse wasn't killed in that smash last night. That man's been dead for two days at least, perhaps longer."

"Good God!" exclaimed Wynne.

"I may be quite wrong," went on Welby. "The onset and passing of rigor is a thing for the experts to argue about. I'd say that rigor had come and gone in this case—but I'm not an expert. I'm telling you this because I think those two bodies have got to be taken for a P.M. at once."

"I quite agree," said Wynne, and Welby went on:

"I've got to go on with the investigation here—that's my duty. I think the best thing to do, if you're willing, is to get the bodies in your van and for you to drive to this side of St. Olwens' bridge with Bowen. He knows the drill; once he's across the river, he can phone our headquarters and report. They'll take over then."

"You're quite right, Inspector. I'm here to assist the law and I'll do all I can. Now you want to load up immediately?"

"That's it, sir. Bowen and I can do that ourselves; we'll back your van into the farmyard, up against the barn door—it'll be easy enough that way. Now if you'd go and tell the Lambtons that Bowen and I are moving the bodies, there's no need for them to come out. They've had enough, anyway."

Wynne looked at Welby's inscrutable, intelligent face, and said: "Do you think they realised—?"

"I don't know, sir. As I tell you, I'm not that certain myself—but the sooner the P.M. is held, the better. You know..." He paused a minute, and then added: "If you hadn't been as determined as you were, if you'd given that river best, as well you might, and those corpses had stayed here a couple more days—well, there mightn't have been much to choose between them, so to speak."

"And I'd like to remind you—though I don't expect you need reminding—that those two young men walked out to my place last night to report what had happened. No one could have blamed them if they'd left it till to-day, Inspector. And by midday, I doubt if I could have reached that bridge at all. Our river isn't the sort of stream to take liberties with."

Wynne's voice was very quiet, but the Inspector was aware of a different note in it.

"I haven't forgotten any of that, sir. Now, if you'll just see the Lambtons stay indoors, Bowen and I will do our part of the job."

"Very good," replied Wynne; "but you won't want to stay here all night, and it's easier for me to provide transport for you than it is for the Lambtons, so I'll drive back again before dusk to pick you up. I can give you a bed. So far as I can see, the probability is that the bridge won't stand much more of this sort of thing, so you may be cut off, too."

"I'll risk that, sir; and I'm very grateful to you for your help."

4

The Colonel felt very unhappy as he walked back to the farm. He liked the Lambtons, and trusted them, but he was also aware of the solidarity that existed between country folk in a remote hill district like this. They would never give one another away. "Did Henry realise how things were?" Wynne asked himself. "He's intelligent; that fellow is much more intelligent than he'd ever let you realise in an ordinary way, and he took the lead in everything last night."

He rapped on the kitchen door and peeped inside. To his relief the whole family were sitting round the table at their midday meal.

"Please don't get up," he said. "I'll come in and sit by the fire for a bit if I may. The wind's still devilish cold."

"Come and join us, sir, 'tis a good meal, and the pie just out of the oven," said Mrs. Lambton.

"Thank you very much, but I mustn't do that—my wife will be keeping a meal for me," he replied; "but if that's a teapot I see, a good cup of tea would just suit me, and one of those good scones of yours, Mrs. Lambton."

He sat down by the fire and smiled at Gwynyth, who sat next to him.

"You've got a bonny rosy face, young lady—no need for the messes the town girls use." He smiled at her.

"I reckon they'd have red cheeks if they'd done my job this morning," she laughed back. "Thirty gallons of milk to put through the separator. The milk lorry didn't come, and the answer's butter—and my arms just about ache. But I'll bring you some lovely butter when Henry's got his old car going again—there'll be pounds of it."

The Colonel's quick ears caught the sound of the engine as his van was backed into the yard. Henry heard it, too, he was certain of that, but Henry made no comment. Instead he said:

"It's hard work making butter. If folks want farm butter when rationing goes, they'll have to pay for it. It wouldn't be worth our while to sell butter much cheaper than ten bob a pound, with milk the price it is and the time it takes to make the butter up."

"Ten shillings a pound. I never did hear such a thing!" exclaimed Mrs. Lambton. "Nobody'd buy it. Butter was eighteen pence the pound last time I sold it in the market—and lucky to get that."

To the Colonel's satisfaction, the whole family started arguing about the economics of butter making, and he drank his cup of tea without worrying whether they would notice what was going on outside. When he'd finished it, he stood up.

"I'm going to drive my van back, Mrs. Lambton. You know what that means—and once again, I'm grateful to you all for all you've done. Now don't get up, please. I shall be back here again before dusk, and if there's anything you're in need of, you can tell me then. It's no use talking about this sad business any more just now. The police have got their part to do and I'm sure they'll do it as considerately as they can. So now you all get on with the day's work and we'll hope things will get back to normal before too long."

"Indeed, we hope they will, sir," said Mrs. Lambton, "and we'd like to thank you for all your thought of us. Without you, I don't know where we'd 'a been."

"And I don't know where they'll be yet, God help them," thought the Colonel unhappily, as he drove cautiously up Hollybanks with the police constable beside him. "Perhaps that damned inspector's just guessing," he added hopefully to himself.

CHAPTER V

I

When Colonel Wynne had set off for St. Olwens, Inspector Welby went back to the Doctor's garage. Welby was an able and ambitious officer, and a very well-informed one. He had expressed himself very cautiously to the Colonel, but he had no doubts in his own mind that he was right. The doctor's unknown passenger had not been killed in the car crash last night: death must have occurred at least two days ago—if not sooner. It was the post-mortem discolouration that Welby had been going by—that wasn't all bruises, he said to himself.

"Two or three days ago," pondered Welby. "Thursday to-day; the thaw set in on Monday night. For a fortnight before that it was freezing hard—twenty degrees of frost there was—enough to freeze any corpse solid… There'll be some fine old arguments as to the time of death, but it wasn't last night."

Welby pulled the garage door to—it was a sliding door, on runners, and the metal groove and overhead rail were rusty. It took quite a lot of strength to move the door, and, as Welby had guessed, it was no longer possible to lock it. There was a spring lock on the door, but the tongue would no longer engage with the slot on the door post—the latter had been knocked out of the upright.

"Might be anybody's murder," he thought.

Leaving the garage, Welby walked on to the cottage where the Derings lived. It was an ancient building, mainly brick and timbering, with a tiled roof yellowed over with moss and lichens. There was stonework round the window frames, and fine stone door posts; the big built-out chimney was stone, too. It was a beautiful little building to anybody with an eye for architecture, but Welby was quick to notice the moss and lichen on the roof, the unpointed brickwork, the old ivy and the sagging roof-tree. "A hovel" would have been Welby's description of it; he had no interest in the picturesque; he liked doors and windows to fit, drains to function and taps to turn on and off, and he was pretty sure that Boars Wood Cottage could boast none of these essentials.

He rapped on the door with his fist, expecting to face "some clodhopper" when the door opened, for Colonel Wynne had made no attempt to describe the Derings. The door was opened by a slim dark girl, in a cherry-red jumper and dark skirt, as neat and trim as any city girl, with a poise which told of a well-exercised body and an independent mind. For all his townsman's bias, Welby was no fool; he recognised "quality" when he saw it, and by "quality" he didn't mean "class." He meant the sort of upbringing which developed independence and the ability to learn by experience.

"I'm sorry if I've come to the wrong house," he said civilly. "I was looking for Mr. and Mrs. Dering, Dr. Robinson's gardener and daily woman, that is."

"You haven't come to the wrong house," she replied. "I am Mrs. Dering; I cooked for Dr. Robinson, and my husband did the garden. He's indoors." She paused and waited for Welby to speak—a tacit demand for his business.

"I'm Inspector Welby. I came out to investigate the car crash last night. Would you and your husband answer a few questions?"

"Certainly—although we didn't see the crash, you know. Please come in."

She ushered Welby into a cottage kitchen which was quite unlike any other cottage kitchen which the Inspector had ever been in; he realised at once that it was tidy—as trim as the girl herself—and not choc-a-bloc with gear. A tall fellow stood by the fire—so tall that Welby had to look up at him.

"I'm Michael Dering," he said. "Please sit down. We're just having a cup of tea before I go out again. Would you like a cup?"

"Well... I wouldn't say no," said Welby. He had had no dinner and he was hungry. "It's still perishing cold, in spite of the thaw."

"Give him some cake, Sue. He's starved," said Michael, and in a moment Welby was sitting by the fire with a cup of tea and a large hunk of good fruit cake.

"We can't tell you anything at first hand about the car smash, because we didn't see it," went on Michael, "though my wife had a word with Bob Parsons when she was trying to tie his head up."

Susan Dering then went on: "The Lambtons had got Bob in the back of their Ford when I spoke to him," she said. "His head was bleeding pretty badly. I said I was sorry—the sort of feeble thing you do say when it's no use saying anything—and Bob said: 'If he'd only braked I could have got by. I think he muddled his brake and accelerator—he just shot out.'"

"That's about what it looks like," said Welby, putting his cup down. He turned to Michael. "Now if you'd just give me your full name, age, and so forth, and where you came from before you lived here, I needn't keep you long—just get all statements into the form the Coroner likes," he added.

"Michael Dering, age 35. Born in Sussex; served in the R.A.F., '39–'45. Farmed with my brother for five or six years—also in Sussex.

Wanted to get married and couldn't get a house—the usual story; tried growing fruit in Worcestershire and lost what money I'd got. Saw Dr. Robinson's advertisement in the *Western Morning News*, offering a cottage and three acres and a wage of sorts—so we took it. That the sort of thing you want?"

"That's it, thank you. In Worcestershire, you said, before you came here?"

"Yes. Greengates, near Upton. The chap I worked with was named Henson. He went to Canada when we went bust—Vancouver, I think."

"Right. Now, about last night. You'd been in St. Olwens?"

"That's it, shopped and went to the barbers. Left about five o'clock. We found the water was over the road this side of the bridge and we waded through—just in time. We were on our bikes. I suppose it was nearly seven when we got to Brynneys' Crest—it'd been hard going. Ken Hobson yelled at us and we got off to see what was up. You probably know the rest."

"Yes, but we like corroboration of evidence," said Welby evenly. "What did you do to start with?"

"To start with," echoed Susan, and the clarity of her voice almost made Welby jump. "We wished we'd got someone like you there, Inspector, someone very strong and reliable. You see, we all had to shove behind the Lambtons' old Ford, so that Henry could get it started on the hill and turn it at the top. We stood behind the Ford and shoved till we bust, Michael and Mr. Lambton and I, because the wheels wouldn't grip and its weight came back on us. That's the first thing we did. Then Michael helped Henry to turn the Ford at the top, on a road like glass with the rain coming down so that Henry couldn't see Mike's torch light at the back. Then—oh, I tried to tie up Bob's head with a wet handkerchief and a wringing scarf, while the others went to carry up the doctor's body—they'd got him out of the car before we came. But Ken had found another body at the back—he saw a hand sticking up from under a rug, in the light of his hurricane lamp—and he didn't like it, poor kid."

Susan broke off and Michael went on relentlessly: "Yes, we could have done with a chap your size, Inspector. Henry hacked his way into that damned car—it was half full of flood water, and he splashed around like a porpoise until he got a grip on Exhibit B. Then Will Lambton and I got hold of Henry's legs and hauled; it wasn't pretty, any of it."

"Just one question here," put in Welby. "The man's head was badly knocked about. Did you notice if he was still bleeding?"

Michael stared at him; then he said: "Sorry, we don't seem to have made ourselves clear. The chap was dead; he'd been lying face down in about two feet of icy flood water. Henry had had to hack away under the water to get him clear. Then we pulled him out—by main force. Dead men don't go on bleeding—particularly after they've been immersed in ice water. How much of the damage was done in the smash and how much by the recovery party I can't tell you. If we did the wrong thing from the police point of view, that's just too bad. If there'd been an earthly of getting the police to do the job, believe me we'd have been very happy to leave it to you."

Welby was silent for a moment; the anger in Michael Dering's voice hadn't been unobserved, but there was something else that made Welby wonder. A gardener—this chap? He didn't sound like any gardener Welby had ever known.

Welby merely observed: "Very good; if my questions sound foolish to you, I'm sorry—but let's go on to the next point. You have both of you seen the body we're talking about. Have you ever seen the man before?"

He looked from one to the other, and in turn they replied: "No. Never."

"Did Dr. Robinson often have any visitors?"

Susan replied to this one: "I have been at Boars Wood every morning for six months. On weekdays I was there from nine till twelve. On Sundays I went in and took a dish containing a meal ready cooked at twelve o'clock, and then came straight back here. I have never seen a visitor there. A canvasser called one morning, for the R.D.C. elections. Dr. Robinson refused to see him and told me he never wanted to see callers—neither canvassers nor parsons nor any other busybodies."

Welby turned to Michael, who replied: "I never went into the house, except to put coal, logs and kindling in the back porch. My job was to get the garden in cultivation, on the understanding I could market any surplus vegetables. The doctor bade me good day if he passed me, otherwise he left me alone. I certainly never saw a visitor."

"About the car," went on Welby. "Did you look after it for him?"

"I cleaned it. Once or twice I cranked it up for him, when the engine wouldn't start," replied Michael; "but he looked after it himself. He kept a lamp in the bonnet to keep it warm, and ran the engine a bit most days. I should think he'd been pretty careful with it—but he'd aged a lot these past few months."

"Where did he fill up?"

"Tennant's—the chap near Brynneys' Bridge. Tennant kept an eye on the tyres and battery, and did any odd job, I believe, but the car wasn't driven for more than a few miles a day, so there wasn't much wear and tear."

"What sort of driver was he?"

"You've heard that already," replied Michael. "He was a bad driver because he was too old to drive. I think he'd been a good driver in his time, but his eyesight was going, he was very deaf, and his reactions were slow. I asked Will Lambton to try to persuade the old man to give up driving—but Will hadn't the heart to do it."

"Have you ever driven the Buick yourself?"

"No. When I first came I offered to drive him; he said that when he needed a chauffeur he'd say so. Neither did he ever offer us the loan of the car when we went out."

Welby looked from one to the other. "He doesn't appear to have been an accommodating employer," he said.

Susan replied to that: "He was a harsh, curmudgeonly old man," she said quietly, "but we were sorry for him. He suffered a lot from rheumatism; old age had cut him off from all the things he took pleasure in—his fishing and shooting and bird-watching. He had no relations who cared about him, apparently. But he wasn't bad to work for. He left us alone and didn't interfere, and he didn't grumble. I think he was grateful—glad to have us here—though he didn't say so."

"Now, about his relations—next of kin," said Welby. "Do you know anything about any relatives?"

"Nothing," said Susan. "He didn't offer any information and I didn't ask any questions. You'll have to find out that from his private papers. We can't help you."

"I see." Welby turned to Michael again. "Did you ever go into the garage for any reason? I see it won't lock."

"I often glanced in after the old man had been fiddling about, and when he'd put the car away," said Michael. "You see, his eyesight was very bad, and he smoked a pipe sometimes. I'd have been sorry to see his beloved car go up in flames—and the garage was built much too near that small barn of the Lambtons'. But I hadn't been in the garage for some days, because the old chap couldn't get out in the snow. I never thought he'd take the car out yesterday. I know the snow had gone, but the roads were still wicked."

Welby nodded, then he said: "You both know the problem we're faced with—identity of the body in the back of the car, and how deceased got to St. Brynneys. Have you any suggestion to make which would help?"

Michael shook his head, but Susan replied: "Bob Parsons once told me that Dr. Robinson did sometimes give a lift in his car, particularly if he saw a man on the top road who was obviously coming to this village. He'd never offer a woman a lift, but he might a man. The only thing I can think of which might explain the mystery is that Dr. Robinson saw this man just as the rain was starting and offered him a lift."

"Well, that's worth bearing in mind, thank you very much, Mrs. Dering," replied Welby. He stood up, adding: "I take it that you have a key to Dr. Robinson's house—can I have it, please?"

Susan took a key from a hook on the dresser, saying: "That's the back door key."

"Thank you. I should like to say that I do realise you had a filthy time last night—and I don't underestimate what you did. Perhaps we C.I.D. men grow thick skinned through hearing too many horror stories, but I don't want you to think we're entirely callous. Thank you for answering my questions. I shall need to keep this key, but I may call in later if I need to ask you about the house—and thank you for the tea and cake, Mrs. Dering."

After Welby had gone, Michael said: "He might have been worse—and he wasn't quite so uppish at the end as he was at the beginning. I'm going to split some logs in the shed, Sue. There's nothing I can do outside; the soil's like a morass."

"All right. I hope he enjoys himself in that house; it's cold as a grave—but I didn't think it was my business to offer to make a fire for him."

"If he wants a fire, he can make it himself," replied Michael.

2

When Welby let himself into Boars Wood House, it wasn't many minutes before the dank cold made him shiver. It was an old farmhouse, and the ground floor was stone-flagged. The uncovered flags in the kitchen were dewed over with damp, and in the two sitting-rooms the carpets were wet to the touch, while the down-draught from the open chimneys filled the rooms with a noisome odour of wet soot and sodden ashes, for the rain had run down on to the dead fires.

"Rheumatism—I don't wonder, it's enough to cripple anybody," thought Welby.

It was very dark indoors, and the rain lashed viciously against the windows, while the pine trees in the shrubbery moaned in the wind. There was no electricity and Welby set to work to light the oil lamp; it was a Mantilla lamp and the town-bred Inspector knew nothing about these admirable objects. Consequently he only succeeded in blacking the mantle and having a proper old flare-up, so that fresh soot deposited itself on his cold hands and face. Welby swore—but he couldn't reconcile it with his dignity to go back to the cottage and ask Mrs. Dering to come and cope with the lamp. He hunted around in the kitchen until he found two old-fashioned lamps which he knew how to deal with, and he took these into the farther room which held a rolltop desk. There were books all round the walls on built-in shelves, a table holding an old-fashioned microscope and some naturalist's gear, a big old-fashioned armchair and a couple of Windsor chairs. It was a dreary colourless room, with a worn carpet and curtains which were obviously left-overs from wartime black-out.

"Hard up? Or past noticing? Unless he was a miser," thought Welby.

He settled down at the desk, unlocking it with the keys he had found in the old man's pocket, and set to work on the contents of the desk. At first he thought he was in for an interminable job, for the drawers were packed with papers, but he soon found that the top right-hand drawer contained all the business documents in a small iron cash-box (also locked). In about half an hour's time Welby had worked out details of Dr. Robinson's affairs as far back as 1940. In the spring of that year he had bought Boars Wood House and the cottage adjacent, together with garden, orchard and paddock, making three acres in all, for the sum of £1000. ("He got it cheap, but prices hadn't risen much then," thought Welby.) The fifteen acres of agricultural land which went with Boars Wood had been sold separately to William Lambton. In 1940, Dr. Robinson's income from investments was £400, all from good non-speculative industrials. Now it was less, because the doctor had been realising some of his capital to pay for the upkeep of the house and cottage, an expensive business in the 1950s—Welby found receipts for such expenses as repairs to the roof, outside painting, repairs to the cottage and so forth. The old man's income was now about £300 a year from investments, and he paid the Derings three pounds a week. Welby found the form of agreement, signed by Michael Dering—three pounds weekly plus the cottage, with the right to market the produce from the three acres of land he was to cultivate—"not a bad bargain for either side," meditated Welby. "The old man had got enough capital to see him through, and he could have mortgaged the property if he'd wanted to."

All this was straightforward enough, but search as he might Welby could find nothing to give him any information previous to 1940, no indication of any relatives, place of origin, or anything which connected Dr. Robinson with any people or places previous to his presumed retirement. The only clue was an entry in the earliest of the Bank statements: "Credit carried over from Stubbs' Bank, £300." Stubbs... that had been one of the few private banks which had carried on independently after the formation of the "Big Four." It had merged with the British Provincial on the outbreak of war, but Robinson had entrusted his account to the Western Counties, mused Welby. "St. Olwens' branch... they'll have his securities and his will," he thought to himself. "All the same, it's funny..."

He was now chilled to the bone, despite his topcoat and muffler, and he got up and stamped his feet, which were numb with cold, but he was an obstinate fellow. He determined to look through the other drawers to see if he could find any personal letters. He found himself examining letter after letter from Secretaries and Members of Naturalist Societies, Bird Watching Societies, Anglers... Fauna... Flora... Geologists... Long debates on the breeding of mallards, the nesting habits of the Red-Backed Shrike, Response to the Earth's Magnetic Field in the navigation of Migrants... Welby gave it best. He got up and decided to have a quick look round the house before the daylight failed completely.

3

Will Lambton was milking Buttercup again when Colonel Wynne looked into the cow house.

"Do you know where Inspector Welby is, Lambton?" he asked. "I said I'd run him back and put him up for the night."

"He went into the Doctor's house," said Will.

Ken chimed in: "He's still there, leastways there was a light there when I came back from the old barn—by the garage, that is."

"Right—I'll go along and find him," replied Wynne.

The Colonel walked along to Boars Wood, noted the gleam of lamplight in the front room and went and knocked on the front door. He got no answer. He knocked again, still with no result. He then tried to open the front door, but it was locked. With a feeling of exasperation he made his way to the back door, but this also would not open. He hammered on it with his fists, but obtained no result. Standing in the rain, the Colonel swore. He'd had enough of to-day. To his relief, a voice hailed him:

"What do you want, there?"

The voice was unmistakable—it was Dering's. The Colonel called back: "I came to fetch the Inspector. There's a light in the front room, but he didn't answer when I knocked—and I've knocked hard."

Michael Dering came striding across the lawn. "He got the key from us a couple of hours ago, sir. If the light's still on, he must be in the house somewhere."

"Devil take it," said Wynne. "He's not in the front room, I looked through the window."

"I wonder if he's fallen downstairs—Sue says they're a death trap—very steep and carpet in ribbons."

"Oh, my God," groaned Wynne. "We've had enough without that."

"I couldn't agree more," said Dering. "Look here, sir. I've got some tools in the shed—shall I force a window? The frames are all pretty rotten."

"Do—the sooner the better," said Wynne.

Michael ran over the sodden grass—Wynne noticed that water splashed up at every step, the ground as saturated as a sponge—and in a minute Michael was back with a big chisel.

"I'll force the kitchen window, sir, then climb in and open the door for you. This is your pigeon."

"I'll take the responsibility—get on with it," said Wynne.

The rotten woodwork crunched as Michael levered back the casement window; he had it open in a trice, got a foot on the sill and then nearly staggered back, as a huge black cat shot out past him and streaked across the grass.

"Confound the brute. How did it get shut in?" he exclaimed.

In another moment he was inside, and Wynne heard him unlocking the door. "The Inspector must have locked himself in, the lord knows why," he said.

"Welby's a townsman, used to locking doors," said the Colonel, switching his torch on. "Gad… what a house," he groaned. "Your wife must have had a job."

He went across the kitchen and into the passage, with Michael behind him. The sitting-room door was open, and the lamplight shone on the floor at the foot of the steep narrow stairs. Welby lay there on his face, looking very big and solid in his dark topcoat.

4

The Colonel's "Damnation" synchronised with Michael's "Oh, hell."

Then Wynne said: "He must have fallen downstairs, tripped over the cat or something…" He bent and moved the fallen man a little and Welby groaned.

"Not dead, thank God… Had about enough of this sort of thing, driving hearses all day long," muttered the Colonel. "Go and get that lamp, Dering—and turn it down. It's smoking like…"

Michael came back with the lamp and Wynne said: "Better turn him over, I suppose. Do you know anything about first-aid?"

"Not a thing," said Michael.

He bent and lifted the heavy Inspector carefully, turning him on his back, and Welby obliged with more groans.

"His legs aren't broken, so far as I can see," said Michael. "His ribs may be, and he's knocked out. What about it, sir?"

"I'll go and get my van and you and William Lambton can lift him in and strap him steady somehow," said Wynne. "I'll take him home with me and we'll see if we can get a doctor out somehow. You've had enough, and so have the Lambtons."

"Well, we'd do our best, sir, but we've only got one bed and we'd hate him to die on us," said Michael.

"I don't think he's going to die; he's a heavy chap and he fell heavily," said Wynne. "Before we do anything else, just go up those stairs and see if he caught his foot in the carpet."

Michael went up, holding the lamp; just before the top he said: "Here's the explanation—carpet's ripped right across. He caught his foot in it and slammed down on his face. There's no handrail and the steps are steep." He came down again, adding: "I'll go and back your van along to the gate and get Henry and a trestle to carry him on… he's a tidy weight."

"Good lad," said Wynne.

Michael ran off into the gathering darkness and the Colonel swore again. He was a humane man, but he was very tired and very cold, and he felt that Police Inspectors should have enough gumption not to fall downstairs. Then, rather ashamed of himself, he added to himself: "I expect that damned cat tripped him up, shot between his legs or something. It was scared stiff…" Then he sneezed, several times in quick succession. "God, what a house… poor old chap."

CHAPTER VI

I

"IT LOOKS A PRETTY KETTLE OF FISH TO ME," SAID THE ASSISTANT Commissioner at Scotland Yard. "They've got one corpse which may, or may not, be a week old, has probably been in cold storage, and came to light in a motor smash; a second corpse of which the one thing certain is the time of death. The remote hill hamlet which is the theatre of operations is cut off by floods surpassing any inundations in living memory, and the county C.I.D. officer who started the investigations promptly fell downstairs, suffering several broken ribs, one broken ankle and concussion."

"Well, sir, it sounds a most promising set-up to me," said Chief-Inspector Julian Rivers (also C.I.D., but Metropolitan Police). "May I add that I find your introduction very stimulating."

"Here it is—and I wish you luck," said the A.C., handing over a wad of typescript. "I also offer you my sympathy. The climatic conditions sound singularly repellent and the whole thing's a mess. But there is one good point; that's Colonel Wynne. I was on the Somme with Wynne; he was my C.O. when I was a sub-loot. He's got brains and he's a good chap to work with. It was he who suggested co-opting the military and using amphibious vehicles. But I believe their river's got completely out of bounds. You've got to cross the river to get to the scene of the incident, but the relevant corpses are this side—however, read it yourself. The fact is I never could understand the Welsh—"

"But it's not in Wales, sir," protested Rivers. "Loucester is in England."

"So it may be, but that report's written by a Welshman. Damn it, Rivers, it's as near poetry as makes no difference. But I couldn't very well refuse to help them: what with the floods and all the rest, they're fairly up a gum-tree."

"A gum-tree sounds a very good thing to be up, sir, judging from the pictures of the River Aske in this morning's paper," replied Rivers.

The A.C. waved a hand towards the typed report. "Read it in the train," he said, "and don't ever send me a report like that, Rivers. It's diffuse—picturesque... And don't get drowned. We're short-handed enough as it is."

2

Rivers read the report of the St. Brynneys case in the train. It was prefaced by a note from the Chief Constable, Major Trevor, who said that the extra work caused by the floods was creating considerable problems in the Loucester area, and that the situation was made more difficult by an accident resulting in the absence of one of his senior C.I.D. officers. "We should be very glad if the Commissioner's Office could investigate this case for us," he concluded.

Rivers glanced at the signature on the last page of the report—Evan Williams. Rivers showed the signature to Lancing, who was travelling with him.

"It was the name which made our old man so flippant," said the Chief Inspector. "It's an extraordinary thing; men of Scots extraction frequently get their hackles up when dealing with Welshmen, and vice versa."

"It's because both lots want Home Rule for themselves and resent the other's claim to attention," said Lancing. "Get on with it, chief. I'm panting to have the gen. It sounds a poem of a case to me—particularly the bit about the bloke who fell downstairs—if he did fall downstairs."

Rivers settled down to read the report, handing each sheet over to Lancing as he finished it. The two C.I.D. men had a first-class compartment to themselves "for consultation," and neither being averse to comfort, they were enjoying their journey—the more so with the prospect of the rigours which faced them at their journey's end.

"Well, I'll leave the argument about precise times of death to the experts," said Rivers, when he and Lancing had finished the report. "They are agreed on the essential point, that the bloke in the back of the car was killed more than twenty-four hours before the car crash."

"So it's a matter of 'Who put him in,'" said Lancing. "The doctor's car had been standing in the garage for a fortnight without being taken out, and for most of that time the temperature outside was at least ten degrees below freezing. The lamp in the bonnet would have kept the radiator from freezing, but it wouldn't have had any effect on the back of the car—or would it?"

"Very little," said Rivers. "The presence of the lamp would have raised the temperature at one end of the garage a few degrees. The bonnet of my car gets just warm to the touch when the lamp's inside, and that heat rises to the roof (you did all that in the fourth form), but I don't think it would have made any difference to the temperature at the back of the car, especially as the door of the garage had warped."

"So our subject was in cold storage to some extent," said Lancing. "Now there was a rug in the back of the car... Let's see... Henry Lambton chucked the rug out when he was coping..."

"Yes, and the rug lay in the flood water until next day, when the thrifty farmer went and salvaged it," said Rivers.

"We won't get much help from that," went on Lancing; "but it's not unreasonable to argue that the corpse could have been shoved in the back of the car while it was in the garage, and covered with a rug. The old doctor was very near-sighted, and he probably didn't go and peer in the back of his car when he went to fiddle with the lamp in the bonnet."

Rivers nodded. "I see you're working on a first hypothesis that it wasn't the doctor who put the bloke in the back."

"Well, don't you agree?" asked Lancing. "We both generally notice the same thing. If the old boy took the corpse for a ride to get rid of it, why was it still in his car when he was facing for home?"

"Yes, I agree with you there," said Rivers. "The track beyond the crossroads—Hollybanks, they call it—led up to a wood. If the doctor's motive in going out that day was to park the corpse somewhere off his premises, why didn't he heave it out and hide it in the wood at the top of the track? The stream which his car bounced into after the collision must obviously run parallel with the track—more or less. He could have heaved the cadaver into the stream and hoped the flood water would help to confuse the evidence before the corpse was discovered. But I can see no point in his turning the car and driving for home again with the incubus still in the back."

"Unless the corpse had stiffened so awkwardly he couldn't get it out," said Lancing. "Then he'd have been in a spot, wouldn't he?"

"I don't think an old medical man would have been beaten by that," said Rivers, "and if those three men are telling the truth, the second corpse wasn't rigid enough to make them suspicious. Welby was probably right in his surmise—rigor had passed off at that stage."

Lancing sat and pondered.

"Have we any conclusive evidence that Robinson *was* a medical man?" asked Lancing.

"None," agreed Rivers. "We haven't any conclusive evidence about him at all, except that he died when he was supposed to have died."

Lancing looked thoughtfully at the neatly typed report. "Evan Williams told us quite a lot," he said; "but why don't they remember that the fingerprint system is about the most foolproof *vade-mecum* the police force ever cottoned on to?"

"I know," said Rivers. "That's why our old man was so terse. It doesn't seem to have occurred to their innocent minds that we may have records of both their corpses at C.O."

3

The train was punctual, and the two Scotland Yard men were met at Loucester by a smart police car in charge of a worried-looking Inspector.

"Look here," said Rivers, after greetings had been exchanged, "you've got enough on your plates without looking after us in addition. We've got to go to the mortuary to see the two exhibits, but after we propose to get out to St. Brynneys somehow. I gather a shuttle-service has been organised by the sappers to get us across the river at St. Olwens, but we can drive ourselves on this side. A hired car would do—you probably need all your own outfits."

"Well, that's very considerate of you," replied the other. "Major Trevor has a car he can lend you if you're willing to drive yourselves. He's out at Wyvern at present; they're evacuating the low-lying houses and there's been some looting—shocking business, I'm ashamed to think of it happening."

"It always happens; it happened even in the blitz," said Rivers quietly. "Empty houses are like a magnet to some folks. Now you drive us to the mortuary, and tell us where we can collect Major Trevor's car, and we'll try not to worry you more than we must."

"We're thankful to have you, Chief," replied the other.

They got into the police car and were given all the information they needed about their route.

"Colonel Wynne knows you're coming," went on the Inspector. "He's going to put you up—there's no available hotel within miles, and the Colonel's house is within a few miles of St. Brynneys—and on that side of the river."

"Colonel Wynne's been very helpful all through," said Rivers, and the other replied:

"I'd say he has. If it hadn't been for the Colonel I can't think what they'd have done at St. Brynneys—dug a couple of graves, I suppose, and waited for the river to go down. All the telephone lines are still down that side of the river. You chaps can't have an earthly what it's like up in the hills there."

Rivers and Lancing eventually stood in the chill of the mortuary and looked down at the two dead faces—faces utterly contrasted, the underlying bony structure being fundamentally different. Dr. Robinson was long headed, and he had a grimly Wellingtonian profile, hatchet like, with a fine high narrow forehead. The other subject was round-headed, plump, with a button of a nose and heavy jowl—a face like a putty model which had spread a little.

Rivers only gave a brief glance at Robinson's remains, but he studied the other for some time.

"I've seen this one somewhere, Lancing... or else a photograph of him. The proportions of the face are infantile—all the features shoved together and a bulging forehead. I think we shall find him in records. We'll take their dabs and get them sent back to C.O."

They examined the clothes of the unknown man—they had been baked dry and were stiff to the touch, impregnated with the mud brought down by the flood water. The cheap shoddy suit, the underclothes, raincoats, socks and worn shoes were all the same reddish-brown now, stiff with the silt of upland sandstone.

"Let's hope we don't have to fall back on those to prove identity," said Rivers; "but I don't think we shall. This chap served time not so very long ago; he's been put to sewing mailbags—look at his hands. They were soft-skinned hands, and the fingers are calloused by the canvas and thread."

They found Major Trevor's car outside the mortuary and drove the twenty miles to St. Olwens, leaving the level arable land behind them as they headed for the hills, intermittently seen through a mist of rain. At St. Olwens the village constable met them, and in the fading daylight they were handed over to the Sappers, to be ferried across the Aske.

"The bridge won't last the night," said the sergeant. "The farther arch has shifted, and the water can't get away because the timber and stuff that's been brought down has dammed up the arch. Perhaps when they rebuild it they'll make a better job of it."

Rivers had seen some turbulent streams in his time, but he had never seen one that looked more vicious than the Aske did that February evening. The water was coming down in swirling torrent, bringing trees and gates and wreckage with it.

"The trouble is that the valley narrows just below—makes a sort of bottleneck, so that the water can't get away," said the sergeant.

"Have you had many casualties?" asked Rivers.

"No. There aren't any houses down by the river between here and St. Brynneys. The country folk know what the river's capable of, and all the farms are well up in the hills. Some of the houses near Wyvern are flooded, and a lot of beasts drowned, but that's because the river has risen higher than it's ever known to have done for centuries. You can see the headlights up yonder—that's Colonel Wynne's chap waiting for you. The Colonel's done a good job of work in this emergency—he ought to be decorated for it; that estate van of his has been a hearse and an ambulance and a travelling grocers all combined."

Half an hour later, Reeves and Lancing were being welcomed by Colonel and Mrs. Wynne in the hall of Maidencombe House, in front of a huge log fire, while Thomas seized their suitcases and the Colonel dispensed drinks "to keep the chill out."

"This is the exact reverse of what we expected, sir," said Rivers. "We were quite prepared to camp out in a barn or sleep in the car. I can't tell you how grateful we are to you for your welcome and hospitality."

"But we're delighted to have you," said Mrs. Wynne. "This house is much too big for us now the children have all got their own homes, and I feel I shall be one up on the grandchildren—they've never had Scotland Yard aces staying in their superior modern houses."

"You'll have plenty of fun and games when you get out to St. Brynneys to-morrow," promised the Colonel. "You'll be wading in flood water and soaked to the skin—no oilskins keep this rain out for long, so you know what to expect. We'll dry you out when you come back here, and give you dry beds—it's the least we can do."

4

"If you'd tell us all that you can about Dr. Robinson, sir," said Rivers. "Not only the bare facts of his residence at St. Brynneys, but the inevitable surmises roused by the fact that he chose to come and live in such a remote spot."

The two C.I.D. men were sitting in Colonel Wynne's study after dinner, and the Colonel was interested to hear Rivers's first approach to the problem which faced him.

"Ah—sounds as though you know a bit about country folk and their reactions to an unexplained newcomer," said Wynne. "You're quite right, of course. Robinson must have given the folks around him an inexhaustible topic for gossip and surmise. But all the gossip would be indoors, so to speak—it always is. They're incredibly careful not to discuss anybody outside their own immediate circle." He paused and then went on: "You've got to bear in mind the period at which he came to Boars Wood—1940. The bombing hadn't started, admittedly, but the word 'evacuation' was a commonplace, and it wasn't long before people were pouring out of the cities. There were no evacuees billeted in St. Brynneys—the billeting officer gave the place best—no school for the children, no buses, no shops, miles away up in the hills—no townsfolk would have stuck it."

"But the old doctor stuck it, sir," said Lancing.

"Yes. He did. Come to think of it, he was pretty shrewd in what he did say; it wasn't much, but it was enough to explain himself to some extent. He'd retired from practice—old age and poor health. He'd always wanted somewhere quiet to end his days; he liked fishing. He said he'd tramped up the Aske valley when he was a young man, and never forgotten it; when he came to retire, he went and stayed at the Angler's Arms in Wyvern and watched the local papers for a property he could afford—all quite reasonable. And he told the Lambtons he was a Londoner. You see, London's too far away for them to take an interest in it. If he'd said Gloucester or Hereford or Cardiff or Bristol, they've friends or connections in those places. They'd have done their damnedest to find out anything they could about him, but London's outside their scheme of things. Nevertheless, I've no doubt the Lambtons debated him *ad infinitum*. You see, he never had any visitors, he told them nothing of his kith and kin and he had scarcely any letters. I wasn't told all this directly, not given chapter and verse so to speak, but it seeped out in odd ways."

"He seems to have been accepted as a retired medical man," said Rivers. "As far as you know, did his neighbours put this to the test by consulting him? They're over ten miles from a doctor, and there must have been accidents and other emergencies when a doctor on the spot would be expected to oblige."

"Perfectly true, but Robinson made it clear at the outset that he had retired from practice and that he would not treat anybody for anything. All that he would do was to tell them if a complaint or injury was serious enough to make it necessary to consult a doctor, and give an unofficial opinion as to whether the remedies they used were on the right lines. So far as I can gather, he never went beyond the commonsense advice that any intelligent educated man could give regarding ailments and accidents, but also it's true that he was accepted as a retired doctor—I never heard any query expressed about that."

"Apart from the Lambtons, who were his immediate neighbours, can you tell us which people he would have had any contact with?" asked Rivers.

"Well, the Lambtons themselves could tell you that much better than I can," said Wynne.

"I understand that all right, sir, but I'm asking you," replied Rivers. "The more information I can get before I start asking questions in St. Brynneys, the better. It will serve as some sort of check and may suggest a line I could follow up."

"Right. I'll do my best. At least I understand the exigencies of life in a place like St. Brynneys," said Wynne. "Anybody living there—and this was even truer during the war—depends on the tradespeople who deliver food, to some extent. All through the war a grocer from Treffham acted as a sort of 'universal provider' to the country people in St. Brynneys, Pine Quarry and Slyne Pike. The grocer is called Davidson, and during the war he brought up all the foodstuffs once a week—bread, meat, groceries, paraffin, chemist's goods—practically anything he was asked to bring. I mention him because he's about the one and only person who has been inside Boars Wood once a week ever since Robinson came there. He'd know about the various housekeepers and married couples Robinson employed—and I gather he had a few questionable characters at one time or another. It was the devil of a job to keep domestics in a place like St. Brynneys."

"Did Dr. Robinson always house his domestics in the cottage?" asked Rivers.

"No. When Robinson bought the place there was an old farm labourer living in the cottage—Dai Owen. He paid five shillings a week for it and did a bit of gardening and wood chopping. Dai Owen died last August and Robinson got possession of the cottage and was thereby enabled to get the married couple who're there now—the Derings. Now, as to other people Robinson had any dealings with: there are the Evanses, at Slyne Pike. They've got a cottage and a couple of acres. Evans helps the Lambtons at haytime and lambing and so on, and both he and his wife have worked for Robinson at various times, but I believe they had a row over something—but it's no use me telling you about it. I just don't know the facts."

"Right—but can you tell me anything about the Evanses, sir? Are they natives of St. Brynneys?"

"No. They came there in 1919. Evans was then a young ex-service man; he couldn't get a job—I believe his home was in Bristol—and he tramped around doing casual labour and looking for a shack and a bit of ground where he could keep pigs. He's kept himself and his wife somehow, mainly by helping the Lambtons and any other farmers who wanted extra seasonal labour."

"What do you think of him, sir?" asked Rivers.

"Not much." The Colonel hesitated, and then added: "I've employed him here occasionally, fruit picking, hedging, walling and so forth. He's a good worker when he wants to be, but I don't trust him. I always believed he took his own rake-off and a bit more—but I may be misjudging him. I never caught him out."

Rivers glanced through his notes. "Now when young Parsons collided with Dr. Robinson's car, Parsons was on his way to the Evanses at Slyne Pike?"

"That's correct," agreed Wynne. "Parsons has a smallholding—he's a very industrious competent fellow—and he employs Evans for odd jobs. Parsons knew the Evanses must be hard put to it to feed themselves and their stock because the snow had prevented them getting supplies, and Parsons loaded up his van with supplies for the Evanses—very decent of him to think of it."

"Very decent," agreed Rivers, "but aren't the Lambtons nearer to Slyne Pike than Parsons is? You evidently think highly of the Lambtons, sir. Wouldn't you have expected the Lambtons to help the Evanses out?"

"The Lambtons would have helped if the Evanses had asked for help," replied Wynne. "I think Will Lambton had a few words with Evans—but you'd better find out about that for yourself."

"Right—all that may be very helpful," said Rivers. "Now, any other contacts, as we say?"

"There's Jack Tennant, the garage man across Brynney Bridge. Robinson used to fill up there, and Tennant serviced his car for him. That's about the lot: the Lambtons, the Derings, Bob Parsons, the Evanses, Davidson and Tennant. I think you'll find Robinson never spoke to the parson and never consulted a doctor, and he had no visitors and never went to see anybody."

"That's all very helpful, sir, thank you very much," said Rivers. "Finally, can you tell me if Parsons would have had any contact with Dr. Robinson?"

"I shouldn't think so," replied the Colonel. "I can't see any reason why he should. Bob Parsons is friendly with young Lambton, and it's probable they do some deals—most of the young farmers do a bit of trading on their own—so Parsons probably goes along to the Lambtons to spend an evening occasionally, but I don't think Robinson would have had any use for Parsons. He's a young chap—under thirty at a guess—and not given to being respectful. That goes for Henry Lambton, too; they're independent, these young chaps—not given to touching their caps or making allowances for their elders."

Shortly after this the consultation broke up and they all went to bed. Rivers, however, sat up for a long time. He had been given the notebook in which the unfortunate Welby had put down notes for his own guidance. Welby, of course, was still unconscious, and expected to remain so. The last entries had been made during and after Welby's visit to the Derings, but the notes were not in longhand; they were in a private shorthand presumably invented by Welby himself. Rivers sat with the notebook held close to the beam of his bedside lamp and puzzled over hieroglyphics whose main virtue was their indecipherable quality. He concluded that one of the characters stood for a question mark, and there were a number of such characters in the entry which was headed, in block capitals, Michael Dering.

Rivers gave it up as the grandfather clock downstairs struck midnight. "Better start again from the word 'go,'" he decided.

CHAPTER VII

I

"WE HAVE FOUND OUT WHO THE OTHER DEAD MAN WAS, Mr. Lambton," said Rivers. "He had been in gaol and we have records of all men who have served prison sentences. What we want to discover now is how he came to be here and who he came to see."

Rivers was sitting in the Lambtons' kitchen, in front of a heartening fire. Mrs. Lambton had said: "If I'd known we were going to have company I'd've lighted the fire in the parlour, but I'm not going to let no one sit in that ice house. Seems to me a thaw always drains the warmth out of a house—'tis the damp, likely—so come along and sit by the fire."

Henry was cutting logs on the circular saw with Ken. Gwynyth and her mother were busy churning butter in the dairy, so Rivers and Lancing were alone with Will Lambton, who rubbed his head in perplexity.

"Well, seems to me the easiest way is the commonsense way," said Will. "He was in the doctor's car so he must 'a come to see the doctor. There's not so many folk hereabouts; he didn't come here, that we do all know. He didn't go to the Derings because they were out. He never got to the Evanses—not in them shoes, he didn't. The roads was wicked and 'twas like glass up that hill to the Pike, and he never went near Taffy Williams—he's the shepherd out on Caerlyon. Drifted up, Taffy's place was, and no townsman'd ever have found a way through it. So it must 'a been the doctor's."

Lambton paused and then added: "You say he'd been in gaol and I'm not surprised to hear it. It's not right to speak against the dead, but when I saw his face—well, I reckoned 'twasn't a good face. And he was a town chap. The only townsman here was the old doctor, so it makes sense to me he came to see the doctor."

"How do you think he got to St. Brynneys, Mr. Lambton?"

"That beats me altogether," said Lambton. "We've been thinking it out—wouldn't be natural not to. At first, we reckoned he must 'a come by bus to Brynneys' Bridge; there's a bus passes the other side o' the bridge Wednesdays, but the bus conductor—he's a St. Olwens chap—I'm told he says there was no one on the bus he didn't know, and by the time the bus passed the bridge the flood was over the road this side, and I don't believe that chap would ever have waded through flood water. No. I think Henry's right. Henry said the chap must 'a come earlier in the day and got a lift from St. Olwens. He could 'a walked down from the pointer top of Hollybanks while we was all having our dinner in here and got to the doctor's without being seen." Again Lambton paused, and Rivers waited for him to finish. Rivers was a patient investigator and he wanted to hear what explanation the Lambtons had worked out.

"In a manner of thinking, it explains why the doctor took his car out with the roads in that state," went on Will. "He wanted to get rid o' the chap and he said he'd put him on the road a bit so's he could get a lift later, maybe. That's the best I can make of it," he concluded.

"And it's a pretty good effort, Mr. Lambton," said Rivers. "I wanted to hear how you explained things for yourselves, because I was pretty sure you'd have a go at it, but there's one fact I haven't told you, and

I think it's better that I should tell you, because I want your help. The man in the back of the car—he called himself Jack Brown—wasn't killed in the car smash. He was killed well over twenty-four hours before the smash. In other words, Dr. Robinson had a corpse in the back of his car when the crash occurred."

Lambton stared back at Rivers—stared without a word. When he did speak he spoke slowly.

"Poor old chap... poor old chap... So that was the way of it."

"You weren't surprised to hear that," said Rivers quietly.

"Well... I didn't know. Maybe I wondered—but 'twasn't my business, and anyhow, if you'd seen how us manhandled that other chap out of the back of the car 'twas enough to explain anything that didn't seem natural. 'Twas a rough business—had to be, him half wedged down and the torrent running through the car." He broke off. "So maybe he did it a' purpose, the doctor did; crashed into Bob as being the easiest way out, poor old chap. Mind you, sir," he added, "we may have wondered why a gentleman like the doctor lived here the way he did. I'm not saying we didn't wonder, but he's lived here nigh on thirteen years and all that time I've had nought against him. He was our neighbour, he treated us fair, and many's the friendly word I've had with him about the birds he was always watching. So it wasn't for us to go thinking unneighbourly, even though we did wonder if there was a bit of trouble behind him. But if trouble found him out, well, I can see the old man going his own way to settle it—and maybe that's what he did."

"Maybe it was," said Rivers; "but I've been sent here to get things a bit straighter, and the first thing to find out is how Jack Brown got here and when he came. He didn't come here on the Wednesday—the day of the car crash—because he was dead by then. The pathologists believed that he'd been dead for three days when they examined his remains on Thursday evening."

"Three days... Thursday, Wednesday, Tuesday..." Lambton counted back slowly. "He never got to St. Brynneys on Tuesday, that I do know," he went on. "'Twas the worst day of the lot, Tuesday were."

"Suppose you tell me about the weather from the time the snow started," suggested Rivers. "You know what the roads were like during that period."

"That I do," agreed Lambton. "Now if you want to get this straight, we'd better go back a bit. January came in wet: poured, it did, up till the last week. Then the wind changed with the moon and blew from the north-east—bitter, 'twas, and hard frost with it—I knew it'd be snow if that wind kept on. The snow started the night of February 1st—a Friday that was. I remember the day because my wife was put out—'Candlemas to-morrow,' she said, 'and how'm I to get a bunch of snowdrops for the churchyard with them all deep in snow?' She always takes snowdrops to put on her dad's grave at Candlemas, him having died that day. And once the snow started, it never let up. Ten mortal days we had of it, and drifts deeper than I ever did see."

"Were the roads impassable all that time?" asked Rivers, but Lambton replied:

"Nay, 'twere not that bad at first. The Council, they kept snow-ploughs going and the milk lorry got through to Brynneys' Crest somehow. Jimmy—he's the lorry driver—he used chains and he brought a mate with him, for they had to dig a way through some days. Henry and Mike and me, we kept Hollybanks clear so we could get the tractor up with the milk kits on the trailer, and a time we had of it, I tell you, no sooner cleared a way than it snowed up again. And it wasn't till last Monday—the eleventh that was—it gave over. The wind changed and it thawed all in a rush. That's what started the floods, the thaw coming so sudden. And Tuesday—that was the hell of a day, that was, begging your pardon. The snow turned to mush and you'd be knee-deep in it before you knew where you were. Jimmy and his lorry gave it a miss that day—couldn't make it nohow—but we stuck the milk kits in the snow and reckoned the milk'd be as good as ice cream for a bit, and Jimmy fetched it all away Wednesday morning. But no one got through on Tuesday, that I'll swear, least of all a chap in shoes like that chap had."

"Well, it's quite a problem, isn't it?" said Rivers. "You say the milk lorry got through every day until the Tuesday. Could a car have got through after the lorry had cleared the way?"

"That it couldn't. The milk lorry's a big heavy outfit, built high, too—it had to reckon with bad going up in our hills and it's got a wide wheel base and powerful engine. No car could've got through. I reckon Henry's a better driver than most, but he wouldn't've tackled it—he knew better. And Bob Parsons with his jeep, he wouldn't try—not after he stuck once, on a drift close to's own back door. He dug the jeep out and put it away, and he walked here that evening—last Friday, 'twas—to get some physic for a sick heifer. But there's not many fellows would ha' done it; hard going, that was, and no mistake."

"All right," said Rivers cheerfully, "I'll take your word for it."

"You ask Henry if you don't believe me," replied Lambton, "or ask Bob Parsons, or young Dering. Ask the Evanses up at Slyne Pike—fair stuck they were, for days. Or you ask Jimmy Wetherby who drives the lorry—he'll tell you what 'twas like."

"Well, what it amounts to is this, isn't it?" said Lancing; he had been taking notes and he read out: "No motor vehicle except a powerful lorry fitted with chains could have got through to St. Brynneys after the night of Monday, 1st Feb., and in order to get the lorry through it was manned by a couple of sturdy chaps with shovels to dig it out when it got stuck. A tractor could get up and down Hollybanks hill, but the snow had to be cleared for it every day. A vigorous man, properly shod, could walk from Parsons' farm... Pine Quarry, is it? How far's that, Mr. Lambton? Five miles?"

"All of five miles—and he'd 'a needed to know the roads and where the drifts was."

"O.K.," went on Lancing. "The first day the roads were fit for ordinary traffic was on Wednesday, the 13th. The previous day the melting snow made the roads impassable."

"That's it—and not only the melting snow, either. The ground was froze solid underneath, and when the snow melted atop in the soft air that froze to ice again before 'twas through. Wicked, 'twas."

2

"Let's put it this way, Mr. Lambton," said Rivers, after Will Lambton had told them a bit more about the state of the roads between 2nd February and 13th February. "It seems pretty improbable that Brown could have got here between the second and the thirteenth. But if it was on the thirteenth he arrived, he was brought here. He was dead on the thirteenth."

"And who brought him?" asked Lambton. "And when did they bring him? I tell you no one drove down Hollybanks Tuesday night. Henry and me and Ken, we went out after milking Tuesday evening and we chucked ashes over the road at the bottom, just to give the tractor a chance when we took the milk up Wednesday morning, knowing Jimmy'd never bring the lorry down Hollybanks. And next morning them ashes showed nobody'd driven down the hill after we spread them. Henry and Ken can both tell you that."

"Good for them," said Lancing cheerfully, "they're the sort of chaps we like—chaps who notice things. But what about coming to St. Brynneys from the other direction? If you come here from

St. Olwens—the way we came—you have to come down Hollybanks to reach these houses, but there's a road from Brynneys' Bridge, isn't there?"

"There is that," replied Lambton; "but you couldn't ha' driven that road between Sunday night and Wednesday morning. The telephone wires came down in the snow and brought a pole with them. 'Twasn't till Wednesday mornin' the Post Office chaps came and cut that clear."

"Well, the only answer seems to be that someone brought Brown's body on Wednesday morning," said Lancing.

Lambton got up, and went and opened the kitchen door and let out a shout. "Hi, there, Henry—and you too, Ken. You come along in here."

Henry and Ken came to the door and rubbed their muck-laden gum-boots on the sacking in the porch, and then took off the sacks from round their shoulders.

"You tell these two gentlemen what we was doing Wednesday morning," said Will Lambton. "Tell 'em quite clear, so's they can see for themselves."

"Carting turnips and oat-straw, and dumping them in the shed where the cutter and grinder stand," replied Henry, answering with the prompt clarity which Rivers soon found was characteristic of him. "We opened a clamp of turnips in the three-acre—just past the Derings' cottage that is. Ken was at the clamp, I drove the tractor and trailer and Dad got some of the turnips stored and some cut up. Then we shifted some of the oat-straw we'd stacked in the three-acre. At it all the morning, we were; back and forth, seeing we were short of fodder after the snow."

"That's right," said Ken.

"Did you see any car on the road, or anybody passing?" asked Rivers.

"So that's it, is it?" asked Henry, and his tone was not complimentary. "Yes; we saw Tom Baines on his bike—the postman, that is. First time he'd got through for ten days and don't blame him—and we haven't seen him since. And we saw Mike Dering and his missis go out on their bikes just before we knocked off for dinner, but there wasn't anyone else. Do you think we wouldn't have noticed?" he asked Rivers. "We hadn't seen a soul from outside for ten mortal days."

"Thanks, that's all right," said Rivers. "We've got to ask questions, you know. It's our job—just as carting fodder's yours. Now, about the Derings, they rode to St. Olwens, didn't they? So if a car had come along that road they'd have met it."

"They didn't meet anything," replied Henry. "Folks wasn't in a hurry to drive over Brynneys' Crest after the packet we'd had. Them as knows these hills don't try hurrying out while the ice is still in the ground."

"Ken," said Will Lambton, "you go and get on with grinding them oats. Henry, you stay here."

Ken did as he was bid without a word of argument, and Will turned to Rivers.

"Tell Henry how 'twas, sir. Henry's a better head for puzzles nor what I have."

In words as terse and succinct as Henry's own, Rivers told the problem of the dead man in Dr. Robinson's car and Henry listened in silence, his intelligent eyes on Rivers's face. There was a moment's silence, then Henry said:

"He was dead afore Wednesday... Well, no one got a dead man down Hollybanks Tuesday, and no one brought him Wednesday because one or other of us would've seen them at it. There's only two ways makes sense. Either the chap was here, living in the doctor's house, since the snow started, or else he was never here at all—and I reckon that's likeliest."

"Go on," said Rivers.

"Dr. Robinson, he drove up Hollybanks while we was milking," went on Henry, "and he went across the top road, same's he always does, to turn his car in the clearing by the wood. My guess is he found the body up there. The chap had set out to walk somewhere that evening the snow started; he took a wrong turn and got to the wood instead of keeping to the main road—and he lay down and died there and he'd been there ever since, under the snow. The doctor, he heaved him in the back of his car somehow and set out to bring him down here—and forgot to look both ways."

"That's a reasonable reconstruction," said Rivers; "but do you think an old man like Dr. Robinson could have lifted the man's body? If it had lain under the snow the body was probably frozen stiff."

"You're wrong there," said Henry; "but one thing at a time. Could the doctor have lifted the body? I reckon he could. He was stone deaf and half-blind, but he was still pretty strong. You try shoving that garage door of his; it's warped and the runners are rusted, and it takes a real shove to get that moving, but he did it all right. He might ha' been stiff in the knees with rheumatics but he was still strong. And that body wasn't frozen stiff, not when I got it out o' the car—Dad knows that, and Michael. They helped carry him. If a body's covered up by snow it doesn't freeze solid—I should know, I've got sheep enough out of drifts. It's—well, it's like chilled meat. Mayn't be a pretty way of putting it, but it's about right. The chill keeps it from rotting, maybe, but it's not frozen through. I've often wondered about that, but I know it's true. Water in a tank'll freeze solid, but a sheep under the snow don't."

"That's right, son," said Will.

Rivers turned to the farmer. "Do you think that's a reasonable suggestion, Mr. Lambton—about the man collapsing and dying up there in the snow?"

"Well, sir, I can't see nought against it. 'Twas killing weather, right 'enow. If he set out before the snow started he might ha' walked from St. Olwens—or got a lift part way—and just got lost in the snow and lain there. None of us had been up to the wood there since the snow started—and we shouldn't a' noticed nothing if we had, not till the thaw came."

Rivers turned to Henry again. "You're thinking that this man Brown set out to see somebody in St. Brynneys," he began, but Henry promptly chipped in:

"I'm not thinking nothing of the kind," he said. "He was on the road and the snow caught him and he turned off—lost, maybe, or thinking he'd find shelter. He may have fallen down, banged his head or somesuch and gone silly, and that was that. He'd not've got up again. You say he was a gaol bird sometime. Likely he was on the run—that sort often is. But I don't see there's a thing to prove he was looking for someone in St. Brynneys." He broke off abruptly, looking at Rivers with his deliberately inquiring stare, quite unafraid. Then he said: "If that's the lot, I'd better go and see that kid doesn't muck the tractor up again."

"Right you are—and thanks very much for answering all my questions," rejoined Rivers.

3

"I'm simply fascinated by Henry," said Lancing. "He's got the sort of mind that makes a good Counsel. If Henry had had a university education he'd have read law and taken silk."

The two C.I.D. men were sitting in the Colonel's Bentley, which, with superb altruism, he had insisted on lending them. "That rattle trap of Hugh Trevor's will never cope with our hills. You chaps want something that'll get you there and bring you back, no matter what," he had said. Mrs. Wynne, as generous as her husband, had packed a picnic-basket, including thermos flasks of hot soup and coffee for the two C.I.D. men. "The Lambtons are sure to offer you a meal, but you may find it more convenient to be independent, and the heater in the Bentley makes it very comfortable to picnic in," she had said.

Rivers could only say "God bless you." And Lancing added "Amen." (Lancing was a very good driver, and he enjoyed the Bentley to the full.)

After leaving the Lambtons, Rivers and Lancing had driven up Hollybanks, crossed the main road and parked in the clearing near the wood. When they had arrived there, the sullen rain had stopped for a while and they had been able to see across the flooded valley to the heights of the Creffyn and Dragon Tor, still capped with snow, but, even as they gazed, curtains of mist reformed and hid the great range of encircling hills, gradually creeping across the valley to settle on Hollybanks and its woods. They retired to the car and enjoyed their picnic while they discussed Henry.

"University education or not, Henry's got a clear head and he's made out a perfectly reasonable case," said Rivers. "It's the sort of case a country jury would be likely to accept, because it's based on common sense—but we can't accept it until we've sorted out the imponderables. Henry says there's no proof that Brown ever came to St. Brynneys or that he had any connection with anybody in the place. My own belief is that Brown came here to blackmail Dr. Robinson. Brown was jugged for attempted blackmail in 1945 and he may well have tried it again. These old lags nearly always repeat themselves."

"Henry didn't offer any explanation of the fact that Brown had nothing on him to identify him by," said Lancing, "tho' I suppose you could get out of that by saying that old lags are chary of carrying identifiable papers. But you know I was very taken with the casual way Henry suggested that Brown had had a tumble or crashed into a tree."

"Yes, I was very much interested in that, too," said Rivers, "and he knew quite a lot about corpses which have been buried under the snow, but I can't believe that Henry knew enough to distinguish between pre-and post-mortem injuries. Brown's skull was bashed in before he died, and the post-mortem injuries inflicted in the car crash were easily distinguishable to the surgeons who examined the corpse—yet Henry is ready with an explanation of the original injuries."

"Henry could have emptied Brown's pockets," said Lancing. "Henry drove down the hill with the corpses ahead of his father and Ken and Mr. and Mrs. Dering—and Brown's body was the uppermost one in the car. It'd have been easy—get Bob Parsons into the house and run back to the car… and afterwards go through Brown's pockets in the presence of a witness when they'd got the bodies into the barn."

"Admitted," agreed Rivers; "but can you see Henry Lambton getting into the sort of mess which would make him a subject for blackmail?"

"I don't know," said Lancing; "but I can see Henry bashing a blackmailer over the head with a spanner, and being very efficient afterwards."

"Possibly—but where could be the connection between Henry Lambton of St. Brynneys and Jack Brown, late of Balham High Road, London?" asked Rivers. "The connection between Jack Brown of a dozen aliases and Dr. John Robinson, once Dr. James Robertson-Barr, is comprehensible enough."

Rivers drew a telegram from his pocket and read it aloud:

"Just to refresh your memory," he said. "Jack Brown, alias Bertram, alias Jones, alias Owen, etc.: Aged 45. First convicted 1935, Central Criminal Court, conspiracy to extort money with threats, sentence, three years. Convicted again 1941, Wandsworth Police Court, looting in blitz, sentence twelve months. Convicted again 1945, Lewes Assizes, attempted blackmail, sentence two years. Last convicted 1949, Reading Assizes, fraud, sentence three years. That's Brown, alias Bertram, etc. Now for Dr. Robinson. Dr. James Robertson-Barr, aged 72, general practitioner, Croydon, Surrey. Convicted 1939 for stealing rare and valuable books from the shop of Messrs. Edmund Blackwater, Friar's Place, St. James's, S.W.1. Sentence, six months, previous good character taken into account. Discharged, September 1939. There, in brief, is the story which led a scholarly old man to take refuge in a remote hamlet on the Welsh border, where no one would ever have heard of his disgrace," said Rivers. "That part's plain enough. His prosecution and conviction would have made headlines in his own locality and it's reasonable to suppose that Brown, who was free at the time, might have read the case, and the rest may have followed. I grant you I'm making an assumption for my own convenience, but the assumption seems to me a more reasonable one than that Brown got on the trail of Henry Lambton."

"Yes. You're being reasonable, or moderately reasonable," agreed Lancing, finishing the last of Mrs. Wynne's excellent ham sandwiches. "You're arguing that Brown remembered the story of Dr. Robertson-Barr over a period of thirteen years and that some chance enabled him to connect up Robertson-Barr and John Robinson. But what on earth could have brought Brown alias Bertram alias Jones to this part of the country?"

"You like guessing—have a go," said Rivers, "and have some more coffee. It's very good coffee."

Lancing accepted the coffee—and the challenge."

"Brown, discharged Reading Gaol just under a year ago," he began; "known to the police in the Metropolitan area and the Home Counties;

decides to give those area a miss and treks westward ho. Tries his luck in places like Bristol and Cardiff… seaports are always happy hunting ground for old lags, don't we know it. Makes Cardiff too hot for him and takes to the road again, hitch-hiking up the estuary—Newport, Monmouth… or perhaps he went north, there's a good main road from Cardiff to Caerphilly, or Newport to Abergaveney, and from there he could beat it back to Hereford… if he hitched he might have passed through Loucester—you can't be too choosey when you're hitching."

Lancing broke off, and Rivers said: "Thanks—you're always helpful, chum. We'll fall back on good old routine again after we've given the other residents here the once-over. If Brown trekked westward ho as you've suggested, I bet he did so to contact some friends he'd made in jug. If blackmail, fraud, and extorting with threats didn't pay good divvies, try some honest housebreaking for a change. N.B.—Ask for list of recent incidents from Loucester."

"That's all according to Cocker, but it doesn't tie up with Henry Lambton," complained Lancing.

"I'm not trying to connect up with Henry Lambton," said Rivers. "I'm going to try to find out if there were any incidents near enough to this neighbourhood for Brown to have had a chance of setting eyes on Dr. Robinson—or variations on that theme."

"Oh, well, if you'll admit variations, let's get down to it," said Lancing.

CHAPTER VIII

I

"Henry Lambton made two suggestions, both very sensible ones," said Rivers.

He was talking to the Derings, sitting in the tidy kitchen which had struck Welby as out of the ordinary. Lancing admired it, and had said so, straight out. The whitewashed walls, blue and white gingham curtains, blue pottery, and bowls of bulbs on the window-sills had the charm of a deliberately composed still-life.

"Henry said, 'Either Brown came here before the snow started and was living in the doctor's house all the time, or else he never reached the village at all, but died in the snow up by Hollybanks wood,'" went on Rivers. He turned to Susan, adding: "From your point of view, Mrs. Dering, was it possible that Brown was living in the doctor's house during the snow-up?"

"It is not *im*possible," she said. "It's quite a big house, and the only rooms I ever went into were the kitchens (including dairy and washhouse), the sitting-room, the study, as he called it, and his own bedroom. I believe there are five bedrooms altogether, but I never went into them." She paused, accepted the cigarette Lancing offered, and went on: "Shall I tell you exactly what I did—daily routine?"

"Yes, please do," said Rivers.

"I went at nine every morning, letting myself in at the kitchen door, put a kettle on the Primus and got the kitchen fire going. Then I cooked breakfast for the doctor and he had it in the kitchen while I did the fireplace and cleaned the sitting-room a bit. Then I went upstairs and made his bed and tidied up as best I could, while he washed and shaved at the kitchen sink. I can tell you I didn't stay upstairs longer than I had to—it's colder than any house I ever imagined—and I never went exploring, it's all too utterly sordid and depressing. By the time I'd given those ghastly stairs a lick and a promise and swept the hall and porch out, the doctor was generally sitting crouched over the sitting-room fire. He never talked to me—poor old man—and I got used to saying nothing, because he only grunted. Then I went into the kitchen, which was warm by that time, swept it out, washed up, and cooked his dinner. I left a meal ready for him in the oven and came home about twelve o'clock. I always saw there was some soup for his supper, and Mike brought plenty of firing in, so he was comfortable enough in his own grubby way."

"Look here," said Michael. "I feel a bit cheap over this. You must think I'm a pretty dirty dog to let my wife in for a job like that."

"You didn't let me in," said Susan indignantly. "I took the job on with my eyes open." She turned to Rivers. "We both want to live in the country and cultivate," she said. "We like it—I can't tell you why. You either do or you don't. We've no capital, and we'd failed at fruit growing. When we saw Dr. Robinson's advertisement in the *Western Morning News* offering a cottage and three acres of land plus three pounds a week, it seemed worth while looking into it. We came here and saw it; the land was quite good land but foul and overgrown; the doctor's house was in the same state as the land, but Mike said he could cope with the land and make a do of it later, and I said I'd cope with the house. It was a dirty job, admittedly, but it might have been worse. Dr. Robinson didn't interfere and he didn't grumble—and I was sorry for him. I thought when the summer came I could get the house properly cleaned. I don't mind housework—provided I haven't got to work for some yattering woman who follows you round all the time and tells you her life story."

Lancing laughed, and she flashed a smile at him. "I didn't mind my part of the job, and we adore this cottage—and we love the Lambtons. We've been very happy here," she ended soberly.

"Well, thanks for telling us all that," said Rivers. "Incidentally, I was country bred myself—I was born in Norfolk—so I do understand about people who'd rather work in the country than in towns. Now getting back to the possibility that Brown was living in the doctor's house during the snow-up, could you tell anything by the food that was eaten? I take it that food must have been rather a problem when the tradespeople couldn't get here."

"Not so much as you'd think," replied Susan. "We had no bread for a week, but I'd plenty of flour and I made scones. We had potatoes, and eggs and milk in abundance, and Mrs. Lambton sent the doctor a big piece of fat bacon, and we'd got things like rice and macaroni. In a place like this you keep a good store of groceries. You want to know whether two men could have lived on the food I cooked for the doctor. I suppose they could—but I'm pretty sure they didn't. The old man hadn't much of an appetite, and whatever I cooked there was always some of it left over. I'm perfectly certain nobody used any of the stores, not even potatoes, because I'd begun to wonder how we'd manage if we were cut off much longer. I almost counted things. And then nobody did any extra cooking—I should have spotted that at once, because I do keep the range and sink and saucepans clean, and very few people do things quite as you do them yourself."

Rivers turned to Michael, who was obviously longing to butt in.

"Look here," said Michael. "You're obviously considering the possibility that Dr. Robinson disposed of this chap—batted him over the head, or whatever it was. I can't see the sense of keeping him in the house for ten days on half-rations in order to kill him later. Isn't it more probable that he killed him early on and hid his body in the car, covered with a rug? Nobody would have ever known. He could have locked the car. Anyway, no one was likely to look in the back of it, and the weather was so perishing cold that there wouldn't have been any aftermath, so to speak."

Lancing asked promptly: "Did he generally lock the car?"

"I don't know, I never tried it," replied Michael; "but even if he did, I bet he was like every other car owner—he locked the door by the driver's seat and sometimes forgot all about the rear doors. Besides, he sometimes forgot to close the windows. I do know that, because I've looked into the garage to see his lamp was O.K., and I've seen the window down."

"So anybody could have put it there," said Susan, her clear voice utterly depressed. Then she added: "I don't believe the old man killed anybody. You haven't seen him, as I have, crouching over the fire; he just wasn't interested enough to kill anybody—not even himself. There was no spirit left in him."

2

"During the time you've been here, did Dr. Robinson ever drive far afield—as far as Loucester, for instance?" asked Rivers.

"Good lord, no!" exclaimed Michael. "He didn't even go as far as St. Olwens. After the first few weeks we'd been here he asked us to go to the bank in St. Olwens for him. He didn't give us the cheque uncovered, so to speak; he gave Sue a letter and we'd hand it to the cashier and look the other way and we were given a sealed envelope to take back. I know that meant he hadn't the nerve to drive in St. Olwens any longer, because he was very secretive and he hated asking us to do anything—and a good thing he didn't drive in traffic. He was a proper terror to pass on the road, you never knew what he'd do. Ask Henry and Ken—they've had some."

"The last time he drove anywhere except on the roads round about here was just before Christmas," said Susan. "He went over Brynneys' Bridge, and he hit the parapet as he turned on to the bridge coming back and buckled his wing. The garage man rushed out and helped get him clear before anyone else came by, so it wasn't reported. Davidson told us about it—the grocer. But he never drove over the bridge again after that. I think he hated driving, but it was the only way he could get out. I suppose he'd got arthritis in his knees and hips—it was simply grim to see him go up and down those awful stairs."

"Did he take the car out every day when the roads were all right?" asked Rivers, and Michael nodded.

"Yes, every day; about eleven in the morning. He would drive past Lambton's and a little way down that hill that leads to the river. He pulled in to the clearing in front of the tractor shed which Henry put up—it's wide enough to turn a car there, and Henry had put down a load of tarmac to have a decent surface when he was working on the tractor. If it was a sunny day he'd sit there for quite a while. Then in the evening he'd go up Hollybanks to the wood at the top to see the sun set—or hope to see the sun set. Will Lambton says he used to have a 'hide' in Hollybanks wood where he watched the birds, but it's a long time since he saw any birds, poor old chap; he couldn't see a white Leghorn in the road in time to avoid it."

3

"Do you know anything about the Evanses?" asked Rivers and Michael shook his head.

"Very little. I don't like him, and they don't like us. You see, Evans is always out to make a bit. I believe he's quite a skilled man and can turn his hand to most things. When we first came here the cottage was in a real muck. Sue and I can paint and paper and colour wash, but neither of us could replaster a ceiling. Evans came along and saw me when we moved in and said he could plaster, so I had him in. He could plaster all right, but he rooked me over the price. I didn't haggle—I don't believe in haggling when you're newcomers to a place—but I wouldn't have any further dealings with him and he resents it. But he's been here a long time and managed to make a living out of that rotten bit of land he's got."

Lancing put a word in here. "I'm rather surprised the Evanses didn't get their foot in here. Wouldn't it have suited them to have this cottage and your potentially fertile three acres—plus three quid a week?"

"Of course it would," said Susan, "and of course they tried to get their foot in, but Dr. Robinson wouldn't have them at any price. Mrs. Lambton told me that. The doctor employed Evans to paint the house when he first came here and they had a row over the bill. Evans always tries it on—he's a silly ass, really, because he queers his own pitch."

"Can Evans drive a car?" enquired Lancing.

"No, he can't even drive a tractor," replied Michael, gazing at Lancing appreciatively. "I can drive a car, if you want to know. Sue can drive a car; so can Ken—though that's off the record, because he hasn't a licence. Will Lambton can drive, though he doesn't really enjoy it, but Evans can't."

"Were the Evanses really snowed up?" asked Rivers, and Michael laughed.

"Feeling hopeful? You've got to remember we've chewed this story over in all its aspects ever since Wednesday night. Query, did Evans bump off your old lag, loot his pockets, carry him down the hill and bung him in the doctor's car for a keepsake?"

"Not 'did he'—that's getting on too fast," said Lancing. "But 'could he have'?"

"I've no doubt he could have bumped him off—anybody could if they'd got a coal hammer handy," said Michael; "but for the rest—I very much doubt it. 'Snowed up' is a relative term. Any able-bodied man could dig the snow away from the door and yard and get to his outhouses and feed his stock. Evans did so, of course—he's no fool. But to reach this place he has a choice of routes: either down the fields—a matter of half a mile—or else along the road to the top of Hollybanks and so down this hell of a hill which Will and Henry and Ken and I sweated to keep clear so that they could get the tractor up the hill with the milk. Well, that route's nearly two miles from the Evanses' to here, and the snow drifted very deep in the dip just by Evanses' turning—he didn't clear any of the road. I'll swear it was impossible to get down the fields with a corpse round your neck—nobody could have done it—the snow was too thick. And I don't believe Evans could have carried Exhibit A two miles along the road, especially with that deep drift to negotiate."

Michael broke off, because Susan had begun to shake with laughter—laughter which, Rivers realised, was not far from tears.

"Oh, it's awful!" she cried. "Michael tried to carry Henry down Hollybanks; he said Henry was about the right weight and he draped Henry round his shoulders. Michael's tough, but he had to give it up; the road was still treacherous and he slipped and they both came down, and Michael was absolutely winded."

"If you added the snow—if you happen to know about snow," went on Michael, "the answer's a lemon. No one could have done it—and certainly not Evans. He's well over sixty and he's not half as tough as Henry or me." He paused and then added: "You've probably heard what I call the Henry Solution—that the poor devil collapsed in the snow up by Hollybanks wood and died there, and the old Doc picked him up and put him in the car. Well, here's an additional guess for what it's worth: the snow had thawed out in that clearing by Wednesday. If Evans passed that way to see if there were any bunnies in the snares he'd set before the snow came down, and Evans saw the corpse lying there, I wouldn't put it beyond him to loot its pockets—wallet and so forth. Thereafter explanation according to Henry."

"Now that's a very intelligent suggestion," said Lancing.

"Why not go and see Evans?" asked Michael. "He'll probably tell you he saw me carry a corpse down Hollybanks, but as I didn't do it, I'm not worrying."

"Again—highly intelligent," said Rivers. "We'll take your advice and go and see Evans."

4

"We've got some remarkably intelligent people in this set-out," said Lancing. "Henry and Mike between them have got most of the answers, *but*..." He paused for a moment and then went on: "Even though the ground was frozen hard, do you think that Brown could have smashed his skull quite as comprehensively as he did by coming a cropper or colliding with a tree?"

The two C.I.D. men were driving up Hollybanks again, en route for the Evanses', and Rivers took his time before answering.

"Not by colliding with a tree," he replied; "but a branch of a tree falling on him might have done it. And I have known some bad head injuries if a chap crashed suddenly and his whole weight was behind his fall when he struck an obstacle—a rock, for instance, or other projection. This is where we get out into this damned drizzle again and search for fallen branches or knobbly rocks—and for God's sake look both ways at the crossroads. This is the most damned awful road junction I've ever seen."

"And no nonsense like Major Road Ahead or Dangerous Bend signs," said Lancing, as he pulled up most Correctly, looked both ways and sounded the Bentley's melodious horn. "Halting's all my eye anyway," he said cheerfully. "You're driving blind till you're right across the fairway. Over we go."

They ran the car up the track to the clearing and Lancing immediately reversed and drove back to the road junction. "I'm not going to risk bogging down in this and having to get Henry to tow me out with the tractor."

"You wouldn't bog down," said Rivers morosely. "The answer's here again. This is a sort of ridge or terrace—the rock outcrops here, that's why this bit's never been cultivated. I suppose the pine trees root in the crevices—and there are fallen branches all right."

"There would be. Trust Henry and/or Mike," replied Lancing.

He strolled on and kicked a rocky outcrop vigorously. "You could pulverise your skull on that," he said. "In fact, you could postulate that deceased was first knocked sideways by a branch which snapped with the weight of the snow, and he then improved matters by accelerating on convenient outcrop. To make matters easier a few tons of snow have melted and several inches of rain have fallen on this ridge, terrace or what have you, erasing, liquidating, or eroding any evidence which may or may not have existed. I suggest we drive on to the Evanses'. We're not going to take 'No' for an answer."

"We are not," agreed Rivers, "and neither are you going to get back into the Bentley quite so soon as you hope. We'll have a good look at the scene of this incident."

"Cripes... it's plain enough, isn't it?" said Lancing disgustedly. He stood at the road junction and faced towards Brynneys' Crest.

"The main road—so called—comes swooping down at a gradient of one in six, executing a voluptuous curve between overgrown hedges; it reaches bottom at the culvert; the crossroads join main road at about a hundred yards before the culvert and the crossroads run downhill to the valley. After the culvert the main road rises again like a switchback at a fun fair. I can't think why anybody in the place is left alive."

He went across to the shattered bridge and looked down at the wrecked Buick. It was half-concealed now, buried in the soil and debris which the torrent had washed down and dammed up against the capsized vehicle.

"The engineers won't be able to tell a thing from either of these wrecks," he said. "The gear boxes and all will be smashed to blazes and the brake drums ditto—but obviously Parsons didn't brake his outfit—he hoped to get past if he stepped on it, never thinking the old chap would step on it too. Every picture tells a story."

"By the time they get a breakdown van to lift the Buick they'll have to excavate it first," said Rivers. "All right. Let's go on to the Evanses'."

5

They drove on up the hill beyond the culvert for nearly a mile. Here was another dip in the road and just beyond it a rough track leading to a cottage, with henhouses and shacks and a couple of ancient Nissen huts set around it, higgledy-piggledy.

"What I should call a rural slum," said Lancing, "and this dip in the road is where the snow would have drifted, as Mike Dering said."

"Yes," agreed Rivers. "I was quite interested in what wasn't said, as well. I'd been wondering why it was that the Lambtons didn't see to it that the Evanses had enough food and fodder, instead of leaving it to Bob Parsons to supply them, but the answer's implicit in the various oddments we've heard. Will Lambton, Henry, Ken and Michael all sweated like heroes to keep Hollybanks clear so that they could get the milk up to the lorry. Evans not only didn't lend a hand in that job, he didn't even bother to dig a way clear to his own cottage. I can hear Henry saying, 'If he wants aught he can bloody well come and fetch it. We're not sweating to cut a way through for him so that he can have a load of spuds landed at his door.'"

"That's about it," said Lancing. "Will Lambton said they kept the road clear for the lorry with the snowplough, but it seems as though the snowplough only functioned between St. Olwens and Brynneys' Crest. That'd have been done so that the milk could be got away from Lambton's. There aren't any other farms along the road until you get to Brynneys' Bridge, so the snowplough gave it best at the Crest and probably reversed at that turn by Hollybanks wood. N.B.—See the bloke who drove the snowplough."

"Go up to the top of the class," said Rivers. "For a cockney you're not doing too badly."

"Cockneys are the most adaptable chaps on earth," said Lancing. "This is where we travel hopefully up yonder loathsome track to consider the Evanses. Incidentally, nobody in this place has been able to cross the river or reach what's called civilisation since Wednesday night. In view of Mike Dering's guess, would it be worth while to ask the Evanses if they've any objection to us giving their cottage the once-over?"

"It might be worth while just to get their reactions," said Rivers. "We haven't a warrant and we're bound to say so."

"Warrant be damned. If they object to us searching it's just what we want," said Lancing.

CHAPTER IX

I

THE DOOR OF THE COTTAGE WAS OPENED BY ALF EVANS; HE WAS short and thick-set, running to fat, but still powerful looking, though Rivers noticed at once that his wind wasn't good; he wheezed when he spoke.

"We are C.I.D. officers, sent from Scotland Yard to investigate the deaths which occurred in the car crash last Wednesday," said Rivers. He said Scotland Yard because he knew that it would convey more than 'the Metropolitan Police.' Scotland Yard was a name familiar to every household in England, no matter how remote. "Are you willing to answer some questions?" he concluded.

"Come in and welcome," he replied. "We'll tell you anything we know—but 'twon't help you much. We didn't see the crash and we don't know a thing about it, bar what's been told us."

There was a porch to the cottage, its two doors set at right angles to each other; the inner door opened straight into the kitchen, which was small and low and dark, almost over-poweringly warm after the penetrating chill of the mist outside. A big iron pot hung on a crane over the open fire, and it needed no powers of detection to realise that onions were boiling in the pot; their aroma in the confined space was most potent.

"Here's the two detectives, Bessie," said Evans as he preceded

Rivers and Lancing round the table which took up most of the space in the small room. "This is Mrs. Evans," announced her husband.

The woman who got up from a low seat by the fire looked enormous in the dim light; she was very stout but also brawny and the arms folded across her chest showed muscles as well as fat under her straining bodice. "She's worth two of him," flashed across Rivers's mind, even as he said: "Good day, Mrs. Evans. We're sorry to bother you."

"'Tis your business no doubt," she replied. "Take a seat."

Rivers advanced to the cushioned seat on the other side of the fire and was about to sit down when he realised there was a huge cat curled up on it; spitting and swearing, the black fury executed a magnificent jump on to the table, where it crouched and spat defiance at Scotland Yard, while other cats emerged from round the fireplace.

"Drat the cats," said Evans, opening the door into the porch, and there was a general exodus of felines, all expressing resentment with remarkable vigour.

"They're nervous o' strangers. Don't see many folks from away," said Mrs. Evans.

Rivers sat down, Lancing perched on the window-seat, and Evans leant against the dresser.

"I can well believe you don't get many chance visitors here," said Rivers amiably. "Do you ever get strangers knocking at your door, Mrs. Evans?"

"Well, sometimes there's a tramp who's missed his road—no tramp ever comes here a' purpose—and I've known gipsies on and off, selling besoms and pegs and such like," she replied; "but that ain't often. There's nought to come for—no bridge across the river, no pickings, no way to nowhere. We're not often troubled."

Evans put his word in. "I can tell you the name of everyone who's come to that door the past three months. There's Davidson, the grocer, and Billing, the corn miller's man; there's the postman and Willy with the egg van, and Hobson with the cattle van. Then there's Sykes, the pig-killer—and that's the lot, barring Mr. Parsons. He takes some o' my stuff into market in his van and gives me a lift meself at times. And I can't see that jeep of his being much use to nobody again—a proper mess that is."

"Mebbe it is, but 'twas a mercy he wasn't killed," said Mrs. Evans. "They didn't ought to've let the old doctor drive at all. If we'd had the looking after of him, 'twouldn't never've happened. Evans, he'd a' seen to it somehow."

"I understood you work for Mr. Parsons," said Rivers, turning to Evans. "Does he come and fetch you?"

"Not him—too busy, he is. He's a worker is Mr. Parsons. No. I go on my bike."

"Then you're on the roads quite a bit," said Rivers. "Have you seen any stranger, recently? Anybody you couldn't place?"

"No. Never a one. I seen the roadmen, and Jimmy with the milk lorry and the Lambtons and the coalman—all folks I know. And I'd remember if I saw a stranger—we don't see so many on these roads."

"Now, about the car crash, Mr. Evans," went on Rivers. "Where were you when it happened?"

"I reckon I was in here with my missis, having our tea," said Evans. "I'd had a day of it, cleaning all them henhouses out and seeing to the pigs. The snow held things up—you can't turn birds out in the sort o' weather we'd had and things'd got left. Reckon 'twas about five o'clock I knocked off—near sundown, that was, and we didn't know a thing about the smash till I went out next morning. Proper upset I was, when I saw Mr. Parsons' van."

"But didn't you hear the smash?" asked Rivers. "The Lambtons heard it, right down the hill."

"Mebbe they did," said Evans; "but we're not so young as we was, and a bit 'ard o' hearing, likely. But there 'tis—we never heard a thing—and nobody came to tell us. I'd 'a been out there lending a hand if I'd known. Proper upset I was—'twas us Mr. Parsons was coming to, with a load o' stuff we wanted bad enough, I can tell you that."

"Were you expecting him that evening?" asked Rivers, but Evans shook his head.

"That I wasn't. Never thought 'e'd come Wednesday, him having been busy like the rest of us and the roads still not fit to drive on—not on these hills. I sent a message to Mr. Parsons Wednesday morning—the milk lorry man took it, him passing not far from Pine Quarry—I said we was stuck a bit for fodder and that, knowing Mr. Parsons had got some turnips and taties to spare, but I never thought he'd 'a come out Wednesday. And I might as well tell you straight, you being police, I went and got that lot out o' the back of Mr. Parsons' van as soon as Mr. Lambton told me the load was for us. We needed that lot, I tell you straight."

"How're you managing now?" asked Rivers, and Evans replied:

"Lambton's helped us out. They've got plenty."

"If they'd thought o' that before, this'd never've happened," said Mrs. Evans; "but Lambtons, they're that close, we don't like asking. If folks can't offer when things is awkward, we aren't the sort to go asking. And I reckon 'twas Lambtons' business to've told the doctor he didn't ought to go on driving. They knew how 'twas—and them Derings knew, too. He wasn't fit to drive, the old man wasn't, and they knew it, the Derings did. But reckon they didn't want him to get rid of the car."

"What exactly do you mean by that, Mrs. Evans?" asked Rivers, conscious of Lancing's still attention.

"Use your head," she said scornfully. "Free all the evenings, aren't they? And the doctor, he never set foot out o' the house after dark.

D'you think they never took that car out themselves of an evening—and the doctor as deaf as a post sitting over his fire with the curtains drawn? You're a London detective—happen you don't know what it's like for a young couple to be stuck in a place like St. Brynneys ten miles from a cinema or a dance hall. And them Derings aren't real country folk, not them."

"Are you suggesting that the Derings did take Dr. Robinson's car out, Mrs. Evans?" asked Rivers. "I advise you to think what you're saying; it may be very important."

She turned to her husband. "You tell him, Alf. It's bound to come out."

Evans shifted uncomfortably. "What's the use of me telling?" he asked. "I've no'but my own word for it and it'd be my word against his."

"You tell him," she insisted.

"Well, 'twas one evening I came back from Mr. Parsons, latish," Evans began unwillingly. "We'd been finishing roofing a shed and 'twas dark before I got on the road. I met a car just before Brynneys' Crest, up the road there. Fair blinded I was, because the driver didn't dip his headlights, and I got off me bike and into the hedge. 'Twas Dr. Robinson's car—and 'twasn't Dr. Robinson driving of it. I knew that, the pace he was going. 'Twas young Dering a-driving—or so I thought. He passed me fast, and I couldn't get a real look, but that's what I thought."

"Who else could it 'a been?" asked Mrs. Evans. "'T wasn't the Lambtons, they've got their own car, such as it is, and I'll say this for Henry Lambton, he's not given to making free with what's not his. But them Derings—too big for their shoes, they are. I wouldn't trust 'em farther'n I could see 'em."

"Now then, that'll do," said Alf Evans. "We don't want no ill blood. That's why I never said aught to anybody about seeing young

Dering in the doctor's car—besides, 'e might've got leave to drive it, you never know."

Mrs. Evans muttered to herself, but Rivers disregarded her and turned to another topic.

"I understand that Dr. Robinson always drove up to the clearing by Hollybanks wood about sunset," he said.

"Not always he didn't," replied Evans. "He'd often have a drive about then, but he might turn one way or another as the fancy took him. When I'm not working away, I'm generally outside about that time, getting the birds shut up and that, and I've seen him go past here, or turn up to Brynneys' Crest—you can see the top of the hill from my garden."

"That's right. I seen him, too. Very slow he drove, poor old gentleman," said Mrs. Evans. "When Alf's not at home to do it, I shut the birds up myself, and I notice like, if there's aught on the road."

"Yes, you and Mr. Evans probably saw more of Dr. Robinson when he drove up here than the people down below could have seen," said Rivers cheerfully. "Now you probably know Hollybanks wood and the clearing pretty well, Mr. Evans. Don't you put some rabbit snares down in the wood?"

"Well, sometimes," agreed Evans reluctantly; "but that's by agreement with Will Lambton, mind. A real pest rabbits is to farmers."

"When were you last in the clearing?" asked Rivers.

There was a perceptible pause this time. Evans rubbed his head and pondered. "That'd take a bit o' thinking out," he said slowly. "Before the snow, that was. If you'd seen the state we was in, you'd understand that. It was as much as I could do to keep the ground clear to get to the henhouses and pigsties, and there was a drift in the road dip there deep enough to bury you twice over if you'd landed in it."

"But you went to the clearing after you'd heard about the crash, didn't you?" asked Rivers. "I wondered if you'd noticed any wheel tracks or other evidence."

Evans hesitated, but he didn't deny the implied statement. "Oh, that," he said. "Yes. I went on my way back Thursday morning, just to see, as you say; but there weren't no tracks. The ground was still hard Wednesday evening and it rained all night. There was nought to see—but if you look at them two cars, you can see how't happened all right."

Rivers nodded. Then he went on: "You saw the bodies of the two men in Mr. Lambton's barn on Thursday morning?"

"Yes. I did. Will Lambton asked me if I knew who the other chap was, but I never seen him before. An ugly sight he was, too."

"You heard that nothing was found in his pockets barring some odd change?"

"Yes. Will told me that."

"That strikes us as very odd," went on Rivers. "We are only at the beginning of our inquiry here—I came down from London yesterday, and got out here with Colonel Wynne's help. Now, owing to the floods, nobody in St. Brynneys can get away—not without help from the military to cross to St. Olwens. I am going to ask for co-operation from everybody in trying to trace any objects which the dead man might have brought with him. It's very unusual for a man to have nothing in his pockets."

Mrs. Evans did not wait for him to get any further; she broke in promptly: "You're as good as saying that somebody robbed him—took away whatever there was so's nobody should know where he came from? Well, if that's what you're looking for, I know where I'd start looking."

"Now then, don't you go talking silly," said Alf. "They don't want no help from you, two London detectives don't."

"You're quite wrong there, Mr. Evans," said Rivers quietly. "We want all the help we can get. Now this isn't a court of law; you're not on oath. You're at liberty to tell me what you like, provided you remember that there's a law of slander. Slander means saying malicious things to damage another person. In any inquiry like this, detectives make allowances for unwise things that may be said in the excitement of the moment, but we don't encourage slander. I've said this to make it clear that we do want your help, but we also expect you to be reasonably careful of what you say."

"That's plain common sense," said Mrs. Evans approvingly. "If you don't want no help, what d'you come asking questions for? You can't think we went and hit the doctor's car over the bank, and you can't think we robbed no corpses—we couldn't 'a done, even if we'd wanted—but I'll ask you a few questions now. What happened to that other detective what came here first? Fell downstairs, I'm told. Where was he when he fell downstairs? Who could 'a got into that locked-up house where he was? And do you believe a grown man'd be so silly he'd fall downstairs on's own?"

"Those are all very sensible questions," said Rivers. "Now can you tell what both of you were doing when Inspector Welby fell downstairs?"

"That I can," she retorted. "We was both here, and Taffy Williams was here, too. Him's the shepherd from Upper Slyne, and he come here for his dinner, having next to no firing left. And that reminds me, Alf," she added, turning to her husband; "we got to get him another sack o' logs out somehow. Even the tractor can't get to Slyne now."

She turned back to Rivers. "Now I reckon you're trying to do your job as polite as you can, and I don't hold it against you asking questions, not if you treat us all alike. That's fair enough, isn't it? Though I'm not going to pretend I like your questions no better than any other honest woman would. But treat everybody alike, I say, and don't go picking on us because we're small folk in a small way and haven't had all that schooling."

"That's all right, Mrs. Evans," replied Rivers. "Everybody is being treated the same."

"I'm glad to hear it," she retorted. "And if you want to search this house, search you can—but you needn't pick on us first. I'm not going to have it said you came to us first believing you'd find whatever it is you want to find. You go and search the Derings' cottage; they was the last to come and live here, and nobody knows aught about them. We been here thirty years—and had no police in the place up till now."

"That's true enow," put in Alf. "Never been no police in St. Brynneys since we had swine fever in twenty-nine—and they wasn't London detectives then."

Mrs. Evans stared at Rivers deliberately, as though challenging him. "Have you searched the Derings' place?" she asked. "If not, you start there. I know me rights. You can't search here without a warrant and you can't have got no warrant if you only came here to-day."

"I haven't asked for a search warrant," replied Rivers. "Neither have I asked to search your house. I only asked for your co-operation—or help, to use a simpler word."

"And I'm doing my best for you," she replied. "You go and search Boars Wood Cottage—and while you're rummaging round, see if you can find any marriage lines. That's one thing no woman mislays—if she's got any."

"Here, don't go talking nasty," protested Alf Evans, but she flashed back at him:

"I ain't said nothing. I told him to look. He wants to search, don't he? Well, let him have an idea the first thing I'd look for, that's all."

2

"I'd certainly say the standard of intelligence is being well maintained," said Lancing, when they had left the onion-laden fug of the Evanses' cottage and returned gratefully to the Bentley, where they both lighted cigarettes. Rivers nodded.

"Yes. Evans is much brighter than he looks—and his wife's a masterpiece. She's the real brains of the outfit. I wonder where she came from. Neither of them were country born; Evans came here after the '14–'18 war, and I should guess he might have originated in Bristol. But what a hell of a lot of mischief they could make if they really got going in a coroner's court. That story of seeing Dering drive the doctor's car—it could be neither proved nor disproved, but it'd be very damaging to Dering. It's the sort of smear story that implants a doubt in honest people's minds."

"Any germination going on in your own grey matter?" enquired Lancing.

"I don't know, laddy. That's the devil of it. That woman's an obese old horror and as venomous as a rattlesnake—but she may be right, you know. I don't think she'd have played the marriage lines card if she hadn't got something. And whereas you can say it's no business of ours if the Derings are lawfully married or not—we're not moral censors, thank God—we've got to admit that if they're not married they've offered hostages to blackmailers."

"I know," said Lancing soberly. "And there was the suggestion about chucking Welby downstairs. It's obvious Mike Dering could have done it—we realised that all the time."

"So could Alf Evans have chucked Welby downstairs," replied Rivers. "He'd worked in the house at one time; he could have got hold of a key—and I don't believe the shepherd chap would have noticed the time. Their clock doesn't go and that elderly radio had been defunct for years by the look of it."

"Could we be back at the Henry–Mike solution?" queried Lancing. "Evans looted the body, then came the car crash and it all looked Bob's your uncle until a policeman came nosing around. And if Welby had died, chief, wouldn't Michael Dering have been very near a capital charge? We can afford to go easy about him, because Welby will soon be able to tell us what happened—but the other would have been a different kettle of fish. Dering was alone in the woodshed all that afternoon."

Rivers nodded. "The Evanses hate the Derings like stink," he said. "The Derings got the cottage and the job the Evanses wanted, and I suppose Mrs. Evans resented Susan Dering because, to put it crudely, Susan's a lady."

"Anything there?" queried Lancing. "Say if the whole job went haywire, chief. Alf Evans murdered some old pal of his own and got it all nicely taped to prove that Dering had done it—bringing off a double—and then old Robinson mucked it all up by finding the body and heaving it into his car and got killed on top of it."

"It's too complicated," said Rivers. "Pull up here again; I want to have another look at that Buick. We ought to get it towed out—and I can't see how to do it."

Lancing pulled up by the culvert and they both looked over at the torrent and morass. "I asked Henry if he could get it up with the tractor, but he won't attempt it," said Rivers. "The tractor'd bog down if he got it on the land—that's obvious—and he says he couldn't get the car up over the culvert without getting it on its wheels again—which can't be done without lifting tackle, and it's the hell of a weight. I'd say it was twenty years old at least—and built to last."

"If you got some troops out here, they could dam the stream the other side—or deflect it," suggested Lancing; "and then we could dig it out and get inside. What a job!"

"I'll talk to Colonel Wynne about it," said Rivers. "I say, didn't you like the way Evans owned up to snaffling the load Parsons brought up for him?"

"'Seeing you're police,' or all on the side of the angels," said Lancing, as they went back to the Bentley. "If my sense of smell is still reliable, Evans is a potential rogue. He stinks."

"I wonder if Will Lambton would open up about the Evanses if I told him what Alf said about seeing Mike Dering driving the doctor's car. Lambton likes Dering."

"I don't know about Will, but I swear his wife would get vocal if you told her about the marriage lines smear," said Lancing. "Mrs. Lambton wouldn't stand for that."

"Yes, that's very sound," agreed Rivers. "Well, we will now go and see if Bob Parsons is awake enough to answer a few questions. He must have a hard skull and well-articulated cervical vertebrae; according to the evidence he ought to have been killed instanter. I reckon he was driving at sixty miles per hour to have shifted that old Buick over the culvert. And after a word with Bob Parsons, we'll concentrate on Boars Wood House and the stair carpet."

"Are you well up in oil lamps?" asked Lancing.

"I was brought up on oil lamps," retorted Rivers. "It's an everlasting puzzle to me that blokes of your generation who can fix radios, and wire houses, and take a car engine down for fun, become helpless in the presence of an oil-pressure stove or Mantilla, and muck them up every time you try to light them."

Lancing chuckled. "I'm petrified by pressure stoves," he said. "How did you know? I've never told you."

"I've watched your face," said Rivers, "and thanked God there are still a few gadgets I can leave you cold at."

CHAPTER X

I

"Yes, you can go up and talk to him—but don't stay too long, sir," said Mrs. Lambton. "He's still a bit weak in the head, but Gwyn and I are real proud of him. If you knew the trouble we've taken—specially Gwyn. She's fed him like a baby. You see, we once had Henry with concussion when he came over the handlebars of his motor bike and rode home afterwards. And 'twas old Dr. Robinson told me, 'Keep him still; don't let him lift his head, and feed him on slops—feed him with a spoon. Keep him still and keep him quiet and he won't come to no harm,' he said. And Henry got better, just like Bob's doing."

"Makes me laugh to think of these hospitals and all the fuss they make," said Gwynyth, her bright eyes on Lancing. "If it hadn't been for the floods, they'd have taken Bob away in an ambulance, and X-rayed him and put him in plaster and doped him with penicillin and M. and B., and all those stuffs—and likely as not he'd have caught something else and died on them. I do hate hospitals. But we've looked after him just using common sense and he's doing fine. He's hungry now—creating because he can't have meat and two veg."

Lancing smiled back at her (Gwyn was easy to smile at). "Jolly good for you. I say, if I come a cropper in the course of duty—fall downstairs or something—will you and Mrs. Lambton look after me and save me from the hospital nurses?"

"That's enough from you, Detective Inspector Lancing," put in Rivers. "If you do fall downstairs I'll have you demoted and you'll be a sergeant again as you hit the floor. Mrs. Lambton, will you take me upstairs to see your patient? And perhaps your daughter will teach Lancing how to light a Mantilla lamp without blacking the mantle, and how to pump a pressure stove without setting the house on fire."

Mrs. Lambton laughed a little as she led the way upstairs and Rivers heard Gwynyth's voice. "Don't know how to light a Mantilla—call yourself a detective…"

"The young ones are freer than me and my sisters was," said Mrs. Lambton; "but Gwyn's a good girl for all her cheeky ways; she's looked after Bob same as she looks after an ailing lamb—no end of patience she's got."

Bob Parsons was still lying flat on his back, his bandages a credit to his nurses. As far as Rivers could see in the greying light, Parsons was near to normal again, though his eyes were still sunken in their sockets and his face drawn.

"Here's the Chief Inspector just wants you to tell him how't happened, Bob," said Mrs. Lambton. "Of course we've told him just how 'twas and how the old doctor ought never to've been driving—we've told him all that—but it's just for you to say that you tried to pass him and he came across you. So I'll leave you for a minute—and don't you get bothering, Bob. 'Twill be all right."

"I hit him all right," said Parsons, as Rivers sat down by the bed. "Mebbe 'twas my fault—I was driving hard. I wanted to get a load of stuff to Evanses—they was short—and I thought I could do it before dark. You see my headlights wasn't much good—the cold got into the battery—and I'd got to get home before dark."

"Yes, I see," said Rivers. "Evans told me he'd sent you a message saying he was short of food."

"Jimmy told me that morning," said Bob. "I thought if I left it till afternoon the roads'd be thawed out better—the frost was still in the ground. It wasn't easy driving, and mebbe I wasn't careful enough, but I reckoned there was nothing on the road—there's a pole down before the bridge—and I never thought of the old doctor. If I'd thought of him I'd never've believed he'd 'a come on such roads."

"That's all right," said Rivers quietly. He realised from Parsons' voice that talking was an effort, and that the memory of the smash still turned him sick.

"I don't want to worry you, but just answer my questions. Had either you or the doctor got your headlights on?"

"No. 'Twasn't dark. Headlights don't help you in the half-light."

"Did either of you sound your horns?"

"No. If he'd hooted I could ha' stopped. He just came out slow, not many yards ahead, and I thought I could pull out and pass him—and then he shot out, right ahead o' me, like as if he'd accelerated hard. I can remember thinking Oh, Christ… we've had it. I couldn't do nothing. I don't remember the crash. I woke up off the road—somewhere down by the culvert—and after I'd tried to open the door of the Buick and couldn't, I made for Lambtons to get help."

"That's all clear enough," said Rivers; "it was your road so far as the law goes. Now the Lambtons have told you about the second man in the doctor's car."

"I saw him. Henry made me look when he brought us back. I don't know who he was." He broke off and closed his eyes for a moment, his brow frowning as though with intolerable headache, and Rivers said:

"All right. We'll leave it at that."

"No, wait a bit… I get muddled when I try to think. He was a town chap, wasn't he? Town clothes and that. The only chap I've seen in these parts dressed like that was a fellow who came round wanting to sell second-hand cars... or he'd sell insurance too, or something. You ask Henry. I told him at the time."

Mrs. Lambton came in at that moment, and Rivers got up.

"All right, Mrs. Lambton. He's done very well. Now I'll leave him to have a nap."

He went downstairs again and found Gwynyth catechising Lancing about the latest films he'd seen. Gwynyth turned her bright eyes on Rivers.

"He's passed his test for the pressure lamp and the Mantilla. He's not that silly—only scared of what a lamp can do."

"If I have any further nonsense about not being able to light and service oil lamps, I'll send him back to you for another lesson, Miss Gwynyth. Congratulations on your patient. He's doing fine. Now do you know if your brother's anywhere around?"

"Yes, he's in the cowhouse. Ken's just taken the cows out to the drinking trough, so if you're frightened of cows, look out. They're all milling around in the yard, and they're a bit fresh when they're shut up all winter."

"Thanks for the warning, but cows are my long suit," replied Rivers. "I was quite a good milker when I was ten."

"Come back and have tea," she smiled at him. "There's hot scones and enough butter for a regiment. It's good butter—I made it."

"I can't imagine anything I'd like better, but I've got to earn my keep," laughed Rivers.

2

"Yes, Bob's right about the chap hawking cars," said Henry. He had driven the cows back to their standings—or rather the cows had returned in their own order of precedence, the "boss cow" leading, the others going to their own places without further direction, and Lancing had watched with a wide grin while Rivers helped to slip the cowbands round broad Shorthorn necks, as though he'd done it all his life.

Now they were standing under the hay loft, with the beams of a hurricane lamp shining on the limed walls.

"These chaps do come round sometimes," went on Henry, "hoping they'll find sillier mugs than they are themselves. They drive up in some rotten old tin pot they've painted up to look smart and try to hustle you into exchanging it for the one you've got. 'Here you are, mate, a car that's as good as new—reconditioned engine, rebored, new battery and good tyres—it's all yours in exchange for that awful old crock you've got and twenty quid cash.' 'You drive home in your own bitch of a thing—and lucky if you get there'—that's what I tell 'em," said Henry. "But"—and he turned to Rivers—"that chap in the back wasn't like either of the blokes I've seen round here. Although he were bashed about and no mistake, he'd got a dial you couldn't mistake. You ask Ken about the last car dealer we had round here. Ken almost got enough practice in one of the old crocks to pass his driving test. Took him for a ride proper, he did. He's got brains, that kid."

Henry went to the door of the byre and let out a yell. "Hi! Ken!"

Young Ken wasn't far away; he appeared out of the gloom outside on the instant. He was a nice-looking boy, fair and slim, with a complexion any debutante could have envied.

"You tell the Chief Inspector about that slimy Joe you took for a ride in the original Ford 8—go on, he won't run you in. He's too busy to ask for your licence."

Ken grinned at Rivers. "He was a little dark chap," he began; "regular Taffy; talk the tail off a dead donkey, he could. 'Son,' 'e says—reckoning I was young Mr. Lambton maybe—'Son, it's time your dad gave you a car of your own. Can you drive?' 'Not half,' I said, and him, 'In you get and give her a trial.' He kept an eye on me until he saw I could drive and then he said, 'Now let her out a bit and see what she can do.' Well, I took 'im at 'is word. Drove him nearly to St. Olwens, I did, and back again. And I told him the bearings was nearly busted, the clutch plate was loose and there wasn't no brakes so you'd notice. And, anyway, me dad died when I was five and I hadn't more'n a quid in the post office. Proper mad, he was."

Rivers laughed, and Henry chuckled quietly. "That larned him," he said. "Coupla gallons o' petrol he must ha' used, these hills being hills."

Rivers turned to Ken. "You say this chap talked to you. Did he ask any questions—about who lived here and so forth?"

"Not half. Wanted to know about every house we passed and who lived there, and if they'd got a car—so's he could try and do business, he said. But I reckon he never wanted to see St. Brynneys no more by the time he'd done with me."

"But he wasn't anything like that chap in the doctor's Buick, was he?" asked Henry.

Ken's face fell and he turned away. "That he wasn't," he replied.

"O.K. Buzz off," said Henry. "You can start on Gwyn's Ayrshire and watch out for her tail. She's a devil with her tail, that cow is—gives you a swipe for love."

Ken went off and Henry turned to Rivers. Much to the latter's amusement, Henry used Lancing's approach.

"Anything in that for us? I'd forgotten how that hopeful pumped Ken. Fact was, I laughed so much over Ken's free drive I forgot all the rest."

"Well, you know, it's quite an idea," said Rivers. "If some fellow wanted to find out who lived around here without drawing attention to himself, he was pretty smart over it. Some second-hand car dealers do go round, just as you describe, hoping for a mug, and offering the boy a ride wasn't a bad idea."

"I bet that kid noticed the number of the car—boys always do," put in Lancing. He went outside to the second cowhouse and called out:

"Hi, Ken! What was the registration number of that Ford you were talking about?"

"Ot something," replied Ken promptly, "and she ran 'ot, too. OT22, that was it. No 'twasn't, 'twas better. OT12. 'Ot one, too."

"Thanks. Very snappy," replied Lancing. He went back to Rivers. "Quite a lad, isn't he? But the registration was probably phoney."

"We can try," said Rivers. "When did this chap call?"

"Martinmas," replied Henry. "Armistice Day, Dad calls it. All the same."

"November 11th," said Rivers. "Well, I'll look into it. Henry, I want a word with Mrs. Lambton, but without your sister there. Can you fix it?"

"O.K. I'll tell Gwyn her Ayrshire's getting mastitis and she'd better milk her herself. That'll bring her. Always pulling Gwyn's leg over that cow of hers. 'Film star,' she calls her. Can you beat it?"

3

"It's plain wicked!" exclaimed Mrs. Lambton. "Wicked, that's what 'tis. I'd like to give a piece of my mind to that great slut. If ever there's dirty gossip going round, it's always Mrs. Evans starts it. I've held me tongue for peace and quietness—we don't like making trouble with neighbours—but that's going too far, that is."

Rivers had told Mrs. Lambton what Mrs. Evans had said about searching for marriage lines, and Mrs. Lambton was so angry she could hardly contain herself.

"Sue Dering's the nicest girl I ever had in my house," she declared. "She's wholesome, all through. I've heard her talking to Gwyn and glad I've been to have her. The young things like Gwyn is all alike—won't listen to their parents; we're no' but the old folks. But Sue, she's different. Gwyn admires her and she'll take from Sue what she wouldn't listen to from me. And to think of Bessie Evans daring to say such a thing and her living with Evans ten years afore they could get married, him having a wife in Cardiff or somewhere." She broke off for sheer lack of breath and then went on more slowly: "I've never said that to a soul before," she said, "and maybe I oughtn't to've said it now, but I'm that angry! Why, Will and me knew how 'twas about the Evanses, not long after they came we knew it, but I always treated her kindly-like, knowing some folks has troubles you can't always understand. I've been up and nursed her when she was ill, and treated her as I'd treat any other neighbour, never letting her think I knew it against her. But I won't stay quiet and let her say things like that about Sue Dering."

"Where did the Evanses come from?" asked Rivers.

It was Will Lambton who answered. He had been sitting silent, with a troubled face, while his wife said her say, but now he said:

"In 1919, 'twas. Alf Evans he was unemployed, like so many o' the ex-service men. He'd been reared Bristol way, and tho' he'd been put into a factory to learn a trade, his dad was a market gardener. Alf set out tramping to find a bit o' land where he could keep chickens, and 'twas Colonel Wynne let him have that cottage and fettled it up a bit for him. It'd been empty for years, farming being bad. It's Colonel Wynne's land, that is. He bought it for the shooting and one time there was a keeper at the cottage and he raised pheasants. Colonel Wynne, he said: 'I don't know if this chap Evans can make anything of it, but he's an ex-service man and I hope you'll help him along. Give him a job or two and see how he shapes,' said the Colonel. And so I did—and

Evans could be a good worker, mind you; turn his hand to anything, Evans can. If we didn't like him—well, takes all sorts to make a world."

"How did you know the Evanses weren't married?" asked Rivers, and Mrs. Lambton took up the story.

"Oh, 'twas a shocking thing, dreadful, 'twas. You see his wife came here—his lawful wife, that was. She traced him somehow, and after she'd been to the cottage she came down here and carried on something dreadful. We'd 'a been sorry for her, but she was that awful—all made up and dirty with it, smelling of drink, and language such as you never did hear. Will got the trap out at last—there weren't no cars here then—and he said, 'You'd better be getting back where you came from, missis, for there's no place for you here, and if you don't get in that trap you'll have to walk to St. Olwens.' She went, thank God… And if I didn't think much of the Mrs. Evans I knew, I thought less of the real one. Enough to drive any man wrong, she was."

"Well, there 'twas," said Lambton. "I'm real sorry that story got spilled again. We done our best to forget it, and it's Mrs. Evans's fault it's come up. I always notice that it's folks who've slipped up themselves is quickest to say hard things about others."

"You say they got married after they had been here for ten years," said Rivers. "Did they tell you about it?"

"Bless you, no," said Will. "You see we'd never named it to them. I should ha' thought Evans must ha' known his wife came down here and let the cat out of the bag with a wallop, but we never said nought. What was the good? There he was up there and 'twasn't for us to try to get him shifted. And Evans he said nought—don't blame him, there weren't much he could say, and 'twas easier all round if we kept our tongues still. But one year—1930 'twas—the Evanses went off for a holiday to Swansea, and they got married there, for Polly—that's my wife's sister—she was at Swansea, too, and she saw 'em come out of register office, and she was that curious she went in and asked—Alfred Evans, widower, to Bessie Huggins, spinster. So there 'twas."

"It's a funny thing," said Mrs. Lambton. "Folks go off to places where nobody knows 'em and thinks it's all secret and somebody always sees 'em. Life's like that."

"That's only too true, Mrs. Lambton," said Rivers. "I suppose you never told the Evanses your sister had been at Swansea?"

"That I didn't," she said. "Least said's soonest mended. I'd never ha' told you about the Evanses if they hadn't said wicked things about Sue Dering. She's a good woman, Sue is, and anybody who says aught else is lying."

"Thank you very much, Mrs. Lambton," said Rivers, who had found out just what he wanted to find out. "I think I'd better go and collect my colleague—they're having fun and games out there."

"That's Gwyn teasing young Ken—they're full of life, those two. Ken's a good lad, for all he came from the home in Loucester, him being an orphan and no folk to care for him."

"He's settled here proper and we'll make a farmer of him all right," said Will Lambton. "He's got the makings of a proper farmer, Ken has."

4

"Curiouser and curiouser," said Lancing. "They say one half of the world doesn't know how the other half lives, but in this place you can't take anything for granted. There was old Robinson, came and hid here—and the lord knows if somebody didn't ferret him out and blackmail him. We just don't know."

"And it's quite likely we shall never know," said Rivers. "The fact about this place is that it's so small and so far away from anywhere that people have come here thinking they're hidden away and nobody will ever notice them—but if they're not indigenous they stick out like organ stops. Everybody wondered about the doctor; the Lambtons wondered about the Evanses, and the Evanses are consumed with curiosity about the Derings. Well, we can't do much in this abode of bliss this evening, but we'll just look at that stair carpet and see if we can find any traces of the unfortunate Welby."

"W.A.H., which is, being interpreted, What a House!" said Lancing.

They were in Boars Wood House; like Welby they had entered by the kitchen door; unlike Welby, they had dealt efficiently with the lamps, so that all the ground floor rooms were illumined with yellow lamplight, and the whiter incandescent light of the Mantilla shone up the steep stairway. In addition to the lamps both men had powerful electric torches.

It seemed to Susan Dering, looking across from her own cottage door, that the house had suddenly come to life. She had never seen lights in all the ground floor windows before. Indeed, she had seldom seen lights at all, because old Robinson had always drawn curtains across the windows. Now the mellow lamplight shone out across the garden, competing with the early twilight, and the upstairs windows gleamed ghost-like as Rivers and Lancing went from room to room with their torches. Michael came and took Susan's arm.

"Come in, Sue. It's no use watching and it's a 'demmed damp unpleasant evening.'"

"I know—but it fascinates me. It's the first time I've seen the house looking alive and attractive. It ought to have a big family living in it, with the children tumbling up and downstairs and yelling all over the place. Gwyn ought to live there. It's all nonsense her saying she doesn't want to marry a farmer. I wonder if she'll marry Bob Parsons after all."

"I thought all that was off," said Michael as they went into their own fireside.

"So it was—they quarrelled over something—but Gwyn's been nursing him. It's easy to get fond of a man you've looked after."

"We can't settle other people's lives for them," said Michael.

5

Rivers and Lancing examined the footprints on the hall floor. The boards were bare but Susan had kept them well swept, and many footmarks showed where wet boots had left soil and leaves and dung on the boards.

"Looks as though an army had been in here," said Rivers. "Those are Welby's boots—he went into 'the study'—so called. This lot are probably Dering's gum boots—yes, he came in with the Colonel—the long narrow prints... and two lots of very dungy boots... Henry—he helped carry Welby out—and Will Lambton. He looked in to see it was all O.K. on Wednesday evening. Now for the stairs."

They went up one at a time, examining each stair. There were fourteen stairs, covered with decrepit haircord carpet, worn down to the stringy warp. On the second stair from the top the carpet was ripped right across and torn away from the tacks.

"If you caught your toe in that you'd do a nose-dive all right," said Lancing, "especially if you were hurrying, and there's no handrail to grab—but anybody could have kicked the carpet afterwards to supply the explanation."

They went up and into each of the five bedrooms; only one was furnished, and that with a minimum of cheap old furniture. The room was tidy, the bed made, the linoleum polished. Susan had evidently done her best. Welby's footprints showed to-and-fro across the floor.

"He'd got his boots soaked through before he came in, poor fool—he ought to have worn wellingtons," said Rivers. "Where did he go from here?"

The answer was plain, for the floors of the other rooms had not been swept for years; the layer of dust showed plainly where Welby had explored; he had opened old trunks and suitcases and packing-cases—all full of books, or the remains of books. Mice and rats, moths and beetles had made nests there and mildew had whitened and rotted old calf bindings. The final room was over the kitchen; one window pane was broken and birds had nested there.

"The cat," said Lancing, pointing to the floor where feathers and the remains of wings showed signs of slaughter. "You can see its paw marks—and Welby skidded here... he made a lunge at the cat. Is he one of those blokes who's got a thing about cats? If he chased it downstairs that explains everything."

Rivers nodded. "Looks like it. He was by himself, of course. He'd sent his constable back with the van; he probably didn't bring a torch and he seems to have been a clumsy juggins over lamps, so we can take it he was up here in the gloaming. I've known many a big chap get rattled quite unreasonably in an old house where rats and mice made inexplicable noises."

"And there may have been other inexplicable noises," said Lancing. "There's a door at the top of the stairs—God knows why, unless it was put there to keep children from breaking their necks on those qualified stairs. It's hooked back against the wall now—but if someone played hide and seek and then slammed the door hard when Welby was on the top step, I think it would have worked. Like to try it? You go back to the dead-bird room, and I'll take cover and organise the door trick."

Rivers went back to the far room and then returned to the stairhead. He was ready for Lancing's assault with the door, one hand against each wall on either side of the narrow stairs, but even so he was nearly flung forward as his foot touched the top stair.

"O.K.?" asked Lancing.

"Yes—small thanks to you. I'm surprised Welby didn't break his neck."

"That's two surprises registered in one day," said Lancing. "Let's beat it. I'll test for fingerprints to-morrow."

CHAPTER XI

I

"We've collected a lot of information, sir, and everybody has been most helpful," said Rivers.

Once again the C.I.D. men were in consultation with Colonel Wynne; warm and well fed, as comfortable as men could be, they were sitting over a blazing fire with a pair of cocker spaniels to complete the party. Before dinner, Lancing had sat at his typewriter, typing to Rivers's dictation, setting down every detail of locality, every answer given to questions, every surmise which had crossed their minds during the day. One copy of the report just produced was to be ferried over the floods by the Duck crew, and posted to the A.C. in London; two carbon copies were kept for reference by Rivers and Lancing.

"D'you feel you're getting any further?" asked the Colonel.

"I don't think we've got much further than Mike and Henry have got between them," said Rivers. "They're both very intelligent fellows, and they have the advantage of local knowledge, and I think they've pieced together a very good theory—although I admit that Lancing and I have developed variations. But let me tell you what Dering calls 'the Henry Solution,' reinforced by extras from all of us. In the event of no further facts coming to light, the Henry Solution may well be put forward as the most probable explanation."

Wynne listened intently while Rivers sketched out the theory that Jack Brown had arrived in St. Brynneys when the snow had just begun to fall heavily, had turned towards Hollybanks wood and had slipped heavily on the frozen ground or been knocked senseless by a falling branch; that his body had lain under the snow until the thaw, and the contents of his pockets been looted by Evans. "Dering added the final circumstantial suggestion," concluded Rivers, "that Dr. Robinson found the body, managed to heave it into his car, intending to drive it down to the village, and then came the collision with Parsons' car."

"It's very neat," said the Colonel. "Almost too neat... But did they supply any explanation of what is the oddest business of the whole thing to me? What was a fellow like Jack Brown doing on the St. Brynneys road at all? It doesn't lead anywhere; the side roads over the hills are some of the worst roads in England and they only get you to yet wilder country and even poorer steadings."

"We've got plenty of answers to that one, sir," said Lancing. "Brown could have come here on the trail of the doctor—to blackmail him. He could have come after the Evanses or the Derings, or anybody else with a secret which they had come to St. Brynneys to conceal."

"I've told you about Dr. Robinson, sir," said Rivers. "I think we can accept that St. Brynneys was his bolt hole, a retreat from everybody who might have known his story."

"Doesn't it strike you as odd that he stuck to his title of doctor if concealment was his aim?" asked Wynne.

"No. Not a bit," replied Rivers. "You've got to remember he was an elderly man when he came to this neighbourhood, and elderly men are creatures of habit. For forty years he'd been addressed as 'doctor.' He was probably afraid that if he called himself 'mister' he wouldn't realise when he was being spoken to. He chose a name which, while very common, sounded like his own. No, I follow all that."

"Very well, that's suggestion number one. What's this about the Evanses?"

"Tell us again all that you know about them, sir," suggested Rivers.

"It's very little. In 1919 Evans tramped out here trying to find a shack and a bit of land where he could raise pigs and chickens. Hundreds of ex-service men did the same. He saw that cottage—it was empty and derelict. He saw the Lambtons and they sent him to me. He showed me his army pay book—it was plain enough. He'd enlisted early in 1915, he'd been wounded twice and demobbed in 1919. His old factory wouldn't take him back, he'd no job, and he was tramping looking for a home for himself and his wife. I couldn't very well have refused him, could I? Whether I liked him or not. I didn't think he'd stay there long, but I was wrong. He made his living, one way or another, and if he'd only been as straight as he was handy he could have had a good job and a farm of his own eventually. But I don't see where a blackmailer could have got him."

"Well, here's the story, sir," said Rivers. He related the Lambtons' evidence, and Lancing capped the brief résumé.

"Alfred Evans. Widower. I wonder. It might be Alfred Evans, bigamist. They say old sins have long shadows."

"Well, I'm damned! That's an eye-opener for me," said Wynne. "To think of the Lambtons never telling me."

"Would you have told the Lambtons if Mrs. Evans the first had come brawling to you, sir?" asked Lancing. "Wouldn't you have said the equivalent of Mrs. Lambton's 'Some folks have troubles you can't always understand?'"

"I expect I should," replied Wynne. "I never pass on scandal unless there's some good purpose to be served. But this opens up a lot of… variations, as you call them."

"Lancing's been doing arithmetic," said Rivers. "Assuming that Evans is in his late sixties, is there a chance that Jack Brown was son of the first Mrs. Evans? I can tell you there's going to be a bit of grousing when Swansea and Cardiff and London get my requests for information. Evans—there must be millions of them."

Lancing chuckled. "Most of our donkey-work gets done by what Mr. Punch called his staff of learned clerks. We send off the questions and the searchers of records provide the answers."

"Good God!" exclaimed the Colonel, as though enlightenment were dawning on him. "You're going to get chapter and verse about everybody."

"I'm only going to try to get it," said Rivers. "I hope that my informants will assure me that there is no truth in Mrs. Evans's Parthian dart; to wit, that if I search for Mrs. Dering's marriage lines I shall not find them."

"Do you mean to say she told you that?" demanded Wynne.

"Not told me; merely raised the question," replied Rivers.

"I'll get the Evanses out of that cottage if I have to pull it down over their heads," declared Wynne wrathfully. "I saw Mrs. Dering when I was there collecting poor Welby; she's a charming girl—as nice a girl as I ever met."

"Yes," agreed Rivers. "Mrs. Dering is the sort of person whom one likes instinctively—and Mrs. Evans is a fat slut, whom one dislikes at sight. But no detective can afford to believe that Mrs. Evans's suggestion is therefore a lying suggestion. I think she made it very deliberately, and she must have known that if her suggestion were entirely wide of the mark she would be likely to suffer from it in the long run."

"It's the hell of a business," said the Colonel unhappily. "I'm bound to admit that when Dering first came here, he had me guessing. I couldn't see him as Robinson's gardener—but when I talked it over with my wife, she was very sensible over it. As she says, no young couple without capital can embark on farming these days—the price of land and stock and gear's too high. A single man can get a farm labourer's job and live with the farmer—that's the usual custom in our hill farms—but it's a long time before he can save enough to get going on his own. But that proposition the Derings took on—three acres of fertile land and three pounds a week—there's possibilities in it, you know. If he's a good cultivator and has market sense, he could build up a sound business. And as my wife said, housework isn't so heavy on a woman as working on the land." He stopped and looked at Rivers with an apologetic smile. "I'm being garrulous, Chief Inspector. You're enough of a countryman to work all that out for yourself, but I'd like to repeat to you what I said to Welby. Welby thought of Dering as the culprit at once; Dering's a newcomer and he doesn't seem in the picture, but you can't get away from the fact that Dering and young Lambton walked out here that night to report what had happened. If they'd left it for another twenty-four hours—and no one could have blamed them if they had, seeing what the roads were like—I doubt if there'd have been any case for you chaps to get busy on."

"Yes. I admit all that," agreed Rivers. "I'd go further than you; Dering's an educated man; if he knew that Jack Brown had been dead for three days at least, he would also have known that the longer he could delay reporting to the police the better chances there were of the accidental death verdict being returned. So there we are."

2

"Are you going to search those cottages?" asked the Colonel a few minutes later.

"I think so," said Rivers; "but we shan't find anything."

"Why not?" demanded Wynne. "If Evans did loot the body—and I wouldn't put it beyond him—he and his wife would have burnt any papers or a wallet, or anything like that, but I have a feeling they wouldn't have burnt pound notes—they'd know from the newspapers that all pound notes are virtually untraceable, but I don't think they'd have thought out the fact that Brown's fingerprints might be on the pound notes."

"Yes, that's a good point," said Rivers; "but the Evanses are cunning." He turned to Lancing. "When I asked Henry Lambton if he'd seen anybody pass through the village on Wednesday morning, what did he say?"

"'Yes. I saw Tom Baines on his bike—that's the postman—and Mike Dering and his missis set out on their bikes,'" quoted Lancing.

"So there you are," observed Rivers. "The postbox was cleared on Wednesday morning, and if Evans did loot the body, my guess is that he did it on Tuesday evening, just after the snow had melted. Any pound notes found by the Evanses would have been put in the post on Wednesday morning. They're too cunning to have kept them in the house. And any counsel for the prosecution would press Mike Dering and his wife very hard as to why they chose to ride to St. Olwens with the roads in the state they were."

Colonel Wynne sighed. "You chaps don't miss much," he said; "but you're going to search, all the same?"

"Searching is often very stimulating to the searched," said Lancing. "It was the mention of a search that made Mrs. Evans come across with her famous last words; the sight of a search warrant may ginger her up to further indiscretions."

"While on the subject of the Evanses, it's worth remembering that Evans had been out to see to Bob Parsons' stock," said Rivers. "Michael Dering went the first day, and Henry and Ken went up and saw to it that his grazing bullocks were all right, but Evans has biked out every day to feed and water the poultry and collect the eggs. I should be interested to see if Evans has been taking the opportunity of giving the house the once-over."

"That's an idea," said the Colonel. "He had to have the keys to get at the gear and cook the potatoes—we all still use some potatoes to make up the hen food; meal and corn cost the devil of a lot to buy, and Parsons hasn't any oats or wheat. How is he, by the way? Ought I to have got a doctor ferried over?"

"No. I should say there was no need; he's getting on all right, and Mrs. Lambton and her daughter have nursed him very well indeed," said Rivers. "He got off very lightly considering the crash. How long did you say he'd been here, sir?"

"About three years; he bought the place, you know, and he's done very well with it. He and another chap worked it together the first year, but the other fellow—name of Vaughan—gave it best—couldn't stand the life, so far from anywhere. Of course Parsons needs a wife; it's no sort of life for a man cooking his own meals and running his own house in addition to working on the land. I thought at one time that Gwynyth Lambton and Parsons were courting—he couldn't have done better—but Mrs. Lambton says Miss Gwyn's set her mind against marrying a farmer. Silly girl, she'll get over it."

"Do you ever see anything of Parsons yourself, sir?"

"Now and then. I first met him at the auction when he bought that property; I remember he was dead set on getting it, and I admired his determination in going on bidding. I went and wished him luck when he'd got it and I've ridden over there once or twice to see how he was getting on. We buy some of his stuff and he's done carrier for me occasionally—marvellous what he carried in that box body he built—calves, pigs, root crops. I'm interested in these young fellows who get going on their own. It's uphill work, you know."

"I can well believe it," said Rivers. "What about the other chap—Vaughan. Was he a worker, too?"

"Not in the same class as Parsons; neither as vigorous nor as purposeful. I wasn't surprised when I heard he'd chucked it—got a job as milk roundsman in some seaside resort, I believe. Riding round in a smart van and no mucking out the pigsties. You need to be tough to succeed as a smallholder, but I think Parsons will make the grade. He's improved his land out of all knowing since he had it." The Colonel broke off a moment. "Of course we none of us know what will be the outshot of this job you're working on, but it seems pretty certain that Parsons will come before the Bench on account of his collision and be charged with dangerous driving. I'm a bit troubled about it."

"Well, he's been perfectly straight about it, sir," said Rivers. "He said he was driving fast, he said he hit the other car—there's no two opinions about that, but there's no speed limit on that road, there are no warning notices, and, though it is a crossroads, the branch of the road leading to the wood is an unmetalled *cul de sac*. The onus is on the driver on the minor road—it's his business to halt, to look both ways, and to sound his horn if he's any sense, because you can't see up the hill. In addition to that, there's plenty of evidence that Dr. Robinson was too old and infirm to have driven a car, so I shouldn't expect a conviction for dangerous driving by Parsons."

He paused, and then added: "Lancing and I were looking at the Buick and wondering how it could be got clear of the flood water. We can't get a breakdown outfit this side until the floods go down, and Henry Lambton doubts if his tractor could lift the Buick until it's right side up. Do you think the military could help us? They couldn't get any big tackle up there, but a gang of toughs with levering irons can do a surprising lot of lifting if they try."

"Certainly," said the Colonel. "I'll see about that. The army are sending out some Signal Corps chaps to-morrow to have a go at the telephone lines this side. The Post Office chaps have got more than they can deal with—I believe it's fair chaos—all the rural lines came down in the snow, and with due respect to the Postmaster-General, those light vans aren't fit to drive over our roads in the state they are now. The Sappers can improvise lines—on emergency connections—until things get better. It's just their cup of tea. I'll send a message to the C.O. at Wyvern and get him to send a fatigue party out to raise that car. May I ask what you're expecting to find in it—or is it just a routine operation?"

"I'm not expecting to find anything, sir, only hoping," replied Rivers. "Brown's body was manhandled into the car somehow, and dragged out of it—somehow. It's possible that there may be some evidence, in spite of the fact that the thing's been submerged for days. Then, as a matter of routine, the car should be examined before any case is put forward; the traffic police generally try to find out if the vehicle was in gear, the state of the brake-drums and so forth."

"I don't think anything useful will come of that," said Lancing. "That Buick was once a very good car, but I should say it's at least twenty years old and had not had much servicing of late. The gear lever has snapped right off and the probability is that the gearbox can tell us nothing—the gears would have been jarred to blazes; the steering column's broken and the axle's gone, too. Personally, I was amazed at the determination of those chaps who got the bodies out—it took some guts."

Colonel Wynne turned to Rivers. "Don't you think the determination shown by the Lambtons—and Dering too—is one of the outstanding factors in this case? If there had been anything phoney, wouldn't they have left it alone? Come to that, they could have said they didn't hear the crash at all."

"Like Evans," said Rivers. "He and his wife heard nothing—they're hard of hearing."

Wynne turned and studied Rivers's face. The Chief Inspector was a big fair fellow, his hair untouched with grey, his skin still fresh and very little lined, his eyes deceptively sleepy.

"I wish I could fathom what you chaps really make of it," said Wynne.

"Well, you've got all the facts, sir," replied Rivers, "and you know the locality and the people concerned. There are a variety of possibilities—say if you list them, for your own satisfaction as well as ours."

"Right," said the Colonel. "I favour the simplest explanation. Robinson was run to earth here by a blackmailer. How the latter traced him in the early stages I don't know, but I think the second-hand car dealer was somehow concerned in the final discovery. The blackmailer came to St. Brynneys on or before February 1st and tried to raise money from Robinson. Robinson temporised—said he'd no money in the house, perhaps. He then offered to drive the chap into St. Olwens—to the bank, possibly. Robinson killed Brown in the garage, with a big spanner or a coal hammer, and put his body in the back of the car and covered it with a rug."

"That's all right so far," said Lancing; "but you're postulating a daytime visit if the bank comes into the argument. Why didn't Robinson promptly take the car out and get rid of the corpse? There are plenty of quiet spots where he could have concealed it—up those hill roads, for instance."

"All right, young fella me lad," retorted Wynne, who was beginning to develop his argument with enthusiasm. "You don't know what being old means. I do. The effort of killing the chap would have left Robinson exhausted—he'd lifted the body, remember. I think he'd have shut the garage door and gone back into the house to recover his wind and nerve. Incidentally, Robinson would have searched the body, too, and destroyed evidence of identity. Well, that's episode one. Episode two was the snow. By the evening it was impossible to take the car out—and it would have been much too noticeable if he'd attempted it. The Lambtons would have stopped him, or followed him. Episode three is the thaw. Robinson took his car out on the very first occasion he had any hope of getting up Hollybanks hill. He was going to get rid of the corpse." Wynne looked at Lancing inquiringly. "What's wrong with that?" he enquired.

"It ignores the one point which to Lancing and me is essential," said Rivers. "Robinson had been up to Hollybanks wood; he had stayed there for at least ten minutes according to the Lambtons; he then reversed his car with the body still in the back and started to drive home. I don't see how that makes sense at all if you're assuming that he set out to get rid of the body."

Wynne gave a deprecatory chuckle. "*Touché*," he admitted. "I didn't think of that one."

"Say if I list the obvious alternatives, sir," said Lancing. "A. The Henry Solution. Speaking with all respect, it's a much better one than yours. It can include the fact that Brown came here on blackmail bent and ran his quarry down through the second-hand car racket. Brown died from combined efforts of a split skull and exposure—and/or Act of God through falling branches. Evans found the body and looted it. Robinson drove up to Hollybanks wood, saw the body and heaved it into his car, the effort exhausting him so much that his driving was more haywire than usual."

"Yes. I admitted it was neat," said the Colonel; "but I still think there's an improbability. Why should he have bothered to heave a corpse into his car? He'd have left it alone and gone back and told the Lambtons about it."

"All right. Solution B," said Lancing. "Dering killed Brown, shoved the body in the doctor's car, being pretty sure the old man was too blind to notice it. Dering went into St. Olwens at the first opportunity to dispose of certain articles which he didn't want to keep in the house, intending to take the car out and get rid of the corpse after dark. On his return home he found the doctor had solved his problem for him. It was all so uncannily fortunate that he decided to be on the side of the angels in future, and accompanied Henry Lambton to report to you."

"You can twist things to your liking," expostulated Wynne.

"We call it looking at things without bias," said Lancing. "I could make out a probable case against every individual we've interrogated—but probabilities aren't any good without evidence. Then there's Solution C. Evans killed Brown in the clearing by Hollybanks wood, intending to bury the corpse when the frost was out of the ground. When Robinson drove up to the clearing he didn't notice the corpse because Evans had concealed it with pine branches, and Mrs. Evans kept the doctor in conversation on one side of the car while her husband heaved the corpse into the car on the other side— the doctor was deaf, remember, and so myopic he couldn't cross Brynneys' Bridge without hitting it. Final tableau, Evans told the doctor the road was clear just as Bob Parsons came speeding down from Brynneys' Crest."

"As an imaginative reconstruction that's not a bad effort," said Rivers. "It doesn't cut across any of the evidence; in fact, it dovetails the facts very skilfully."

"Well, I'm not going to ask you to outline the case against myself, although I'm pretty sure you could do it," said the Colonel, "and I'm glad you've left the Lambtons out of it." There was no reply from either Lancing or Rivers, and Wynne said sharply: "Well? Out with it. You might as well tell me."

"We've nothing against the Lambtons, sir," said Rivers; "but there is one fact I haven't told you. Dr. Robinson's will was with his securities at the bank. He left everything he possessed to be divided equally amongst the Lambtons—all the four of them, including Henry and Gwynyth."

"I'm delighted to hear it—and I don't regard it as relevant to this case at all," said the Colonel firmly.

CHAPTER XII

"WE'LL GO AND HAVE A LOOK AT BOB PARSONS' PLACE before doing anything else," said Rivers the next morning. He was standing on the steps of Maidencombe House; the Bentley was purring softly with Lancing at the wheel, and Thomas (who had taken a fancy to Rivers) was standing holding the car door open for him, after giving a final loving polish to the gleaming bodywork. The spaniels, after the manner of their kind, were making every effort to get taken for a ride. Rivers waved to the Colonel—who was vociferating at the dogs—got into the car and Thomas slammed the door.

"In the best traditional manner, and very nice too," grinned Lancing. "It would have done for a 'still' of the Squire, God bless him."

"If you could refrain from being facetious immediately after breakfast I should be indebted to you," said Rivers. "My forebears worked—as the Lambtons work, not at all like the Colonel—who, incidentally, is one of the best chaps I've ever struck in my life. And now by way of returning to the job, you follow the St. Brynneys road for four miles, and then turn left."

"By the pine quarry," said Lancing. "For once the name of the property is apposite. I suppose you've remembered that Evans will probably be there—he's doing the livestock chores. It'd be rather a lark if we caught him snooping at the boss's papers."

"No such luck," said Rivers. "Evans is one of the eely variety, harder to catch than you'd think. No one would be better pleased than I should to have an excuse for putting Evans under lock and key. He's the type who makes it hard to practise the no-bias attitude."

"Damn all, what is bias, Chief? Using your nose is bias. Using all the experience you've gathered in years of contact with wrong 'uns is bias. Or isn't it? If a cop can't use his judgment, what's the good of his training and experience? We both know Evans is a potential bad lot—and so's that great slut of a wife of his."

"We don't know, and our opinions aren't evidence," said Rivers, "and the turn by the quarry is a hairpin bend of a turn, so watch what you're doing. If you mark these bumpers Thomas will be out for your blood."

"If I mark these bumpers I'll never drive again, so help me, God," replied Lancing.

The awkward corner was negotiated in the best traditions of police driving, but Lancing swore bitterly at the road surface. It wasn't a properly metalled surface at all, more like a rough farm track, on which loads of stones had been used to fill in the pot holes and ruts, without having had a steam-roller over them afterwards.

"It's blue murder, Julian," he cried (and Lancing only used his superior officer's front name in moments of real stress). "We can't take a car like this on such a hell of a surface. It's only about another mile—look, there's space to park there, without getting bogged down, and space to turn, too."

"All right. Have it your own way," agreed Rivers. "Colonel Wynne drives up here himself—he told me the way to get to Parsons' place—but I suppose the road's been a watercourse since the thaw, and the frost before that didn't improve matters."

Lancing drew the car in to the "lay by" (probably a widening made so that hay carts could pass), collected a case from the back and locked the car (not forgetting the back doors and windows), and the two men continued on foot. The rain had ceased at last, and it was a still, grey morning. All around them, as they climbed the bends of the hill, was the sound of running water; every ditch was a torrent, every runnel a cascade. Apart from that, the silence was entire; it seemed as though even the hedge sparrows had no energy to chirp, and the rough pastures had no stock grazing in them for the grass was a morass of mud.

"You can't blame the bloke who gave it best—Vaughan or whatever his name was," said Lancing. "It must be about the most solitary place in England—those fields are hedged, but they're not cultivated. There's not enough grass on them to keep a rabbit going."

"This isn't Parsons' land," said Rivers. "The Colonel said he'd done well by his land, so you'll probably be able to see the difference."

At the summit of the next hill Rivers said: "That's the place. He's got it shipshape all right."

A small grey house, a long grey barn and a variety of hen huts stood in the middle of fields which were still green—betokening well-drained and well-tilled land. The hedges were layered, the gates painted, the ditches cut sharp and deep, and Rivers nodded approval.

"Yes. He's making a do of it. Hallo—the hens are making a din. They've not been fed. Evans can't have got here yet. Listen, that's the pigs joining in the general complaint; they're all hungry and thirsty and they've heard our footsteps."

"Lazy oaf, that Evans is," said Lancing; "but he may be about the place somewhere."

"He may be," said Rivers. "If so he'll be in one of the outhouses; let's go and look."

The outhouses were all secured, the barn padlocked. A further stone building, some hundred yards from the dwelling house, now held standings for cattle.

"It was once another dwelling house," said Rivers. "They nearly always built two farmsteads together in lonely places like this. Let's get back to the house—I'll tackle the lock."

Lancing suddenly stood still as they were passing the barn. "Cripes... look at that," he said.

A rusty trickle of reddish-brown liquid was seeping under the barn door. It brought Rivers to a halt.

"That," he said, "is blood—unless I'm very much mistaken. We'd better tackle the barn first after all."

He drew a set of picklocks out of his pocket and got busy on the padlock; it was big and strong, but a mass-produced article, and Rivers had no difficulty with it. He removed the padlock and pushed the barn doors in to free the wooden bars which clamped them on the inside, then he pulled the two halves of the great door outwards. Lancing was the first to see inside; Rivers heard him catch his breath and utter one brief profanity; then Rivers looked inside himself.

"That got you on the wrong foot," he observed. "It's the carcass of a pig—a long, fat, pink pig."

The carcass hung from a beam in the barn; it was, as Rivers said, very pink and very long, and in the dim light it looked quite horribly human. Lancing broke out laughing.

"You can quote that against me for a long time, Chief; but it's quite a sight."

"It's interesting," said Rivers. "Lambton never said anything about Parsons having had a pig killed... I wonder now. Was Mr. Eel-y Evans snaffling some ham and bacon to cure on his own? Ham's worth money—and that's a fine carcass. I wonder how long since it was killed—it's all neatly de-gutted."

"Onions," said Lancing. "Pork and onions."

"Pig's liver, pig's fry, pig's trotters and black pudding first," said

Rivers. "Well, this isn't our affair, but I'll certainly tell Mr. Lambton about it. I haven't assisted at a pig killing since I was sixteen. I wonder if that carcass has been hanging there since last Wednesday."

Lancing began to laugh again. "In reverse," he murmured. "The first cadaver was too old, is this one too young?" He looked resentfully at the pink carcass; it was swinging gently now, as a result of Rivers's pinch. "It's a horrible sight," Lancing protested. "I've never batted an eyelid at the nastier exhibits of our trade, and now I've lived to be shattered by the sight of a long pink pig."

"You're not the first," said Rivers. "I've known quite strong-minded people rush screaming from the barn at home just from the sight of a well-prepared pig. In fact, I've been leathered for enticing nice-minded people into the said barn. Oh, well, let's get on." He shut the barn doors and refitted the padlock. "If it's going to be part of our job to prove that Evans murdered a pig, it'll be a new one on me," he said. "I think the local chaps had better cope with this one. We haven't the technique for it."

The house was a small, low, stone house, obviously ancient, with small windows and immensely thick walls. A porch stood in front of the only entrance, and the lock on its door was so large that Rivers observed you could almost pick it with your fingers. Slender long-nosed pliers did the job, and the house door inside was equally easily dealt with.

They entered a long low kitchen, sparsely furnished, though there was a well-cushioned Windsor chair and an old settle by the fireplace. Hams hung from nails in the beams, and there was a sourish smell of stale food. There were plates, a teacup and a teapot on the table, as well as a breadboard and a large dish.

"Mice," said Rivers, "and probably rats as well. I expect Parsons left the loaf out and probably the bacon—yes, and a jam pot—all scraped clean—in a manner of speaking. Problem, how did the mice get out of the jam pot again? But get they did. Where does he keep his papers? Got your gear ready? We'll see if we can find some nice prints of Alf Evans on Parsons' desk. He must have a desk somewhere, just to lose Government forms in. Oh, the parlour's at the back here."

"How long does farmyard mud take to dry?" asked Lancing. He had been examining the stone flags—"because there's a hunk here that's still tacky. Lord, this place does stink."

"Sour milk—or to be more correct, putrid milk," said Rivers. "The jug's in the sink. A pump—oh, well, a pump over the sink is quite a refinement; they're generally in the yard."

He moved across to the far door and went up a step straight into the back room. It held a rolltop desk, which stood open, a chair, and a round table in the middle of the room (covered with buff Government forms). There was no carpet on the floor; a few books lay on a built-in shelf, and some newspapers on the window-seat. There was a big gaily coloured calendar on the wall above the desk (presented with the compliments of William Staple, corn miller), and above the fireplace was a photograph of a beautiful old stone house, embowered in trees.

Rivers stood and gazed round the stark little room. "He hasn't much idea of comfort, poor chap," he said. "His interests are outside, not inside." He walked across the room and looked at the photograph. "Somewhere in the Cotswolds, at a guess. Was he born there, I wonder? Well, I'll leave you to your fingerprint stuff—try everything, papers, furniture, doors, windows. You'll be able to eliminate Parsons' own dabs after a while. They'll be on the china on the kitchen table—you can generally see enough to get the pattern if there are a lot of identical prints. It's variations you can't spot so easily."

"If Evans has touched anything I ought to be able to spot it," said Lancing. "He's got enormous fingers, fat and podgy, and he sweats like a pig."

"Parsons has thin hands, very strong but bony," said Rivers. "I'm going to have a look round upstairs and in some of the outbuildings."

Rivers left Lancing setting out his gear—insufflators, powders, camera, flashlamp, all neatly packed in his case.

There were two rooms upstairs; both were furnished after a fashion with iron bedsteads, chests of drawers, boxes to serve as bedside tables, and rickety chairs. The room in which the bed was made up was clean and tidy, the floor swept, the bed decently made. Clothes were hung up in an improvised hanging cupboard and cleaned shoes stood against the wall. There was a candlestick and a big old-fashioned alarm clock on the box beside the bed, and the clothes in the chest of drawers were laundered and folded.

"Nobody's fiddled around in here," thought Rivers. "Parsons is a tidy chap—much tidier than most chaps who pig it by themselves—but I can't see young Gwyn coming and sharing love-in-a-cottage here. She's been too comfortable at home."

He went downstairs and out into the yard, and the pigs and hens raised their voices again in hungry protest. It was now ten o'clock—hours later than their normal feeding time.

"I wonder where that lazy old devil is," thought Rivers, his mind going back to Alf Evans. "Did he figure out that we might be coming here this morning and decided he'd give it a miss till this afternoon?"

He went round the outbuildings, noting the gear—a motor cultivator and other implements, the metal bins of grain and meal, the potatoes and turnips stacked under straw, the buckets and troughs, ladders and barrows, scythe, hay rakes and pitch forks—all the tools that look so nondescript and which cost such a surprising lot to buy. There was no cart—Rivers, brought up on a Norfolk farm, thought it odd to have no cart. "He has meadowland—there's a haystack in the yard," he thought. Then he glanced at the bright green of what was obviously cherished meadowland behind the house. This was hill country, and the meadow was on a steep hillside, dipping to the south. "Too steep for a horse and cart," thought Rivers, noticing things because observation was second nature to him. "How does he cart the hay—uses that jeep and a trailer perhaps, or even a sled, like they do in the Yorkshire dales. He'll miss that jeep. That'll never pull a load again."

There was a packing shed for the eggs—wooden boxes holding hundreds of washed eggs, and some buckets full of unwashed eggs. ("Evans again, lazy oaf," thought Rivers.)

In short, since the place was empty in the absence of Parsons, there was a great deal which was very well worth stealing, and all the time in the world to steal it.

"It's three miles from any neighbour; if a tramp got wind of it he could take his pick," thought Rivers. He went back into the house, and because he was practical by nature he went into the dairy—used as a larder—and considered the "left-overs." Three mouldy loaves; another quart of stinking milk, the remains of a leg of mutton smelling distinctly toxic and a nasty-looking mess which might have been a not too successful suet pudding plus a large saucepan of sour porridge. "The pigs might as well have the lot—barring the defunct joint," thought Rivers. "Pigs aren't particular—and those fellows are hungry."

He went and glanced at Lancing, immersed in his own technique. "I'm going to feed the pigs with the left-overs," said Rivers, "and maybe dole out some grains to the hens. I think better when I'm doing something."

Lancing chuckled. "This is the first time I've ever really believed you were brought up on a farm," he said. "You always seemed a hundred per cent urban before."

Rivers went and collected a fodder bucket, and then looked round for something to save his trousers from contact with the pigs—fortunately, he knew exactly what to expect when he opened the pighouse door. It was odd, he pondered. What he had said to Lancing was true—in this country environment he could think better when his hands were busy with country activities. He found a revolting-looking old mackintosh which had obviously been used for "mucking out" byre and pighouse, and having filled the fodder bucket with swill he went and opened the pighouse door. The uproar within rose to a crescendo reminiscent of pig-killing as Rivers investigated the entrance cautiously, but he found that Parsons' pighouse was as efficient as his husbandry. There were five fine porkers, but they were restrained from rushing forward by strong boarding which kept them from the concreted alley-way. Nevertheless, they made a concerted effort to rush the boarding and get at Rivers and his fodder bucket. He hit their snouts vigorously to drive them back, so that he could get at their troughs, and was surprised when they retreated with piercing screams. Then he suddenly realised that the old mac he had borrowed must have been used in the recent pig killing and that the pigs had scented it. They didn't like Rivers at all, but they found no fault with the swill.

Going outside again, Rivers glanced at his watch. He was puzzled because Evans had not put in an appearance.

"Surely he's never done a bolt," flashed across the C.I.D. man's ever-suspicious mind. "If that's it, the rest should be simple... or shouldn't it? Query, will the floods help him or hinder him? But we'd better go along and see."

He went back to the house and found Lancing busy with his camera. "I think Evans has pawed this lot over," he said, nodding to some papers which he had clipped inside the cover of his case. "We can take them away and return them later. It'll be jam to ask Evans if he went inside this house and hear him deny it with smug virtue."

"I'm wondering if Evans has waited to be asked anything," said Rivers. "We shall look a proper pair of mugs if he's disappeared—beaten it up to the hill and mucked in with matey rogues who'll hide him as the Dutch hid escaping prisoners. This is a secret sort of country."

"'Venture to the Interior,'" murmured Lancing. "All right. Give me ten minutes to photograph the doors—there's a lovely superimposing of dabs various on this one. How were the pigs?"

"Like us—suspicious," said Rivers. "All right. Ten minutes. We can come back later. I've got a chain and padlock I can fix the front door with—and if anybody picks that one I'll run him in on the strength of it."

CHAPTER XIII

I

"MAY I COME IN, MRS. LAMBTON?"

Susan Dering stood in the porch, her hands full of snowdrops and winter aconites, with a Christmas rose in the centre of the posy.

"I found these in the doctor's garden. Isn't it marvellous how the snow kept them quite perfect? There's not a petal spoilt. I knew you'd like to have them." She held the flowers out and Mrs. Lambton said:

"You're right there—I do love the first flowers; they seem like a promise of all that's good. Come in, my dear—never mind your shoes, we're used to mud by this time, and who worries, anyway. Thank you for the flowers, Sue. I'm glad to have them and glad to have you bring them. Come and sit down. My head's in such a whirl I don't know if I'm in my right mind or not."

"Oh, dear!" cried Susan. "Not more trouble?"

"No, my dear, 'tisn't trouble—just such a surprise. I can't take it in. You know they sent the letters across with those army lads who're working up there—the postman can't get through and the Colonel, he had the post sent out to us."

"Yes, I know. We had some letters, too. I hope it's a nice surprise you've had."

"Well, I don't know I'm sure. Will had a letter from the bank in St. Olwens; the doctor left his will with the bank and made them his executors. Sue, the old doctor left all he'd got to us—to Will and me and Henry and Gwyn—his money, whatever it is, and his house and land."

"Oh, I'm glad!" cried Susan. "How sensible of him! You were such good neighbours to him, and he hadn't any children of his own, had he? I once told him how kind you'd been to me, and he said, 'They're the salt of the earth'—and you know how seldom he said anything. That was one of the things which made me like him, crotchety old man that he was."

"Poor old gentleman!" said Mrs. Lambton. "I do wish I could feel happy about this, Sue, but it almost frightens me. Whatever will people say? But there's one good thing about it: you and Michael can stay here now. You can have the cottage, or have the house, and settle down properly. Mike will soon get some crops off that land, and if he wants a part-time job to make out—well, Will's not getting any younger, and he'll be glad enough to have more help; especially with Henry bent on going to one of them training colleges—as though he couldn't teach all them professors more about real farming than they're likely to know themselves."

Susan laughed, though there were tears in her eyes. "How like you to think of Mike and me. We had a letter from the bank, too, warning us we must quit when our month's up. Oh, I shall be so glad to stay here. I *love* St. Brynneys. I never want to go away."

"Well, we mustn't count our chickens too soon, Sue. The bank did put in a lot of stuff about 'pending' something or other, but it was a proper will the doctor made, and witnessed proper, too, so they say it's all in order so far as the bank goes. And he did always say he'd no kith and kin of his own. But I do wish it hadn't happened like it has. It's such a dreadful old muddle, and there's poor Bob upstairs worrying himself sick. I know it's a dreadful thing to've killed the old doctor, but 'twas an accident, and Bob might well have been killed himself."

"Indeed, he might. I can't think why he wasn't," said Susan. "Michael says the hood of the jeep saved him—broke the force he went flying with."

"It's a mercy it did—and the state he's still in, poor lad. Black and blue all over, and his elbows and knees cut to ribbons—he must be one big ache, and he's on at me all the time to let him get home and see to things."

"Mr. Evans is going there every day, isn't he?" said Susan; "but if Bob's worrying, Mike and I would go and stay there—there's nothing to prevent us."

"No, dear; better let Evans do it, or that'll be another grievance for them. You know they were that jealous when you came, Evans always counting on getting that cottage of yours himself." Mrs. Lambton broke off, her plump face flushed and worried. "Sue, dear; there's something I ought to tell you. It goes against the grain to say it, but it's better you should know, so you can put it right at once, the Evanses being such liars. You'd never believe the lies they suggested to that nice Scotland Yard Inspector—and a decent gentlemanly fellow he is too, thank God for it."

"What did the Evanses say about us?" asked Sue, her voice very quiet and steady.

"As good as said you and Mike aren't married. Oh, I was that angry. I just flew off the handle and said things I never should ha' said. I knew the Evanses was mischief-makers and I knew they was jealous of you and Mike, with you having the cottage and us liking you as we do, but I'll never forgive them suggesting a wicked thing like that."

"Mrs. Lambton, I'm terribly sorry—but it's true," said Susan Dering. "Michael and I aren't married. We can't get married, because I've got a husband living and he won't divorce me."

Mrs. Lambton put her head in her hands and wept; she tried to speak but sobs choked her, and she picked up her apron and hid her face in it.

"Don't cry," begged Susan. "You've been so good to us. I wanted to tell you, but Michael wouldn't have it. I hate to think I've made you unhappy, for I've loved you so much."

"Whatever did happen?" gasped Mrs. Lambton.

"Oh, I can't tell you about it. It was just unbearable. Jock—my husband—he was one of those men who are insanely jealous—and he was cruel, like a madman. I couldn't bear it—I was going mad, too—and Michael took me away. I know you think I'm wicked... it's true... I am, but there are some things no woman can stand."

She got up. "I had to tell you, didn't I? I'm terribly sorry, but we'll go away and you must try to forget about us."

"That I won't," said Mrs. Lambton, "and I won't have you go away neither. I'm fond of you too, Sue, and I won't have it you're wicked. But, oh, deary me, the trouble there is in the world."

Susan came and dropped on her knees beside Mary Lambton. "Do you know, when Mike and I came here, we felt we'd found somewhere so safe. It's such a happy place, with you and Mr. Lambton and your children and Kenneth, and no one from outside coming and fussing and grumbling and upsetting things. We both like working, and we thought we could be useful in a very small way, and just live here in peace. I was silly, wasn't I? I suppose we didn't deserve peace—but I've had so much in my life that was sheer hell, I just jumped at the chance of being happy."

"Dear sakes, don't ask me to sort out the rights and wrongs of it," sighed Mrs. Lambton. "I know I've got real fond of you both and

I'm not going to say none other, no matter what. But when I think of them Evanses…"

"Don't think about them. I'm no business of theirs," said Susan. "You and Mr. Lambton are the only ones we mind about, and we'll do just as you wish—go or stay. Whatever happens, I shall always be grateful to you and always love you—and St. Brynneys as well."

She got up and went, and Mary Lambton sat and cried again over the fire. She was still sniffing when her husband came in and gave one look at her face.

"Lord a' mercy, Mother. What 'tis now?" he asked.

"'Tis Mike and Sue—they're not wed, Will."

"Didn't you guess as much the first day you saw them?" he said simply. "They're as nice a young couple as ever I did meet; they're handy and thrifty, and good neighbours and got heads on their shoulders, too. But why should a bright pair o' youngsters come and do a job like that in a place like St. Brynneys if there weren't some'at they wanted to be quit of? Oh, I know—you'd 'a set about me with a rolling-pin if ever I'd said the same to you—but think it, I did."

He paused, and then said slowly: "B—them Evanses."

Mrs. Lambton wept anew, but her husband went on: "What's the just cause and impediment, as parson says?"

"It's Sue. Got a husband, she has," replied Mary.

"I'm sorry it's that way," said Will heavily. "I only hope the husband wasn't that 'un we had in the barn. That'll be the first thing that detective'll be wondering about."

"Never!" cried Mary Lambton. "Never! Can you see Sue Dering married to a man like that?"

"You couldn't see her not wed to Mike Dering yesterday," said Will. "It's a sorry mess, Mother, but don't you go grieving. Mebbe it'll sort itself out in time."

"All the same," he added a moment later, "B—them Evanses."

And even at his second use of that forbidden word Mrs. Lambton did not rebuke him.

2

Rivers and Lancing walked back to the Bentley and drove on to St. Brynneys. As they reached the top of Brynney Crest they saw that Colonel Wynne had already used his influence with the army. A gang of men was busy around the culvert and down by the Buick, with spades and cables and levering irons and other gear. Lancing grinned.

"I like to see the boys doing a spot of useful work. They'll have that outfit on its wheels and drained out by the time we've finished with the Evanses."

"We'd better stop and warn the sergeant—or whoever's in control—not to interfere with anything once they've got it right side up," said Rivers.

They found a sapper captain directing operations; the men were digging and dam building, deflecting the running water into another channel before they started digging the car out.

"Quite a smash, wasn't it?" said the captain. "That jeep must have been going at the hell of a lick to bounce this thing over." He pointed to the Buick.

"According to the evidence, the driver of the Buick had just accelerated, presumably in error," said Rivers, "so his own momentum may have helped the nose dive. It's a wicked bit of road anyway."

"Oh, shocking—not fit for motor traffic at all, it's a plain death trap," agreed the other. "All right, Chief Inspector. We'll only get the Buick on to its wheels and out of the water. It'll bog down again of course—sink to its running-board, but we can't help that. A tractor couldn't get it out—the ground's simply a quagmire. It'll stick in the mud like a limpet." He glanced at the Bentley. "I think I shall join up with your gang," he said enviously. "They don't give the army outfits like that."

"It's not ours. It's Colonel Wynne's," said Rivers.

The other grinned. "Seems to me you're in clover," he said.

They drove on and Rivers said to Lancing: "Did you notice the Evanses' cottage as we came over the top?"

"Yes. No smoke from the chimney," said Lancing. "I can see Alf Evans beating it," he added; "but not his missis. She's a mountain of a woman, and there was no transport—not even a moke. She couldn't walk far, Chief."

"Henry Herbert Asquith," retorted Rivers. Lancing had learnt what that meant—Wait and See.

"The best authorities say that Asquith never said it, Chief. It's apocryphal—like Up, guards, and at 'em. Here we are: Yoicks. They haven't let the poultry out—and it's the first decent day this month."

There was no sign of life at the Evanses' cottage—not even a cat. The outer door of the porch was on the latch, the inner one locked. Rivers lifted down an old horseshoe which hung in the porch and used it as a knocker. The Sapper officer at the culvert heard the unexpected sound—it travelled faintly as far as Brynneys' Crest, which echoed it—a double knock, made by iron on an ancient oak door, almost as hard as iron. Nobody in the cottage seemed to have noticed it, however.

"If they didn't hear that, they're either not at home or incapable of hearing anything," said Rivers, "so here goes. The mixture as before."

He got out his tools, first using the long-nosed pliers to find out if the key were in the lock on the inside, but it wasn't. Then with a pick lock and pliers Rivers forced the wards back and lifted the latch. Three cats streaked past him like smoke as he opened the door.

3

Mrs. Evans lay face downwards on the rag mat in front of the fire. She was a grim sight. Her tousled grey hair, sodden with blood, lay across her shoulders; her bodice was split, and one huge bare shoulder was streaked with blood. Lancing's voice was strictly matter of fact when he spoke.

"She's not dead—though I wonder she wasn't suffocated the way she's lying."

"She's not suffocated; she's breathing like a grampus," said Rivers. "We'd better turn her a bit—get those cushions to keep her head steady, and a clean handkerchief if you've got one. O.K."

They stood up, both panting a little, for the woman was a formidable weight.

Rivers sighed. "What does A do now? No ambulance handy, no doctor for miles, no district nurse."

"I'll go and get Mrs. Dering," said Lancing promptly. "Mrs. Lambton's had two corpses and one casualty already."

"That's a good idea," said Rivers; "or is it?"

There was a moment's silence as they looked at one another.

"In my opinion it's all right, Chief," said Lancing very soberly. "Mrs. Dering didn't do this; she's not the sort who'd bash an old woman's face in with her fists—and that's how this started—fists; it ended by the woman crashing her head on the mantelpiece as she fell. And I might imagine Dering going for Evans in a bate, but I don't think he'd have bashed Mrs. Evans. Some sorts do, some don't."

"You think Evans did this himself? Got in a rage with the old woman and beat her up. Well, maybe. We've seen plenty of it in London slums. All right. Go and fetch Mrs. Dering. You'll probably find her husband will insist on coming too—if so, bring him along."

Lancing hurried out and Rivers had a look at Mrs. Evans's wound. There was a deep cut on her scalp, but the blood had clotted and Rivers decided to leave it alone until Sue Dering arrived. He went into the scullery at the back of the house, found the oil stove he expected to find and put a kettle of water on to boil. Whether Mrs. Dering was good at binding up head wounds or not, she certainly wouldn't bathe a wound with the water from the Evanses' pump until it was boiled, he meditated. He then went over the rest of the cottage—two rooms up, two down; a parlour, cold, frowsty, plushy and mildewed, locked on the outside. Two bedrooms, the one over the parlour used to store fruit, herbs and junk; the other almost filled up by a double bed, piled with feather mattresses until it looked as though a step ladder was needed to get into bed. Swiftly and thoroughly Rivers searched, prodded, opened drawers and boxes, examined floor and chimney. No signs of disturbance upstairs; no signs of papers or letters or money or account books downstairs, save for a few circulars pushed behind the tins on the mantelpiece.

"All transactions strictly cash," thought Rivers. "No banking account, nothing written down, no proof of what is sold to whom—and they probably make quite a lot of money one way or another—pigs and poultry pay if you know how to go about it. Well, if Evans did a bolt, I've no doubt he pocketed all the cash there was to pocket—or put it in a sack over his shoulder."

His survey was cut short by the return of the Bentley; Lancing, with Susan and Michael Dering, came into the porch, and the two latter stood by the door and stared for a few seconds.

"Lord, what a nasty sight!" said Mike. "More like the morning after the night before in an East End slum than a cottage interior."

Susan came into the room armed with a basket laden with old linen, bandages, Dettol, and surgical plaster.

"Good girl," said Rivers approvingly. "I've put a kettle on to boil, and I'll help with the bandaging if you need a hand."

"I'll do my best," said Susan; "but you'll be lucky if I'm not sick. What do you propose to do with her when I've got her strapped up?"

"I should think if your husband and Lancing and I all helped, we could get her upstairs," said Rivers. "I'm sorry to land you in for this, Mrs. Dering. I didn't like to ask Mrs. Lambton to help again."

"I should jolly well think not. She's had enough," said Susan, going down on her knees beside Mrs. Evans's grotesque bulk.

Rivers turned to Lancing. "Will you and Dering go round outside? Let me know if there's anything to report."

"O.K.," said Lancing.

Rivers went into the scullery, found a large china bowl and collected his now boiling kettle and returned to Susan.

"I think it's the pastry bowl, but it looks clean," he observed.

"Thanks," said Susan. "Put the kettle on again, will you?"

Her face was very white, but she was working away skilfully, cutting the matted grey hair from the wounded scalp. "Please go and find something to cover her up with," she went on; "blankets, or something. I don't think the head injuries are as bad as they look, but she's dead cold. She'll probably get pneumonia. Has she been lying here all night?"

"I don't know, but I should think so," said Rivers. "The hearth stone's cold—the fire hasn't been lighted to-day."

He went upstairs and collected blankets from the bed and came down again and helped Susan in her grizzly task.

"You're very skilful, Mrs. Dering," he said.

"I worked in 'Out Patients' once," she said. "We had plenty of this sort of thing. If you'd empty the basin and bring some more water—and then cut the plaster for me. Thanks."

She plastered and bandaged, bathed the contused face and wrapped the now snoring woman in a blanket.

"Can you get a doctor out here?" she asked.

"I'll try. I'll send one of those army lads down to Colonel Wynne. He'll see to it."

Susan gave a critical look at her work and then sat back on her heels and looked up at Rivers.

"Mrs. Lambton told me what this woman said to you about Michael and me," she said steadily. "I don't know how she knew, or if she was guessing, but it's quite true. Michael and I are not married. I thought it'd be simpler if I told you straight out."

"Thank you," said Rivers. "I—"

She broke into his sentence: "You might as well understand—I hate her. But I'll do my best to nurse her till you can get someone else. And I didn't attack her, neither did Michael. You've probably realised that someone hit her face with clenched fists—you can see the knuckle marks." She broke off and got to her feet. "I'd rather have died than touch her," she cried. "Perhaps it's poetic justice that I had to bandage and wash her. Now go and fetch the others and get her upstairs somehow. You can't leave her on the floor here—unless you want her to die. The draught under that door cuts like a knife."

Rivers went outside, to the back of the cottage, and whistled. Lancing came at the double.

"Bearer party," said Rivers. "Have you any theories about how we get her upstairs?"

"A trestle's the simplest, isn't it?" said Lancing. "There's an old door on one of the huts that I can bust a bit more to make it narrow enough. We can't do a bandy-chair lift, the stairs are too narrow, and fireman's lift isn't recommended for head injuries, and if one takes her shoulders and one her feet, she'll buckle in the middle."

"May I laugh?" asked Mike. "I know it's indecent to laugh, but decency seems rather lacking, anyhow."

Lancing grinned. "All right. Laugh like a hyena if you like. Only don't laugh when we shoulder the trestle; you're going to be in the middle in case it breaks in half. It's that door on the left. Come along."

It was often like that in police work, thought Rivers. The grim and the grotesque, the indecent and the dutiful, the intelligent and the lunatic, all jumbled together on the instant.

"That chap Dering doesn't know the Evanses blew the gaff," pondered Rivers. "He wouldn't be laughing if he did. He'd be seeing red."

Lancing and Dering lifted the door off its hinges and wrenched away one of the long-wise planks and brought it along.

"I think it'll do," said Rivers. "The wood's fairly sound."

"Right. We shall have to get the kitchen table out somehow," said Rivers. "It looks impossible, but it got in so it must get out."

"It wouldn't be easier to bring the bed down, would it?" asked Michael.

"No. It wouldn't. You haven't seen the bed," said Rivers.

4

They got the job done at last. They jammed their fingers and skinned their elbows, strained every muscle in their bodies and swore bitterly in grim silence, but they got Mrs. Evans upstairs on to her accumulation of feather beds. Sue, white faced and terse, said:

"All right. Clear out, all of you. I'll cope."

"Look here, I'll help..." began Michael, but she retorted:

"No, you won't. Clear out."

The three men went downstairs and Michael asked: "Have you the foggiest what happened? And where's Evans?"

"I don't know," rejoined Rivers. "Dering, will you go and see to the livestock? Lancing and I are going to search the cottage and fingerprint everything. When we've done, you can come and stay inside with your wife until the doctor comes. Then we'll think again."

"Right-o," said Dering; "but if Evans has made off, what about Parsons' stock?"

"They'll have to take their chance," said Rivers. "I gave the hens some water and grain, and the pigs some swill when I was there." He looked across at Michael and added: "I'm asking you to stay here—let's get that perfectly clear. And I'm going to search your own cottage. I've got a warrant if you want to see it."

Michael Dering stood very still, his eyes on Rivers's face. "You're welcome," he replied. "I'll go and feed the stock and then I'll come back to the cottage and stay here until you want me—if you do want me."

He walked out of the porch and Lancing collected his gear from the car and the two C.I.D. men began on the usual routine of searching.

"Do you think Evans thought his wife had cackled too much and might cackle some more?" asked Lancing, busy with his insufflator.

"Search me," rejoined Rivers. "It may be the late Evans, you know. If they were both the sort of nosy-parkers who collect all the gen about their neighbours, anything might have happened—another Henry solution, for instance. But I'm disposed to think you're probably right. If Evans is a bigamist, as you suggested, he may have thought his wife was a fool to start mud-slinging, and told her so. After that a free-for-all and a bolt on the part of Evans, with the spare cash in his pocket."

"Which way would he have gone?" pondered Lancing. "Not St. Olwens—the bridge is barred off. I suppose he could have waded the floods at Brynneys' Bridge. The water's gone down quite a bit."

"Not he. That's a main road—meaning a main road," said Rivers. "If he's bolted, it's up into the hills. If he hasn't bolted—well, perhaps the chaps outside will do a bit more digging. They can also stand guard over the cottage while Dering and his missis are here. We haven't got any spare constables and troops are used to sentry-go."

"I should love to hear Henry elucidating this packet, Chief. He'd say quite a mouthful."

"Damn Henry. He's too lucid altogether," said Rivers. "It's not too easy, chum. You'll have to work nonstop all the evening getting those films developed. There's Bob Parsons down at the Lambtons' and ourselves still guessing like lunatics—and not an earthly of any useful reinforcements unless we co-opt the Colonel. The county men are still running round chasing their own bits of trouble. I only hope they'll manage to lay hands on a doctor. If that old besom upstairs dies while the Derings are in charge, it'll be just too bad."

"Cheer up. Things always start sorting themselves out when you get really gloomy," said Lancing. "I'm about through here. Are you going across to see how the army reacts to civil police work?"

Rivers turned and looked across the kitchen. The table was in the garden; every pot and pan and box and tin had been examined with swift competence, cushions prodded, sofa upended, junk re-piled.

"Either Evans did a bolt with the spare cash in his pocket or the place had been looted," said Rivers. "Folks like the Evanses always hoard some cash. It's not here. All right. I'll go and talk to the blokes over there; after that we'll go down to the Derings'."

He went outside and found Michael Dering busy refixing the door on the henhouse. He turned to Rivers quite calmly.

"Habit's a funny thing," he said. "I don't know what the hell's happened, or what you think I've been busy on, or even if you're proposing to run me in and charge me with murder, but I still can't leave a henhouse open ready for the foxes."

"As you say," agreed Rivers. "I have habits, too. I've asked you to stay here with your wife; we can't leave the old woman alone. I don't want to bring Mrs. Lambton up here—she's got Bob Parsons to look after. And there may be a lunatic about or there may not. I don't want anybody else knocked over the head, so I'm going to do my best to ensure security for all. In other words, I shall ask the chaps over there to stay and keep an eye on this cottage. Then, if Evans does show up, you won't have to cope with him on your own."

"Highly efficient," said Michael dryly. "Thanks for telling me—and you might shut my hens up, just to show there's no ill feeling."

"I'll see to it," replied Rivers.

CHAPTER XIV

I

BEFORE RIVERS AND LANCING LEFT, MICHAEL DERING MADE A roaring fire in the open chimney. Susan came downstairs when she heard the sticks crackling.

"Thank heaven! I'm frozen stiff," she said. "There's nothing more I can do upstairs, except pack her up with hot bricks. I think she's had a stroke, it's not ordinary unconsciousness." She turned to Rivers. "D'you think they'll get a doctor over?"

"I don't know, Mrs. Dering. I'm sure Colonel Wynne will do his best. Now can you two manage? There's tea and food and so forth in the pantry."

"We'll manage, thank you," she replied; "but if you want us to stop the night here, you might send up some of our own blankets and a tin of D.D.T."

Michael Dering turned from his activities with the bellows. "We're worrying about being eaten rather than eating," he replied. "You chaps must have met similar conditions before. You'll find all the appropriate counterblasts in our washhouse. We coped in our own cottage when we first moved in."

"I'll collect the needful and bring it up," said Rivers. "I'm honestly sorry about this."

"It's not your fault," said Susan. "We've nothing against you—you've been as decent as cops could be."

"Heaping coals of fire on our heads," groaned Lancing, as they went outside. "Glory—that's Colonel Wynne."

"Thank the lord—he's just the chap we want," said Rivers. "Has he collected a G.P.?"

But no doctor had been found who was able to spare the time to come out on the awkward journey to St. Brynneys to deal with one casualty.

"They're run off their feet and nearly frantic," said the Colonel. "The Signal Corps have got an emergency line working and I got busy on the phone immediately your message reached me. The doctors have got two major epidemics and pneumonias galore. The hospitals are bung full, and they've got an emergency one opened in the Institution—there's been a landslide on the Loucester–Wyvern road and a bus overturned, so I'm afraid there's no help likely to arrive up here. Is there anything I can do?"

"You can help me to explain things to the C.O. of the working party down there," said Rivers. "I want two reliable chaps to volunteer to keep an eye on the Evanses' cottage. Lancing and I can't do it—we've got too many other jobs on hand." He explained the situation to the Colonel, who nodded.

"They'll help," he said. "I've never been in any emergency when the men haven't volunteered to help. I'll go and talk to the C.O., and then you can explain exactly what you want them to do."

In a few minutes Rivers was talking to two volunteers. "An old woman in that cottage has been attacked," he said. "I don't know who did it, but your job is this. No one is to go into that cottage, and no man is to be allowed off the premises. We've searched, but whether we've searched all those shacks successfully, I don't know."

"That's O.K.," said the older of the two volunteers; "but if anyone does make a break, what do we do with them?"

Colonel Wynne made a suggestion here. "Get the birds out of one of those hen huts—shove them into another one—and impound the prisoner in the empty hut. I'll take the responsibility. There's been one murder and one attempted murder here, and I'm a magistrate. With conditions as they are, we've got to treat this affair as a dangerous emergency. We'll warn the people at the farm, so that they don't come up here—and nobody else is likely to come here on any lawful occasion."

"Very good, sir," rejoined the sergeant. "No one to go in and no one to come out—and if they try, march 'em to the lock-up."

"That's it—and use your common sense, Sergeant. No rough stuff that isn't strictly necessary."

"O.K., sir. My dad's a police constable—I ought to know."

Lancing laughed, and the sound of his laughter brought grins on to all the men's faces. "I don't know which I respect most—constables on the beat or the army lending a hand, but they're both a hundred per cent," he said. "We shall be up and down and round and about, Sarge, so if you have any incidents you won't be left holding the baby for very long."

2

"Now is there anything else I can do to help you two chaps?" asked Wynne. Rivers glanced at his watch. It was now two o'clock and he knew the winter afternoon would soon be greying to twilight, for the skies were leaden with clouds and mist.

"I think it would be most help if you went and froze on to your emergency line, sir. It's a relief to know there's a telephone working again this side. I want a description of Evans sent to the county police and I'll code a message if you'll put it through for me—we don't want the army listening in to see if the line's working. There are several inquiries I've got to get going which it's nobody else's business to know."

"Right. You get in the car and get busy. I'll go and have a look at the excavations down there," said Wynne.

Rivers and Lancing went and sat in the Bentley, Rivers coding, Lancing making a fair copy, both munching sandwiches in the intervals of what Lancing called "higher thought."

"If we'd brought a transmitting set, would it have helped?" said Lancing.

"No. It's been getting evidence that mattered, and I don't think we've wasted much time on that," said Rivers. "No transmitting sets would have stopped whoever it was from laying Mrs. Evans out, and that's the only contretemps so far." He paused and munched, and then added: "We're sorting 'em out. We've got Evans on the run—or else buried not very far away. We've got the Derings safe—and isolated, except for the bed bugs. We've got Mr. and Mrs. Lambton looking after Bob Parsons, and I'm going to tell Henry and Ken they're to stick together like limpets. I have an idea that if I tell Ken he's not to let Henry out of his sight—and vice versa—it'll work. And now we'll give this to the Colonel and get cracking down at the Derings' cottage."

"Let's have a look at the excavations first," said Lancing. "I want to know how they'll lever the Buick up, considering there's nothing but mud to lever against."

"They'll use the stones from the bridge," said Rivers. "There's plenty of masonry lying about."

Rivers was right; so was Lancing, for as soon as the stones were placed to act as a fulcrum, they sank into the boggy soil. The army was certainly earning its pay; the men sank up to their knees when they hauled on the cables to help right the car, and the whole party looked as though they'd been in rugger scrums on a field pulped to mud.

"It's moving, though you might not think it," said the sapper captain cheerfully. "We shall get it on its feet somehow."

"A triumph of mind over matter," said Rivers, "or guts over mud."

"Guts, undoubtedly. The trouble is that there isn't any firm ground to get your feet on; even planks get sunk—but we shall do it eventually."

"I'll go and have a word with the Lambtons," said Rivers to Lancing as they turned away, "and you can go straight to the Derings' cottage and get the fingerprint stuff done before we search. I shall have another nose-round in the garage so you'll know where to find me if you want me."

When Rivers reached the Lambtons, he found Henry busy on the engine of the Ford and Ken watching him. Will and his wife were in the kitchen, deep in consultation.

"Oh! I'm that glad to see you!" cried Mrs. Lambton. "Henry saw Susan and Michael in that car of the Colonel's you're using and I'm that upset I couldn't eat no dinner."

"The Derings are both up at the Evanses' cottage," said Rivers. He told the Lambtons about the state he'd found Mrs. Evans in, adding: "I couldn't get an ambulance, or a doctor, or a nurse, and though Lancing and I are used to coping with casualties, it was a woman who was needed. So I sent Lancing down for Mrs. Dering—and her husband came, too. All to the good from our point of view, because I wouldn't have left Mrs. Dering alone up there."

Mrs. Lambton, hands on her hips, turned on her husband. "Will, 'tis twenty-six years come midsummer you and me was married, and I've never slapped your face yet—but 'twas as much as I could do to keep my hands off you when Henry said they'd taken Sue and Michael away. You and your 'I was afeared o' this'—you did ought to have more sense at your age."

"No one's gladder'n me if I was wrong," said Will. He turned to Rivers. "Reckon that'll be Evans did that. He's knocked her about before, that I do know—not but what she likely earned it," he added.

"Now I'll get Henry to take me up there in the Ford," said Mrs. Lambton. "Sue's a sensible girl, she'll do what's best, but another woman can always help."

"I'm sorry, Mrs. Lambton, but I've got to tell you to stay here, in your own house," said Rivers. "The Derings can manage up there; we've got Mrs. Evans to bed and nothing else can be done until a doctor gets out here. You see, I don't know what's going to happen next," he went on. "We don't know where Evans is; he may come back. I've got a couple of army lads outside the house keeping a look out, and I've told them no one is to go into the cottage. I'm sorry if you think I'm being high-handed, but I consulted with Colonel Wynne and he agreed with me. In fact it was he who took the responsibility for giving orders to the troops."

"Why, whatever d'you expect to happen next?" cried Mrs. Lambton, but her husband answered before Rivers could speak.

"Look here, Mother. There's been one chap murdered, maybe at our door, and none knows who did it. There's been Mrs. Evans nigh on murdered, and robbed too. Maybe Evans did it; maybe he's knocked out, too." He turned to Rivers. "That's about the size of it?" he asked.

"That's it," said Rivers.

"And it's a fine old mix-up," went on Lambton. "The Chief Inspector here, he doesn't know who did it—and he doesn't know us, neither. Any of us might 'a done it; me, or Henry, or Mike, or Evans, or the postman, or Davidson, or—yea, damn it—or the Colonel his self. It's no use saying 'None of us done it,' because done it was."

Mr. Lambton was flushed and sweating from the effort of so long a speech, but he stuck to it manfully. "There's only one thing for us to do now, and that's to obey orders," he said. "The Inspector here, he's been fair all round and friendly with it, but he's acting for the law of the land, and what he says is going to be done. We don't want no more of what's been happening here, and that's flat."

"Bravo, Mr. Lambton," said Rivers. "You've hit the nail on the head every time. It's perfectly true that I don't know—I'm still guessing—but it's my business to safeguard everybody, as far as I can." He turned to Mrs. Lambton. "You've got Parsons to look after—he's your responsibility."

"Sakes alive, you don't think no one's going to try to murder Bob?" cried Mrs. Lambton, and again her husband answered.

"Bob Parsons knows more about them Evanses than we do. I said all along maybe when he's hisself again he'll be able to remember summat that'll help straighten things up. And when us is all workin' outside, what's to hinder someone coming in here and doing what they will? You stay in the house, Mother, you and Gwyn—and I shan't be far away, I promise you."

"And quite right, too," said Rivers; "and now I'm going to see Henry and Ken, and tell them to keep together, the pair of them, and not to go off the premises unless they've got to. If I want help from them, I shall expect to find them here."

"That's all plain and above board," said Will. He looked at Rivers with surprisingly shrewd blue eyes. "You don't know Henry. I do," he said. "Henry's all right, he's a proper worker—always has been. But he's too smart—always has been. When I heard him being clever over this mix-up, I said to myself, 'Better not to be so smart. Someone'll be looking old fashioned at you before you done.' And there's this to it," added Will, "if so be Henry's smart enow to spot who did what—and he's no fool, mark you—it might be worth someone's while to put paid to Henry."

"Who's being smart now?" demanded poor Mrs. Lambton, but Rivers replied:

"Your husband's put the whole thing in a nutshell, Mrs. Lambton. He's said everything I ought to have said—and should have hated saying. He's looked at things straight in the face."

"And if I might put me word in over something that's not rightly my business," added Will; "there's Parsons' place and no one living in it. If anybody's lying low—well, they might find it handy. And there's food an' firing there."

"Yes, I hadn't forgotten that," said Rivers. "Mr. Lambton, did Parsons tell you if he'd killed a pig the last day or so? There's the carcass of a pig hanging up in his barn."

"Killed a pig? Not the last few days he hasn't," said Will. "Bob killed a pig for his self before Christmas and cured his own hams and bacon. He'd not kill another—sells 'em to Wall, the butcher, live weight, Bob does." He stopped and stared at Rivers. "I don't like that," he said. "There's summat wrong there. Someone's been chancing their arm. Bob never killed no pig, I'll tell you for why. The licensed pig killer, he comes and does the killing. That's the law. And the pig killer couldn't 'a got to Bob's place since before the snow—that's the answer to that."

3

Rivers spent some time in Dr. Robinson's garage. He had examined it before, when he first arrived at St. Brynneys, and found nothing there to interest him. It had still been open—nobody had touched it since Welby left it. The concrete floor had been neither swept nor washed; it was dirty with the dirt of years, for, apart from the oily deposit which had seeped out of the old car, it was obvious that the cows had wandered inside when the car had been out. Wisps of hay, oat straw, dead leaves and feathers were stuck in the messy amalgam on the floor, and the shelf at the far end was piled with the junk which so easily accumulates in a garage, and it was plain enough that none of it had been moved for months.

The Bentley stood in the road outside, looking incongruous in these humble surroundings. Rivers considered its length and breadth—longer than the doctor's car, certainly, but not broader—the Buick was a big car. Rivers went into the cottage to ask Lancing for the ignition key, and found him busy with his insufflator.

"The answer's a lemon here, Chief; a predestinate lemon. That girl's a terror for cleaning; what she doesn't scrub, she polishes."

"*Ça se voit*," murmured Rivers, glancing round the immaculate kitchen. "We mustn't forget to take up their blankets."

"I've taken them—plus D.D.T., Flit, Keatings and Lysol," said Lancing; "likewise a basket of cups, plates, etc., bread, butter, cheese, apples and bacon. I wrapped the blankets in a sheet, likewise the pillows, and sprayed the lot with D.D.T. Dering gave me an Alpha Plus. I told him I'd lay a bet he'd been a schoolmaster once, but he said, No takers. They said we could eat as many eggs as we liked and to remember to shut up the chickens."

Rivers stood for a moment in silence, and Lancing said: "Do we know? Or don't we?"

"I think so," said Rivers; "but we've not enough evidence to hang a pullet. I can tell you where Henry gets his brains from, though—his father."

"Well, you do surprise me," said Lancing. "I should have guessed that Mrs. Lambton had the wits in that outfit."

"You're wrong. Mrs. Lambton's biased by likes, dislikes and habit. Her husband's a slow starter, but once he's cranked his mind into action, it works—and he can argue clearly from one step to the next.

I'm going to run the Bentley into the garage. I don't believe anybody could swing a cat in there once the car's inside—let alone a spanner."

"I never thought they could," said Lancing, "nor yet get a body in the back. The car doors would touch the walls when they were open and the Buick doors are big ones."

Rivers went out and ran the Bentley into the garage, considering the space left on either side of the car—too little, he judged, to negotiate a body. He then put his shoulder to the car to push it backwards, and found, as he had expected, that it moved easily. The floor was not dead level, it sloped down a trifle towards the door end. "That means a heavier shove to get it back," he thought; "but they're adepts at manhandling cars in this place."

He stood and thought for a moment, shoved the car back (and it took some strength to do it) then stood and stared at his own fingerprints on the high-glaze cellulose. Fingerprints were surprisingly enduring—he knew that. The secretion from the sweat glands was oily and water did not always remove it.

He then went and stood by the garage door and considered how he would grip it to close and open it. Pulling his gloves on, he pushed the door to; it made quite a lot of noise on its rusty runners, but went more easily than he had expected. Then he stood in position to reverse the process and gave a soundless whistle. You couldn't open this door from the outside; the handle grip originally supplied for the purpose was still there, but the wood into which it was screwed was rotten—it would break away if any force were used. To get the main door shifting on its runners you had to go inside by the small hinged portion where the now useless lock was; this section opened inwards. Once inside, you had to grip the wooden uprights which reinforced the main door on the inside and tug until the door moved on its runners—and you had to use your finger-tips to grip it at all.

"Did they wear gloves?... Of course they wore gloves..."

Rivers looked at his own gloves in the fading light—wash leather gloves, which he always carried in his pocket when on a job. They had been clean when he put them on; they were clean no longer. "Did he grease the runners a bit to lessen the row—and then kick some muck into the groove to hide it?... If he did that with gloves on they'd take some washing."

Leaving the garage, Rivers went back into the cottage (noting the lamplit windows with a grin—Lancing had learnt all about lamps on this trip). "Found any gloves?" asked Rivers.

"Quite a selection," replied Lancing; "he has hedging gloves—I expect they all have those—and some decent gauntlet gloves for biking. She has gardening gloves, housemaid's gloves, fur-lined mitts for biking and doeskin gloves for Sundays."

"Bung all his in your case," said Rivers. "You can only close that garage door by getting inside and gripping the uprights—which I did, putting my hands in the most inconvenient places—and this is the result."

"Tractor grease?" said Lancing, sniffing. "If it's that—not so good. Still, nothing like trying. I'll go and try my luck on those uprights. Walk round this cottage while you're here. It's as pretty a little cottage as ever you did see."

Rivers walked round the small house, musing. "Two up and two down"—like the Evanses. There the likeness ended; the Derings had put a lot of work into those four rooms—walls, paintwork, ceilings—all white and spotless; floors stained and polished, windows crystal clear, gay curtains, skilfully hung; in the bedroom a patchwork quilt and hand-made rugs which even Rivers could recognise as expert. There were flower prints on the walls—Dürer columbines and grasses in the parlour, Van Gogh apple trees in the bedroom, but not a photograph anywhere. There were a few books of Michael's—mostly text books on poultry rearing, fruit growing, soil analysis and the like, and some Penguins and Pelicans which were Susan's—novels, poetry and translations from the classics.

"Everything new; bought, made, or improvised," thought Rivers. "They neither of them brought anything with them to remind them of 'all that'—whatever 'that' was. They cut adrift and started afresh at the bottom of the ladder—except for their minds. Nobody can ever dispose of the property the mind has acquired—knowledge, tastes, skills, even habits…"

A moment later Lancing came back. "I've tried," he said; "but it's all smudges, not prints."

"Well, you ought to have enough to keep you busy for this evening," said Rivers. "We're neither of us experts on reading prints. Can we trust our own judgment?"

"I don't know if we can, but I think we will," said Lancing. "And now?"

"Now we'll go back to Maidencombe and organise a dark room or whatever it is you need for developing and printing," said Rivers. "That's your job. I shall come back to St. Brynneys. I've got a hunch that this place had better not be left on its own to-night."

"Well, I shan't be more than a few hours," said Lancing. "I'll come back, too, and we can take shifts—unless you'd prefer me somewhere else—Pine Quarry, for instance."

"Pine Quarry," echoed Rivers. "Lambton says that Bob Parsons didn't kill that pig; it seems that official pig-killers are *de rigueur*, and no pig-killer could have got to the place."

"A pig in a poke—we hope," said Lancing, "and for the love of Mike don't let's forget to shut up the chickens."

CHAPTER XV

I

RIVERS AND LANCING DROVE UP HOLLYBANKS HILL AGAIN IN the greying light. Mist was forming in the valley—not the wraiths and drifts that settle when the earth cools after autumn sunshine, but a slow thickening of the whole atmosphere. Lancing turned on the windscreen wipers and rubbed the window in front of him, but it wasn't condensation on the glass which was the trouble. "Fun and games," he said. "I noticed it was getting colder. With everything at saturation point and no wind, it's going to solidify. All in the best tradition of hill country—and it's not going to help us any."

"It's the damned weather that's been the trouble all through," said Rivers. "Steady on at the crossroads—the army's moving and going home to tea."

Lancing switched on his headlights in warning and the air in front of them became a white dazzling opacity. "Thank the lord there are fog lamps," he said, "otherwise one of us would have to get out and walk in front. I'm not going to land this beauty in a ditch. There they are."

The army Duck was just on the move, and the captain called to them as they halted at the road junction.

"Will you go ahead and give us a lead? Your fog lamps are a damned sight more efficient than ours. We've got that wreck back on its wheels again, but it's half-full of mud and stones and what have you."

"Thanks a lot," called Rivers. "It'll have to wait till morning—searching in this would be a mug's game. We'll go on ahead—and don't ram us if you can help it."

They crawled on up the hill as the mist settled round them, more and more opaquely. The Bentley ran silently, even in bottom gear climbing Brynneys' Crest, for Lancing was taking no chances and drove as slowly as though he were making his way through Coronation week crowds in the Mall, but the army vehicle behind roared and groaned like a tank. Rivers leant out of the side windows and kept his eye on the rough grass edging the ditch, marvelling that Lancing kept the Bentley at such an accurate distance from the verge in the thickening mist.

"Go straight on to the Maidencombe turning—if you can call it straight," said Rivers. "We can't risk mucking around by Pine Quarry. I'll walk back later; walking's safer than driving on a night like this."

They went on steadily, their chief reason for uneasiness being the vehicle behind them, for though the Bentley's rear lights blazed superbly, the two outfits were uncomfortably close.

"They can't miss the indicator lights on this," said Lancing a few minutes later—more perhaps to convince himself than to inform Rivers. "We've passed the Pine Quarry turn, we shall be at the Maidencombe one quite soon."

"I'd better get out and signal to them," said Rivers, "otherwise that bloke who's driving behind will follow us right on to Maidencombe House."

Lancing braked and hoped for the best, and Rivers scrambled out and warned the driver behind: "We're turning right here. You go straight on to St. Olwens' Bridge. Don't overrun it or you'll be waterborne for miles."

There was a groan from the long-suffering crew behind them. "A lot you care," groused the driver. "We've had a lovely day, we have, and this puts the lid on it."

"Sorry, chaps—and thanks for doing that job for us," called Lancing. "Don't forget we're turning right, across your bows. Don't ram us."

Ironically the army cheered as the Bentley turned off and left them to make their own way through the mist.

Maidencombe was warm and welcoming. Rivers explained that he had only come back to see if there were any reports for him, and that he intended to go back to St. Brynneys on foot and stay the night there, possibly calling in at Pine Quarry also.

"Lambton thinks there's a chance that Evans may make for Parsons' house to-night—if he's still capable of making for anywhere," he said.

"That's reasonable enough," said Wynne; "but I've already sent two very competent chaps out there—Len Jackson, who used to be a gamekeeper, and Thomas. They volunteered for the job when I told them how things were, and I think they won't miss much. But if you want to go there yourself, I'll drive you to the Pine Quarry turn. The mist's thick, but I know that road so well that I don't think I shall come a purler."

"That's a very handsome offer, sir," said Rivers. "May I think it over in the light of the report that's come in?"

2

Rivers eventually accepted Wynne's offer to drive to the point where the Maidencombe road joined the St. Olwens–St. Brynneys road—three miles on the straight.

"After that, I'll walk, sir. I'm guessing all round, but my belief is that, in spite of the mist, there won't be any move for several hours. If anybody is planning any activity to-night, I have an idea they'll wait until midnight—or they will if they have their wits about them.

There are two chaps watching at Evans's cottage and your two at Pine Quarry. All four of them have done a day's work. It's very hard to keep on the alert all night when you've been working all day, and this infernal mist will make it harder. Nothing to see and nothing to hear—almost inevitably they'll get sleepy."

Wynne nodded. "True enough. Is your idea to alert the sentries—see if they spot you?"

"Something of the kind, sir. Also to encourage them. In conditions like these it's a real help if somebody comes along and has a word with you—and if they don't spot me, it will make them all the keener not to slip up again."

Rivers and Lancing had reached Maidencombe House just after six; by seven o'clock Rivers set out again, the Colonel driving him this time. A good meal, a good warm and a modest toddy had put the C.I.D. men into good fettle again. Lancing was busy developing his films, and Rivers had found no relevant information in the report which had been telephoned through to him, so he decided to follow his hunch. As he drove, Wynne talked about the mists which are so familiar to all dwellers in hill country.

"If you're not acquainted with these mists, you tend to misjudge them," he said. "The mist isn't uniformly thick, though it appears to be so at ground level. It lies in strata and pockets, depending on the formation of the ground to some extent."

"Yes, I realised something of the kind," said Rivers. "If you fly over hilly or mountainous country you bump into air pockets—and the conditions which cause the air pockets condition the mist also. I'm quite willing to believe that anybody farther up in the hills might see the glow of a car's headlamps in the mist below them. That's why I choose to walk this evening—I shall be less likely to advertise my goings and comings."

"You C.I.D. fellows must get some varied experiences," said Wynne; "but you can't often have to work in conditions similar to these."

"The snow and the floods have been abnormal even for these parts," said Rivers. "I've had several investigations in country areas, but I admit I've never struck anything quite like St. Brynneys. It has a secret quality, and its remoteness affects all the people who live in it. The Lambtons are the only people in St. Brynneys who are native to the spot, and their environment has conditioned them. Townsfolk would expect them to be dull and slow. They're the reverse; the very limitations of life in that place have developed their faculties to a keenness which is remarkable. In short, they're experts in a limited field."

"That's absolutely true—but I never expected a Scotland Yard man to realise it," said Wynne. "Live and learn—I'm learning a lot from you two fellows."

Rivers left the car at the Pine Quarry turn, having used his powerful torch to help the Colonel reverse the car. As the glowing red of the Bentley's tail lights was engulfed by the mist, Rivers stood still for some time to discover how much—or how little—his eyes could help him. It was not nearly so dark as anybody driving in a car might have judged it to be. Somewhere above the swaddling clothes of mist which lay thick between the hills a moon was shining, and Rivers found that his eyes could at last pick out the darkness of the hedge close at hand against the nebulous pallor of the empty mist above. This would enable him to keep on the road without using his torch and he set out at a steady pace, his eyes on the wavering darkness which defined the hedgerow.

It took Rivers an hour to reach the crest whence he and Lancing had seen the stone farm buildings that morning, and he occupied the hour in examination of opportunity, method and motive, considering every contact in his case in the light of those three factors, and eventually thinking himself into the position of each individual concerned to assess possibilities and the reverse. If it couldn't be said that he enjoyed the walk, it was true that his mind was too busy for any awareness of tedium.

He slowed down when he guessed he was near to the five barred gate which shut off the first of Bob Parsons' paddocks from the road. Having found the gate, he climbed it, to avoid the sound of opening it. Now he had no hedge to guide him—and every opportunity of wandering round in circles. There was a track across the paddock and at least he could feel when his feet left the comparatively hard track and sank into the soggy grass. Very slowly, by trial and error—and a large degree of luck—he kept to the path and found himself at the next gate, which he also climbed. Quite near at hand, he knew, was the first of the poultry huts, and he saw its ridge just before his outstretched hand touched the cold clammy wood. He made no sound as his hand reached the door but a bird inside sensed the movement and Rivers realised this was the duckhouse, for an agitated quack sounded from within.

"Oh, well, that's done it. Now they'll all wake up," he thought. "If one duck quacks, all its fellows follow suit."

They did—and in addition to the agitated sound of muffled quacks there came the sound of running footsteps.

"Now, then, you, stay where you are or I'll put a charge of shot into you," came a voice from behind the curtain of mist.

"All right, Thomas. It's Inspector Rivers," said the latter quickly. "I've come along to see how you're getting on."

"We're O.K., sir," replied Thomas. "Nothing to report. The only thing is it's hard to keep awake if we don't keep moving. I never heard you, sir—only the ducks. They get hysterical, them birds do."

"Very useful of them—they may hear an intruder before you do," said Rivers. "What about that gun, Thomas?"

"Bless you, sir, we haven't got our guns—the Colonel wouldn't have it. He gave me a Verey pistol instead—very good flares they makes."

"Where's your mate?" asked Rivers.

"Len? He's in the house porch, sir. We're taking it in turns to do the rounds—ten minutes on, ten minutes off, more or less. No object in barging into one another, so to speak."

"All very sensible. Do you think you'll manage to keep awake, Thomas?"

"Well, I shan't go to sleep on me feet, sir, and the one that finishes patrolling shakes the other when he gets back to him."

"Well, that's champion, as they say in Yorkshire. I shall probably be back again in a few hours' time—so keep your ears skinned. I'll do an owl hoot to let you know who it is."

Rivers gave a very passable imitation of an owl calling—and the ducks quacked in protest.

"That's O.K., sir; and I'm glad to know you're around. It's the blanked nothingness gets you down. I wish I'd got a sheep dog here—good watch dogs, them is—but I've no opinion of them cockers, not for this sort of thing. Too excitable, they are."

"The trouble about sheep dogs is they'll only work for their own masters," said Rivers. "Well, I'll leave you to it. It's very decent of you to take the job on."

"Glad to lend a hand, sir; and if I gets me hands on to that Evans, I'll be gladder still. I always knew him for a rogue."

"I'm going to walk round just to make sure I can find my way," said Rivers, "so you can go and rest your legs for ten minutes."

Very slowly, checking his memory for the position of the different outbuildings, Rivers moved round the farmstead. It was lighter up here in the hills than it had been lower down in the valley, but there was still no wind and the mist was opaque enough to prevent sighting anything until you were within a yard of it. He checked every door and entrance to ensure that all were fastened on the outside, whether by bolt or latch or chain—his fingers did the checking, for he used no torch. Eventually he made his way back to the porch of the house.

"Thomas?"

"Here, sir. Lawks, you gave me a proper start. Ghosts couldn't move quieter."

"They train us to be quiet in our job. I'll be off now—and try to catch me out when I come back," said Rivers.

He went back the way he had come, satisfied on several points. No one was hiding in any of the buildings for they were all fastened on the outside. No one could find their way cross-country through this mist—it would have to be the roads—and it was an advantage rather than otherwise that the two watchers had no dog. A dog might bark when an interloper was too far away to catch. Rivers knew that Michael Dering had taken Parsons' sheep dog down to St. Brynneys, rather than leave it chained up by itself for days on end. "The dog must know Dering—she'd never have gone with a stranger," thought Rivers.

He walked steadily down the road at the deliberate pace of a constable on point duty, his rubber soles making no sound. Every now and then he stopped and listened intently, but the only sound was that of running water, chattering over stones, swooshing over banks, murmuring in the ditches; water pouring down from the hills to add to the spate in the river, five hundred feet below. By the time he reached the St. Brynneys road he was warm enough, and eyes and ears were alert to every variation in the mist and every gurgling note of stream and runnel. Another forty minutes brought him to Brynneys' Crest and he could hear the louder note of the cascade by the culvert. Glancing at his watch, he found it was still only ten o'clock and he decided to go up and visit the other two watchers.

When he reached the dip below the Evanses' cottage, it came as a positive shock to see the diffused yellow light irradiating the mist in front of the cottage windows. He had been for so long in an emptiness of just-off darkness that this manifestation of life seemed almost startling. He lifted the latch of the gate and waited; if the two soldiers were alert, the sound of the latch should have been just enough to tell them that somebody was moving. Rivers listened intently, and presently heard that most informative of all sounds—a man's heavy breathing. So often a man who takes the utmost care that no footfall shall give him away forgets that his own slow-drawn breath can be all too audible in the silence of the countryside. This man was crawling—the breathy sound came from the ground. Rivers flicked a tiny torch on for a fraction of a second.

"Sergeant? Rivers here."

"Christ—what a have," panted the other as he got to his feet. "You never heard me, sir."

"I heard you breathing," murmured Rivers. "Did you clear a hut for shelter?"

"Yes, sir. Bill's patrolling at the back. I've just made a pot o' char in the hut to warm us up and keep us awake. Fancy a cup, sir? It's O.K. in the hut—don't let any light through."

"I won't say no," said Rivers. "There'll be nothing doing here yet with all those lights showing in the cottage."

He followed the now upright (though crestfallen) sergeant to a hut redolent of a Tommy Cooker, hens, mouldy straw and waterproof capes. In the gleam of a carefully-shaded torch he was handed a mug of strong, sweet, scalding tea—and was glad to put it down. The sergeant had but one grouse:

"I can see their fire through the windows, sir, piled up the chimney, it is. It's enough to give you the pip to see it, for it's as cold as a graveyard outside."

"It'll seem colder when they put those lamps out—if they do put them out," said Rivers. "Thanks for the tea, Sergeant, and if you go stalking anyone else, remember to breathe quietly, or you'll get one on the boko when you least expect it."

"I won't forget, sir. I never done none of this Commando stuff meself; quite in a class of its own, that is."

"I believe it is, but speaking as a policeman, I've generally found it pays better to stand still and wait if a suspect's approaching you. You're ready and he isn't, and it's better if he gives himself away than if you do. Well, all the best and keep trying."

3

Back again over the culvert and left turn down Hollybanks hill. It was a hill, too, thought Rivers, all the steeper when you couldn't see the ground you were treading on. Turn left at the bottom by the wall of Lambton's farmyard; there was no light here; Rivers peered up and about, crept a little closer and finally decided they were all in bed. He went on, slowly and silently, past the doctor's garage, and turned in at Boars Wood House, examining the fastenings of front and back door, running his fingers along the edges of casement windows. From there, after listening for a spell, he went to the Derings' cottage and felt the seals he and Lancing had fixed before they left that afternoon. Everything was as they had left it.

"Eleven o'clock; seven hours before the Lambtons get up. It's going to be another of those interminable nights when nothing happens except that you get colder and colder and swear you won't indulge in hunches in the future," thought Rivers—who had known many such nights. He decided to patrol up and down the road at intervals, turn in to the doctor's garage, using the small door, for occasional rests, and visit the cottage and the doctor's house for variation. He dared not go into the farmyard, nor to the back of the Derings' cottage lest the dogs heard him.

It was a cold, weary, monotonous business; up and down the road, counting his paces, listening, arguing with himself.

It was just after midnight that the first sound occurred to break the dreary sameness; a dog barked at the back of Derings' cottage. "A fox poking round," thought Rivers. He walked back to the cottage gate and listened; the dog, chained up in the outhouse, was growling. Every sense alert, Rivers listened. That was Parsons' dog—the Derings' collie was chained to its kennel, higher up the garden. Then the second dog barked—just once.

"Can they hear something I can't hear?" thought Rivers.

Again he waited, concentrating on the door of the cottage, fearful to move, lest he gave himself away. Then, quite unexpectedly, he heard a sound from a different direction—nearer to the farm; it was the creak of a door or gate.

"Have they woken up and are coming to see why the dogs barked?" thought Rivers.

There was no sound of boots on cobbles—no sound at all. Suddenly Rivers decided the cottage would have to look after itself; he must find out what caused the sound at the farm. He dared not run—nothing is more audible than the slap-slap of running feet—he walked, noiselessly, as fast as he could. He was twenty yards from the entrance to the farm when an unmistakable sound made him throw caution to the winds—the whirr of a self-starter. Someone had opened the door of the shed which housed the Lambtons' Ford, had pushed the car out on to the road, perfectly silently, and was now busy on the self-starter.

Rivers had a vision of Henry cleaning the plugs, adjusting the carburettor, topping up the battery—only yesterday.

"It won't start… it can't start first go off," he thought. But it did. Rivers could see nothing—the daredevil driver had not even switched his spot lights on, but the car was in gear, moving away towards Hollybanks faster than Rivers could run. Because he was a very obstinate investigator, he didn't give up; he remembered the gradient of Hollybanks and the age of the Ford, and he plodded on. Once round the corner, clear of the farm, the driver switched the nearside headlight on, dipped it, and put his foot down on the accelerator. Rivers guessed that there was now thirty yards between him and the rear of the car. The light was switched off for the straight piece of hill, and the car moved more slowly—very slowly for a car, but it kept going. So did Rivers; panting, flat out, he managed to gain on the ancient vehicle. The light was switched on again for the next bend and Rivers saw the old-fashioned luggage carrier at the back. He was very near the car now; the engine was making much too much noise for a pursuing elephant to have been heard by the driver, and the latter's eyes were too much occupied with keeping on the road to glance in the driving mirror.

"If I jump on the back now I shall be the last straw—it'll stall," he thought. He didn't want it to stall; he wanted to know where the driver was going. He kept on, his hand on the luggage carrier, jogging behind, until the hill eased a little, and then clambered on, painfully and insecurely. The car slowed, slewed, and then picked up again—it had taken the extra weight behind and its powerful old bottom gear was grinding on.

Rivers's main preoccupation was to get a grip; his hands clutched the wide rack and he shoved hard against the bodywork, achieving a painful balance. If the driver had been able to accelerate, it would have been all up with Rivers, but four miles an hour was a generous estimate of the speed on the bend. The C.I.D. man found the strap which Henry had fixed behind to safeguard the crates and sacks which he so often piled on the carrier, and the strap was a great help. "If only the carrier doesn't fold up…" thought Rivers. But it was a very strong carrier. It had to be, considering what Henry used it for. The light came on again at the bend and they swung round, heading for St. Olwens. Rivers thought of the sergeant up the road, pricking up his ears at the sound of the roaring engine. "He'll be asking, 'What does A do now?'" thought Rivers, "and the answer is there's nothing he can do. Once this thing gets to the top of Brynneys' Crest he'll be able to drive at ten miles an hour anyway… if it does get to the top."

Of course it got to the top; the combination of a pre-war Ford engine and Henry Lambton's servicing of it determined that. It might be making as much noise as a tank, but it was going strong.

4

Rivers remembered that ride as one of the most painful experiences in a life not devoid of physical hazards. The road was rough, the springs of the car as old as springs could be, and the grid carrier was a torment—but it held. They went on, chugging along, with the one light dipped to the verge, and the mist swirling round them. Even in his own discomfort Rivers thought, "This chap can drive: he must know the road like his own farmyard—and he's got eyes like twenty cats… Pine Quarry turn coming up. What's it to be?"

The Pine Quarry turn it was. Rivers gave a sigh of relief. Lancing and the Bentley (by arrangement) would be parked in the roadway where they had parked that morning.

"I hope to God Lancing doesn't switch his headlights on," thought Rivers. "I want to know what this chap's doing. The bay's on the far side of the road and this blighter must be keeping his eyes glued to the on-side verge. So far as I can make out his dipped headlamp isn't any stronger than a number eight torch battery, so he oughtn't to spot the Bentley."

Apparently he didn't—and neither did Rivers; he was far too much occupied with holding on. There was no sign from Lancing, and the Ford chugged on for perhaps another quarter of a mile before it pulled up.

They weren't at the farmstead yet, and Rivers stayed put while his ears diagnosed the next move. The driver had switched off the engine and the light, got out, and with a tiny torch light was examining the on-side hedge. Rivers twisted round painfully so that he could see the tiny gleam through the rear window of the Ford, and then realised there was a stile in the hedge.

"Back entrance," he thought. "Can I stand, or am I gridded to immobility?"

He set his feet down, holding on to the carrier lest cramp should cause his ankles to give, found himself competent to move and slid round the car after the wavering gleam of light. Thereafter it was blind man's buff, for the torch went out and left pursuer and pursued in a maze of curdling white mist.

5

Lancing, standing close in by the hedge, had watched the Ford go by and the faint light from the dipped headlamp had reflected back from the ground sufficiently to show him the huddled shape of the carrier, and he was pretty certain that shape was Rivers. Lancing had been using his own wits; he was to wait with the Bentley in case he and the car were needed, but he had an idea that it would be much better if he were unseen—also the big gleaming car. He knew he couldn't risk running the car behind a hedge in the sodden state of the ground, so he consulted with Colonel Wynne. The latter promptly produced the ideal answer to the problem—a big old camouflage tarpaulin, which was, in fact, used to cover a car when a number of visitors were staying in the house and garage accommodation was strained. It covered the Bentley completely, and its faded browns and greens did nothing to attract the attention of the driver of the Ford, as the gleaming coachwork might certainly have done. Lancing was satisfied that neither he nor the car had been spotted, but he was a bit uncertain what to do next. He walked slowly along the road after the Ford and then heard it stop, but his ears told him nothing else. He walked on until he came up with the Ford and then he examined the hedge and found the stile. Like Rivers, Lancing decided that this was another route to the farmstead, but he couldn't see any point in trying that way himself—he would inevitably get lost in the mist.

"I'll risk going on," he thought. "If I hear any sounds of battle, I can use a torch and hare back."

Keeping to the road, he walked on to the first gate; stood and listened—not a sound. He climbed the gate and walked on, feeling with his feet, a step at a time, to keep to the track. He had walked along that track this morning; he knew that the next gate was straight ahead, and remembered noticing that the track had been made up sufficiently to give some sort of surface for a car. "A white gate straight ahead and the first of the huts beyond it to the right," said Lancing to himself. He had a theory—not shared by Rivers—that if you visualise a thing accurately, you ought to be able to find your way to it blindfold if you start from a known point. He went on cautiously—and then had quite a shock; he not only reached the white gate, he could see its whiteness contrasted with the black thorn hedge in which he stood.

"Glory, the mist's moving—or else it's much less thick up here than it is down there," thought Lancing.

He leant against the gate and listened; beyond, less than a hundred yards away, were the house and the barn and the outbuildings; he could visualise the position of each, though he couldn't see them. The silence was complete and Lancing had a moment of near panic; had he slipped up? Should he (*a*) have remained by the Bentley? (*b*) Have followed the two men over that stile? Then came a sound which banished his qualms—the sound of measured footsteps on the ground nearer the house.

"Not the Chief," thought Lancing, "and not a murderer. Altogether too calm and stolid—that's Thomas or his mate."

He drew back behind the hedge until the footsteps faded out, and then climbed the gate.

"I'll go as far as the barn and then turn back," he thought.

Standing with his back against the gate, he turned half left, visualising the position of house and barn, and went cautiously forward; he had covered about half the distance before he broke into a run. A faint light shone out through the mist, and Lancing knew that it came from the barn door. He heard Rivers's voice, the abrupt note of challenge, saw two figures lit by the beam of a torchlight—and then Lancing threw his own heavy torch with all the force he could muster—threw it, overarm, with a vicious jerk of his elbow. He had seen the glint of torchlight on a pistol in the hand of the man facing Rivers. It was a good throw; it hit the man full in the face and as his pistol was fired the shot went wild, up into the barn roof, and another and another as the finger pressed the trigger of the automatic. Lancing saw Rivers leap forward and heard the crash as both men went down together; both torches went out, their bulbs shattered as they were kicked aside, and Lancing heard Rivers's voice:

"Show a light—a match, anything."

Lancing snatched out a tiny pencil torch and held it steady. He saw Rivers with his knee on the other man's back, his hands gripping the spreadeagled arms.

"He's flat out—for the moment, anyway," said Rivers. "Get the bracelets on him."

Lancing put his torch on the floor, and in the tiny beam of light he pulled the man's arms behind him and handcuffed him, just as running footsteps came thudding over the ground towards them.

"Who is it?" asked Lancing. "Henry?"

"No. Not Henry. Bob Parsons. Surely you knew?" said Rivers.

Lancing stood up. "I didn't…" he began, and got no further, for a cold clammy weight swung against his face. He leapt round, fists at the ready—and lashed out in sheer exasperation; it was the carcass of the pig which had swung against his face—a long, cold, pink pig.

CHAPTER XVI

I

"Well, sir, let's take them in order and consider the case against each," said Rivers. He and Lancing were talking to Colonel Wynne, before they made their final journey by amphibious vehicle over the still foaming Aske. Rivers went on:

"Robinson himself, Dering, Evans, Henry Lambton, Parsons—in that order. A blackmailer had been murdered and his body was found in the doctor's wrecked car, the corpse being a corpse of several days' standing, to put it that way. First, Robinson. It could be argued that he was susceptible to blackmail; that he could have killed Brown with a coal hammer or spanner in the garage, and left the body in the car until the first opportunity of taking the car out and concealing the body. Lancing and I both queried this obvious explanation, because when the collision occurred, Robinson was heading for home, still with the corpse in his car."

"Yes, I realised that was a good point," said Wynne, but Rivers went on:

"You didn't hear Mrs. Dering say, 'I don't believe the doctor killed anybody. You haven't seen him as I have, sitting crouching over the fire; he hadn't enough spirit to kill anybody—not even himself.' I thought that rang true," went on Rivers. "Robinson was old, weary, and alone. What would it have mattered to him if Brown had spilled the story of his disgrace? The only people Robinson ever spoke to were Mr. and Mrs. Lambton, and he said they were the salt of the earth; he knew they wouldn't turn against him." Again Rivers paused. "The salt of the earth," he echoed. "Why? Because he'd told the Lambtons. They knew. They never let us know they knew, though I half-guessed it when Susan Dering quoted that phrase. Dr. Robinson wasn't given to such phrases."

Wynne gave a long slow whistle and Rivers added: "I said St. Brynneys was a secret place. That's what I was thinking of. Well, we didn't believe it was Robinson. Next, Michael Dering. Dering is an educated man and an intelligent one. Was he going to leave the body of a man he had killed almost opposite his own gate? Dering knew perfectly well that the police would soon find out that he and Susan were not married, and he knew that that fact constituted a motive of sorts. I was convinced he wouldn't have left the body there. He could have buried it or hidden it. Nobody saw the man come there, nobody could have proved he came there. Dering can drive; he could have got hold of Robinson's ignition key on some pretext, and driven the body miles away up into the hills. He wouldn't have left it at his own gate to ensure a police inquiry and the disclosure of everything he had tried to hide. Or at least—we thought he wouldn't."

"I went further," said Lancing. "One of my strongest points against the Evanses was that I believed Evans was trying to land Michael Dering with the corpse—and how wrong I was."

"Evans would have loved to land the Derings with a corpse," said Rivers. "He hated the Derings—but we found that Michael as good as proved that Evans couldn't have put the corpse in the garage. Michael insisted (quite correctly) that Evans couldn't drive. He said that Evans couldn't have carried the corpse down the fields because of the state of the land. Michael staggered down Hollybanks hill with Henry Lambton draped round his shoulders to see how easy it was—and it wasn't easy, even for Michael. Evans is a fat bronchitic old lazy-bones—he simply couldn't have done it, not with the snow and ice on the hill."

"And if Michael Dering did the job himself, why was he so prompt to prove that Evans couldn't have parked the corpse in the car?" put in Lancing. "It was all to Dering's interest to point out that Evans could have come down over the fields by the short route."

"That's true enough," said Rivers; "but I also bore in mind that Dering was backing the Henry Solution—and the Henry Solution was the most intelligent of all the explanations offered to us; it first took the incident farther away—up the hill. It also precluded any capital charge and suggested death from natural causes or misadventure. As I said earlier, I think a Coroner's jury composed of country folks would have accepted this theory."

"Why didn't you accept it?" asked Wynne.

"Partly because I was beginning to formulate another theory, but also because the Henry Solution involved Dr. Robinson getting out of his car, finding the body and lifting it into the back of his car. On that particular evening—it was a dour bitter evening—I didn't believe that Robinson would have got out of his car at all; he would have stayed inside, and if he stayed inside, the chances of his seeing a body on the ground in that fading light would have been very small—if he were as near sighted as everybody said he was. Henry said he was half blind. Dering said he couldn't see a White Leghorn on the road in time to avoid it—so why should he have seen a body in a soaked dun-coloured raincoat, which must have been almost the same colour as the withered grass, among a confusion of fallen branches and outcrops of rock? Henry couldn't have it both ways; either he was right when he said Robinson was half-blind—in which case he wouldn't have spotted the body—or Henry was wrong, in which case I should have expected Robinson to see Parsons' car in time to avoid the crash."

"Robinson was very myopic indeed, poor old chap," said Wynne. "I ought to have realised that for myself—he wouldn't have seen the body unless he'd tripped over it."

"And even if he'd tripped over it, I don't believe he'd have lifted it into his car and put a rug over it," said Lancing.

"Ken said the only part of the body which showed was a hand; the rug was over the rest. I don't think the rug spread itself out over the body in the collision; rugs just don't behave like that."

The Colonel sighed. "How much one takes for granted," he said. "I could have worked all that out—but I didn't."

"It's our job not to take things for granted," said Rivers soberly.

2

"Well, we've considered Robinson and Dering in the light of a capital charge," said Rivers. "Next, Evans. Evans is the sort of bloke who so often turns up in an investigation—the obvious suspect. He's the bane of a detective's life. Nobody had a good word to say for Evans; he was a go-getter, a probable pilferer, a slanderer, a liar, with a past that was far from blameless. Of course we suspected Evans—and his wife. But if Evans did the job, he had an incredible amount of luck. Michael Dering used his own intelligence to prove that Evans couldn't have shifted the body to the garage. Henry and the rest of them proved—to my way of thinking—that Robinson was too blind to have seen a body on the ground in that dull light. Ken gave evidence about the body being wrapped in the rug. The only other alternative was the suggestion that Mrs. Evans held the doctor in conversation while Evans bunged the body in the back—but that omitted one factor."

Rivers glanced at Wynne but the latter merely looked puzzled. "What's wrong about it?" he asked.

"The doctor loathed the Evanses. He wasn't given to being chatty to anybody. I refused to believe he'd have let down the window and chatted happily to Mrs. Evans, and he was much too deaf to have heard what she said anyway. If Robinson was fifty per cent blind, seventy-five per cent deaf, and a hundred per cent curmudgeonly, then he didn't have a nice chat with Mrs. Evans."

Wynne chuckled over that one. "Yes," he said. "I pass that. The Evans wouldn't have tried being chatty with him, anyway. He was quite a formidable old man. I agree with you the Evanses had luck—but wasn't their luck partly due to the fact that impartial and highly trained investigators looked at the thing all round and refused to accept the obvious?"

"Thank you for the kind words, sir," said Rivers; "but it wasn't that at all. When I said 'If Evans did the job, he had incredible luck,' I mean the collision with the jeep. How many murderers have had such a glorious coincidence happen to them as for their victim to be involved in a motor smash which promised to throw all the evidence haywire? It must have seemed just too marvellous. That's what I thought, anyway. I hate glorious coincidences—and this one was so exceedingly apropos."

Wynne took out his handkerchief and mopped his brow. "Damn all, Rivers. Are you trying to persuade me there wasn't a collision?"

"No, sir. The collision was obvious—it was the hell of a smash. And it was apropos—it very nearly provided an explanation of everything—very, very nearly. Now can you remember the first thing you thought when you saw the wrecked jeep?"

"That I couldn't imagine why Parsons wasn't killed," said Wynne.

"So did I. So did Lancing. So did Welby. We all know that injuries in collisions are incalculable, but when that jeep struck the Buick, the jeep must have been travelling about fifty miles an hour, and the deceleration from the collision was terrific. Yet the driver suffered only surface cuts and bruises and no broken bones. He was hurt—bruised all over and cut about the head—but he was on his feet, some distance from the crash, when the Lambtons found him, and he was perfectly lucid. He told them just what had happened—told it quite clearly."

There was a moment of silence. Then Wynne said: "Go on."

"The first thing you told Welby about Parsons, sir, was that he'd been a Commando. The Commandos were taught some peculiar tricks—I taught them a few myself. And when I was co-opted to tell them a little about shadowing, evading pursuit, escaping, and so forth, I saw some of their exercises. Many of them were taught parachute jumping, of course, including how to protect their limbs and their heads in an awkward landing. They were also taught how to 'roll jump' from a moving vehicle, with their arms round their heads and their knees up. That's what I believe Parsons did—at the last moment. He rolled out of the jeep just before impact. It was a dangerous, daredevil thing to do—but it was a chance. He'd have had no chance at all if he'd been in that jeep at the moment of impact. The steering-wheel would have smashed every rib in his body before he'd been flung through the hood." Rivers paused again and then added: "What I am telling you is my own opinion—no more. But Lancing and I have both seen cases of crashes at high speed. As the car is decelerated on impact, the driver's body goes forward on to the steering-wheel at the speed at which the car was travelling before impact. And the driver's body is smashed every time, whether he's flung out or not. That is my experience."

Lancing nodded. "That's true, sir. I've never seen a crash at high speed when that didn't happen."

"Good God!" groaned Wynne.

"I don't want to get ahead of myself in telling you how we worked things out, sir," said Rivers. "I did have two immediate first impressions. First, that the collision was an extraordinary coincidence which might well have confused all the evidence; second, that Parsons had got off very lightly considering the nature of the crash. But I put all that to the back of my mind until I had collected all other available evidence. I was told by both the Lambtons and Dering that Dr. Robinson always drove up to Hollybanks at sunset. I was told that the road to Brynneys' Crest had been kept open by the snowplough to enable the milk lorry to get through, and that the Lambtons and Dering cleared Hollybanks hill enough for the tractor to get up with the milk—that is to say, they cleared a way through the deep drifts. This being so, it was probable that Dr. Robinson would take his car out up Hollybanks as soon as a thaw made it possible. He had been housebound for ten days, so it could be assumed that he would go out at the very first opportunity."

"You are saying that there was a strong probability that Robinson would drive across the road to the clearing about sunset on that evening?" put in Wynne.

"That's it," said Rivers, "and everyone knew what his driving was like. It seemed to me that it was a pretty safe bet he would do what he did, and if the corpse were put in the back of his car, a daringly contrived collision might be a very good way of getting a murderer out of his chief difficulty. It was an idea—no more—until I could find evidence to support it."

3

"Parsons had been a Commando," went on Rivers slowly. "That is to say, he might be one of the very few men who had been trained in the hazards of falling to limit the probability of broken bones. What else did I learn about him? He was a smallholder who had bought his own land, and he had had another chap working with him to begin with. Parsons was a very hard worker and obviously ambitious—he meant to succeed. Now all these facts roused questions in my mind. Had Vaughan, who worked with Parsons, been his partner? Had he paid a share towards the holding? Had he taken his money out when he left—and if so, how had Parsons repaid his share? We found no documents or agreement indicating a mortgage, but it's very hard for a smallholder to repay a partner's share in the first years of developing a property."

"I see," said the Colonel slowly.

"These were questions, no more, sir; but I did put an enquiry through about Vaughan immediately I heard of him. The Inland Revenue Inspectors are very zealous in finding out where agricultural workers were last employed. There is P.A.Y.E. and, in the case of a smallholder, property tax to be considered. I knew I could trace Vaughan's home address. *If* it turned out that Vaughan was happily working a milk round—well and good. Nothing in it for us. If he had disappeared, or met with an accident—well, that is what blackmailers batten on."

"That one never occurred to me," said Wynne; "but I can see the strength of the argument."

"It was hardly an argument to start with," said Rivers. "It was more in the nature of a speculation, but there seemed enough substance in it to spend time on fingerprinting Parsons' house pretty carefully. Well—how far had I got by that time?"

"You'd considered the collision," said Wynne. "You'd interviewed the Lambtons... Incidentally, what did you make of Henry?"

"Henry has the makings of a first-class mind," said Rivers. "He's intelligent all along the line. I admit frankly that I was watching Henry all the time, expecting him to put over a fast one. I thought—and I still think—that Henry could diddle us on his own ground, if he wanted to do it. He is logical, quick-witted and industrious. But if Henry were the culprit, his methods defeated me. I couldn't see what he was getting at."

"As, for instance?" enquired Wynne.

"As, for instance," echoed Rivers; "if Henry killed Brown and put him in the car, why didn't Henry see to it that Brown's body was so thoroughly concealed that Ken didn't catch sight of a dead fist sticking up from the rug? Henry was the first to get busy on the wrecked car; it was he who reached through the roof to get Robinson out. If Henry had seen to it that the corpse wasn't observable and the Lambtons had taken Robinson's body home and left Brown's in the car, in the flood water—well, that would have made the perfect plot. Brown's body might well have lain there, unsuspected, for days—and that would have stalemated the investigators properly. And Henry isn't careless," concluded Rivers. "He's got a sense of detail, Henry has."

"Neither of us could make sense of Henry's methods if Henry had murdered Brown," agreed Lancing. "He'd taken the dickens of a lot of trouble to get the second corpse home, and he then walked to Maidencombe to report to you, sir. In short, he was all on the side of the angels—yet all the time I expected Henry to pull a rabbit out of a hat."

"And when I heard the Ford start up that last night," said Rivers, "I was obsessed with the idea it was Henry driving it—up to some smart trick. It wasn't until I turned my torch on Parsons in the barn that I knew it was Parsons—not Henry."

4

"I think we've cleared away the preliminaries, sir," went on Rivers. "Now to the evidence we'd collected the last evening. We'd photographed for fingerprints in Parsons' house—but the film hadn't been developed. We'd found the carcass of a pig in Parsons' barn, and we didn't know if Evans had slaughtered it. We had found Mrs. Evans lying in a coma, her face showing the marks of somebody's fists, but we didn't know whose fists. Evans was not in evidence; he might have bolted; he might be dead. We searched the Evanses' cottage and fingerprinted all likely surfaces. We got the Derings up to tend Mrs. Evans and put a guard on the cottage. We went to Dering's cottage and did our routine stuff there. Eventually, about half-past ten, I returned to St. Brynneys and patrolled. I had plenty of time to think and I will now tell you what I thought—I wasn't very far off the beam in any particular.

"Working on the assumption (then unproved) that Parsons had been blackmailed and had murdered his blackmailer, I guessed that the murder had taken place in Parsons' barn, probably on the very cold evening preceding the snow. Brown was killed by a bash over the head, and head injuries bleed a lot. Since the experts can identify human blood on most unpromising material, Parsons killed the pig to cover up—and dilute—the human blood. Brown's body was put into cold storage under the snow. Probably two nights later, when the snow on the roads was considered impassable, Parsons put the body in his jeep. Using chains, and shovelling when necessary, he got his vehicle up to Brynneys' Crest. That road had been cleared by the snowplough and the lorry men every day. I was certain if a lorry could get through, a jeep with chains could also do so. He then put the body on to the small sled he used for bringing hay down from the steepest part of his meadows (the sled having been strapped on to the top of his box van), and took the sled down Brynneys' Crest and Hollybanks hill—which had been kept clear by the Lambtons and Michael Dering." Rivers paused, as Colonel Wynne gave an exclamation at the mention of the sled.

"It'd have been so easy, sir," Rivers added. "He wouldn't have had to pull the sled, only to hold it behind and steer it, and he was accustomed to a sled."

"All right," said Wynne. "Easy it might have been—but he was a clever devil."

"The whole thing was clever—it was too clever," said Rivers. "However, he got his loaded sled silently down Hollybanks hill, put his load into Robinson's car, covered it up with the rug, and went home, knowing the snow would have covered his tracks long before it got light. In short—he'd got rid of the corpse very neatly."

Rivers took another cigarette and lighted it leisurely. "You see," he went on, his voice on the diffident note which Wynne found so likeable, "I was convinced the car crash was phony. Parsons *couldn't* have survived that crash as he did; but he could very easily pretend to be a lot more ill than he was. No doctor could get out to say he wasn't really concussed at all—and I doubt if any doctor would have said such a thing if he'd seen the smashed jeep first."

"So there was Parsons, very virtuous, tucked up in bed, saying, 'I hit the doctor's car. I was going fast and he just came right across me,'" said Lancing.

"That's anticipating," said Rivers. "I'm saying what I thought when I padded up and down, up and down, in that infernal mist. I thought of Parsons, calculating that old Robinson, semi-blind and very deaf, would take his car up to Hollybanks wood at sunset the first day the roads were clear, without looking in the back of the car first. Why should he have looked in the back? And the doors were jammed, anyway. Parsons would have seen to that. A really good smash, at the best speed the jeep could do, and the culvert handy. It looked a cert, didn't it—if he could still do his rolling technique? And my last great thought, before I heard the dogs bark that night, was that Lancing and I would search that torrent by the culvert until we found what must be there—a crash helmet and a padded coat and the other items which would lessen the hazards of letting yourself down from a fast-moving vehicle."

"And you found them?" asked Wynne.

"Yes. We found them. They had probably been jammed under the culvert, but the torrent washed them down and they were mixed up with the rubble around the car. But we've found a lot of other things as well. Item, Brown's fingerprints on the back of the settle in Parsons' kitchen; traces of blood belonging to the same blood group as Brown's on Parsons' old mac—which I put on when I fed the pigs. We also found Parsons' driving-gloves, still marked with the tractor grease and muck he'd picked up when he greased the runner-grooves in Robinson's garage to lessen the noise of the door opening. He had to push the main door back because the small door was too narrow. We found those gloves in the wreckage of Parsons' jeep when we got the sappers to lift it. We have learnt that Vaughan—Brown's partner—was killed in a traffic accident within a week of leaving Parsons and going to work in Newport. As the B.B.C. repeats so often, 'the car did not stop,' or the jeep, as the case may be. And Vaughan's money was never repaid. He and Parsons both made wills—leaving their share to one another."

5

"Go back to the time you were patrolling—and thinking—in the mist," said Wynne. "When you heard the Ford start, what did you really think?"

"I'm afraid I thought 'Henry,'" replied Rivers. "You see I'd been toying with the idea of Henry as accessory. Henry liked Bob Parsons.

I was wrong, of course. Quite wrong. Henry takes after his father, he's honest all through. But I was right in guessing what the journey was for—to deal with that pig carcass."

"But why the hell..." burst our Colonel Wynne.

"Well, sir, I'd told Will Lambton about the pig-killing; I'd told him about Evans's disappearance, and Will Lambton correlated the two. I knew he would—"

"So did I," said Lancing; "at least—I did at first."

"Of course Will Lambton would tell his family about the illegal pig-killing and Evans's disappearance," said Rivers, "and he'd tell Parsons, too. It was Parsons' pig, wasn't it? Well, if anybody could get up to Pine Quarry unobserved, cut up the pig, get rid of some of the ham and bacon portions, and get back home unobserved, it was next door to hanging Evans. It proved Evans was the snake in the grass, the thief, looter—and most probable murderer. It was a very good idea. And though I thought it was Henry in the Ford, because he got it started so quickly and drove so well, I did have time—while I was on that bloody carrier—to remember that Parsons was quite as snappy with cars as Henry was. Parsons was quite well enough to get on his feet and shove the Ford out of the garage, because he'd never really been concussed at all, only shaken up."

"And what a glorious alibi for him," said Lancing. "The one person who couldn't have meddled with the pig was poor Bob, who was in bed ill, and couldn't stand up because he came over dizzy. He could have come back down Hollybanks with the engine shut off—the brakes on the Ford are good—and slid it back into the garage without a sound and got back into bed."

Colonel Wynne gave a long whistle, and Rivers added: "After all that, Parsons really did crack his skull—on the stone threshing floor of the barn, when I brought him down; but it was him or me, and

I wasn't feeling 'nice,' as Mrs. Lambton puts it." There was a long silence; then Lancing said:

"We haven't mentioned poor Welby. He fell downstairs all by himself, chasing the cat. Welby's allergic to cats."

"And Evans?" asked Wynne.

"Oh, we picked up Evans without too much difficulty," said Rivers, "complete with £137 9s. 6d. in cash in a sack over his shoulder—the savings of many years, I imagine. Evans will be charged with assault. He quarrelled with his wife because he said she'd get them both into trouble for talking too much. You see, her allegations about the Derings' marriage lines were guesswork, and her story about Michael Dering driving Robinson's car a lie. Evans says she went for him first and he acted in self-defence. He'd certainly got a well-scratched face. I don't think he'll be charged with manslaughter—his wife had a stroke, and she might have had it any time."

"And he wasn't a bigamist after all," said Lancing; "only a wife-beater, and a picker up of unconsidered trifles. Which shows you how logical assumptions can go astray."

"We strayed all over the place," said Rivers. "We always do—but we picked up the beam eventually."

6

"I should like to say a word of appreciation about your very brilliant investigation," began Colonel Wynne. Rivers chipped in promptly:

"It wasn't us who made this case solvable, sir. It was you. It was your determination in getting across the river and co-opting the army and amphibious vehicle that made the investigation possible. If you hadn't done that, and the investigation had been held up for a few days, I doubt if Lancing and I could have done much about it."

"Then go back a little further," said Wynne. "It was Henry who earned the credit—Henry with his obstinate determination to report to what he calls 'authority.' And he was nearly asleep on his feet. That's a good lad, Rivers; a very good lad."

"'The salt of the earth'—perhaps old Robinson was right," mused Rivers, and Lancing chuckled a little.

"So the Henry Solution comes into its own eventually," he said. "Hats off to Henry."

ALSO AVAILABLE

'I hate murders and I hate murderers, but I must admit that the discovery of a bearded corpse would give a fillip to my jaded mind.'

Vivian Lestrange—celebrated author of the popular mystery novel *The Charterhouse Case* and total recluse—has apparently dropped off the face of the Earth. Reported missing by his secretary Eleanor, whom Inspector Bond suspects to be the author herself, it appears that crime and murder is afoot when Lestrange's housekeeper is also found to have disappeared.

Bond and Warner of Scotland Yard set to work to investigate a murder with no body and a potentially fictional victim, as E. C. R. Lorac spins a twisting tale full of wry humour and red herrings, poking some fun at her contemporary reviewers who long suspected the Lorac pseudonym to belong to a male author.

With copies of the first and only edition incredibly rare today, this mystery returns to print for the first time since 1935.

ALSO AVAILABLE

Another Julian Rivers Mystery

In Bloomsbury, London, Inspector Brook of Scotland Yard looks down at a dismal scene. The victim of a ruthless murder lies burnt beyond recognition, his possessions and papers destroyed by fire. But there is one strange, yet promising, lead—a lead which suggests the involvement of a skier.

Meanwhile, piercing sunshine beams down on the sparkling snow of the Austrian Alps, where a merry group of holidaymakers are heading towards Lech am Arlberg. Eight men and eight women take to the slopes, but, as the C.I.D. scrambles to crack the perplexing case in Britain, the ski party are soon to become sixteen suspects.

This exciting, and now extremely rare, mystery novel was first published in 1952, one year after the author's own excursion to the Austrian Alps.

ALSO AVAILABLE
IN THE BRITISH LIBRARY
CRIME CLASSICS SERIES

Death of a Bookseller	BERNARD J. FARMER
Death of an Author	E.C.R. LORAC
The Progress of a Crime	JULIAN SYMONS
Green for Danger	CHRISTIANNA BRAND
The Port of London Murders	JOSEPHINE BELL
The Seat of the Scornful	JOHN DICKSON CARR
Death on the Down Beat	SEBASTIAN FARR
Murder's a Swine	NAP LOMBARD
Two-Way Murder	E.C.R. LORAC
Due to a Death	MARY KELLY
The Chianti Flask	MARIE BELLOC LOWNDES
The Edinburgh Mystery	ED. MARTIN EDWARDS
The Widow of Bath	MARGOT BENNETT
Murder by the Book	ED. MARTIN EDWARDS
Till Death Do Us Part	JOHN DICKSON CARR
These Names Make Clues	E.C.R. LORAC
Murder After Christmas	RUPERT LATIMER
Murder in the Basement	ANTHONY BERKELEY
The Story of Classic Crime in 100 Books	MARTIN EDWARDS
The Pocket Detective: 100+ Puzzles	KATE JACKSON
The Pocket Detective 2: 100+ More Puzzles	KATE JACKSON
How to Survive a Classic Crime Novel	KATE JACKSON

Many of our titles are also available
in eBook, large print and audio editions